TO KILL A KILLER

A TANNER NOVEL - BOOK 16

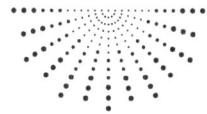

REMINGTON KANE

Year Zero

INTRODUCTION

TO KILL A KILLER – A TANNER NOVEL –
BOOK 16

The two greatest assassins in the world collide and only one can survive.

Tanner's quest to hunt down the legendary assassin Maurice Scallato turns into an adventure across Europe.

With Sara Blake at his side and the mysterious Jacques Durand lending assistance, Tanner tracks Scallato even as Scallato plots to kill him.

To kill Scallato, Tanner must first survive Scallato, and Maurice Scallato is as ruthless a man as Tanner has ever faced.

Although Tanner's mind is on death, his heart beats to a different drum, as he and Sara Blake grow closer.

It's a battle of the two greatest assassins in the world, and in the end, only one can walk away.

Has Tanner met his match, or will he take the art of assassination to a whole new level?

ACKNOWLEDGMENTS

I write for you.

—Remington Kane

I COME FAIRLY, TO KILL HIM HONESTLY

Beaumont and Fletcher – The Little French Lawyer

PROLOGUE

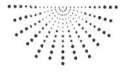

NEW MEXICO, DECEMBER 1997

Cody Parker listened with rapt attention to every word his mentor, Tanner, said to him. Cody was believed to have died during a massacre committed by members of a drug cartel. To avoid discovery, he was going by the name of Xavier Zane. Only Spenser knew his true name.

An exceptional marksman with rifles and handguns, Cody was having difficulty mastering the longbow. Cody stood in a field wearing a sweatshirt with the sleeves cut off, his arms and shoulders were lean and muscular, but weary from the hours of practice he'd already put in. Nevertheless, Cody was resolute in his goal to be a marksman with the bow.

He was one of two protégés that Tanner had taken on. A boy named Romeo was the other apprentice in the art of assassination. Romeo was standing five yards to Cody's left and was firing at a similar target and doing far better at it. Despite the innate rivalry that existed between the two teens, Cody thought of Romeo as a friend.

But friendship aside, Cody was determined to prove himself worthy of someday wearing the appellation of Tanner; toward that goal he sought to be the best of the best.

The current Tanner, a man named Spenser Hawke, smiled at his student's enthusiasm, then sought to temper it with wisdom.

"Never try to be the best of the best, Cody; try to be the best *you* that you can be. If that turns out to exceed everyone else, then so much the better."

"But someone has to be the best, Spenser. Like you, you're the best."

"I like to think so, but we're all only as good as we can be. Maybe there's someone out there who is better than I am."

Cody shook his head. "You're a Tanner. From everything you've told me, the tradition of Tanner gives you an advantage that others don't have. You know the things that the other Tanners knew and tons of tricks and all those different languages. You must be the best."

"Yeah, I know a lot, but so do others. There's a family in Europe named Scallato, they're Sicilians and they've been assassins for generations. They must also be passing down their knowledge and tactics."

"Did you ever meet one of them?"

"I did. His name was Carlo and we were both after the same target. Carlo was about sixty, and he told me that his oldest son was an assassin as well. The Scallato's had been in the assassination business before the first Tanner ever held a gun.

"So, they've been around a long time, but are they any good?"

"They're excellent, Cody, and they're responsible for several seemingly impossible hits that have gone down over the years in Europe."

"Who got to the target first, you or that guy Carlo Scallato?"

Spenser smiled. "I did, and I won a friendly bet we made too."

"So, they're like our competition or something?"

Spenser considered the question, then nodded. "They could be. And if the day ever came that we went head-to-head against each other, our best better be better than theirs, or there will be no more Tanners."

Cody's young face became set into a look of determination as he raised the longbow again, to take aim at the target.

"Make that your last shot and we'll pick things up again tomorrow," Spenser said. "It's time for dinner and Romeo wants to check out that new burger joint."

"Let me keep going a little longer. I'll grab something to eat later."

Spenser looked at his young charge with eyes that reflected pride. "You're determined to get good at this?"

"Better than good, much better."

"Romeo!" Spenser called. "It's just you and me for dinner. Xavier is going to keep practicing."

Romeo walked over. He had shoulder-length blond hair and the look of a surfer.

"Xavier, dude, the waitresses at the restaurant we're going to wear like these short-shorts and tight tank tops, come with us, dude."

"Bring me back a burger, okay?" Cody said.

Romeo grinned at him. "Dude, I'll bring you back a blonde if I can."

All three of them laughed, then Spenser and Romeo

piled in a Jeep to head into town. As he drove, Spenser watched Cody Parker via the rearview mirror. The teen fired off another arrow at the target and came within an inch of hitting the bulls-eye.

Romeo had been turned around in his seat, watching. When he turned back toward Spenser, he was smiling. "He won't be happy until he hits the bulls-eye every time, and I bet he does it someday."

"I think you're right," Spenser said, and once more a sense of pride swelled in his breast.

❧

CATANIA, SICILY, DECEMBER 1997

BERNARDO SCALLATO LAY ON HIS STOMACH ON A ROOF AND took aim at his target, a man named Raffaele.

Raffaele's murder would be the seventh hit of the young assassin's career. As his father's natural successor in the long line of assassins within the Scallato family, Bernardo had been trained well.

Although Bernardo's younger brother, Maurice, was better than he was in all aspects of killing, Maurice *was* the younger brother, so Bernardo would carry out all hits, while Maurice acted as a backup shooter and a lookout.

The target, Raffaele, had been discovered to be in contact with the authorities. Bernardo's employer didn't know what type of cop Raffaele had been selling him out to, but he was convinced that the man was cooperating with authorities to bring down his drug empire.

Bernardo was certain of it as well, because he had just watched Raffaele pass an envelope to an authority type who had the look of a federal agent. They were standing in an alley in a desolate part of the city. The buildings around them were all empty and slated for the wrecking ball. As they talked, the setting sun began casting shadows. They thought no one was watching them, but they were wrong, dead wrong. Despite the heat it would bring, Bernardo planned to kill both the snitch and the cop. Bernardo knew it would intensify the search for him, the killing of a cop, but he hated cops of any stripe.

Pressure on the trigger of Bernardo's rifle ended Raffaele's life, as a slug blew his heart to pieces. The federal agent gaped at Raffaele, and as the body settled onto the debris on the alley floor, the agent turned to flee.

Bernardo fired a shot that caught the agent in the right leg. It was a bad wound, and Bernardo placed another like it in the other leg. Taking the time to make the agent suffer wasn't the best play, but Bernardo despised authority in all its forms, and the federal cop was a handy target.

A voice came from behind Bernardo, startling him.

"See, this is one reason why I'm better than you."

Bernardo, who had been lying on his stomach, swung the rifle around as he flipped over and took aim where the voice had come from. No one was there.

"You don't recognize my voice, Bernardo?"

Bernardo jerked his head to the left and saw his younger brother leaning against a wall and smirking at him. Maurice Scallato had dark good looks and had just turned twenty. He had been training with his father and older brother to learn the art of assassination since he was a boy and was without doubt Bernardo's better.

Bernardo's face grew flush with anger. Maurice was his little brother and needed to be reminded of his place. Had Bernardo looked closer at Maurice, he would have seen that his brother was keeping one hand out of sight.

"Maurice, what are you doing here? I told you to be on watch at the end of the street."

Maurice Scallato walked over to the edge of the roof and looked down at the wounded agent. The agent appeared to be in agony and was bleeding copious amounts of blood from the leg wounds. There was a revolver in one hand and a radio in the other. The agent must have thought the shots came from the roof at the rear of the alley, because wide and fearful eyes were locked on it. The agent shouted into the radio to summon backup, but Maurice knew that help wouldn't arrive for several minutes. That gave him plenty of time to do what he came there to do.

"You couldn't control yourself, could you, Bernardo? You had to make the cop suffer. Me, I would have blown the cop's brains out and been headed home by now."

Bernardo rose from his prone position and pointed at Maurice. "I run things, not you, Maurice. The sooner you get that in your head the better off you'll be."

Maurice smirked as he brought up a gun and took aim at Bernardo. "I think I'll put something in your head instead."

The slug entered precisely halfway between Bernardo's astonished eyes, causing him to topple backwards off the roof. As the body landed several yards away from the wounded agent, there was a cry of fright as the agent's head jerked up. The wounded cop fired off a string of panicked shots that either went wide or chipped the side of the building. Once the gun was empty, the cop attempted to crawl away.

Progress was slow, and Maurice Scallato made it down to street level as sirens could be heard faintly in the distance. Maurice removed a thin metal ring from his brother's right hand and smiled as he slid the band onto his own finger. The ring held a special significance for the Scallatos and had been passed down through the generations. After flipping the wounded agent over to frisk for more weapons. Maurice studied the credentials he found, they signified the agent as a member of Interpol. He then placed his gun against a temple drenched with the sweat of fear.

"You can die, or we can make a deal."

When the agent spoke, Maurice was surprised by the French accent. "I want to live! I want to live!"

"And you will if you remain useful to me."

Maurice glanced over at his brother's body, then back at the agent. "I need the name of one of your fellow agents. My father will want blood for my brother's death."

The agent wore a mask of gritted teeth and clenched eyes from the agony of the leg wounds. When the wave of pain subsided, there was shock and uneasiness showing in the eyes.

"You want me to sell-out a friend?"

"Why so surprised? I just killed my brother to better my own situation, but I never said they had to be a friend."

Those words placed a flicker of glee in the agent's eyes. "Lance Robear, he's a son of a bitch and he stole my last promotion from me."

Maurice laughed. "You and I will work well together. We're both willing to do what it takes to thrive in this world."

The sirens were much louder as Maurice began walking away, but he heard the agent call out and turned to look back. The agent's eyes were tearing up from pain but retained enough clarity to look at the dead man, Raffaele, then over at the body of Bernardo, finally, the watery eyes gazed into the eyes of Maurice.

"Who are you?"

"My name is Maurice Scallato. I am the greatest assassin in the world."

1

DAMN DELECTABLE

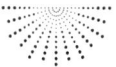

NINETEEN YEARS LATER, LOS ANGELES, CALIFORNIA

WHILE SITTING IN A HOTEL LOBBY, TANNER FELT HIS HEART rate increase as Sara Blake came into his line of vision, and what a vision she was. She had been making his heart beat faster for a long time, although, on more than one occasion, it had been fueled by adrenaline and the will to survive.

They had been enemies who had sought to kill each other and who had come damn close on both ends. She had triumphed over him, had brought him to his knees, and had him where she'd wanted him, beaten and at her mercy. In typical female fashion, she had used love to conquer him.

Not love for her, oh no, but love nonetheless, and he had sacrificed himself to save another. But it had been a pyrrhic victory for Sara, for the gaining of it had cost her not only a lover, but also her sense of honor. That's when fate stepped in and offered them both a way to put the past behind them, and to save the lives of innocents. During that adventure, a respect grew between them, and even, amazingly enough, the faint beginnings of a friendship.

But then, they parted, with a new peace in place, only to reunite months later over business concerns.

The friendship blossomed, the respect deepened, and hearts once cold as ice were on a slow simmer. They were friends, true friends, and if Tanner were to be honest with himself, he wanted more from Sara Blake, and not just sex.

Sara walked toward him wearing a black skirt with a simple yellow blouse. Tanner knew she had grabbed the clothes off a rack in the boutique located in the hotel's lobby. Maybe a dozen women had bought the same outfit that week alone, but Sara's curves and the contours of her body made the look her own.

Her blue eyes found him, and she smiled. A year earlier, the sight of him would have produced a sneer. But she was smiling a genuine smile, and now the heart that was beating faster threatened to melt from the rise in temperature he felt. She was one damn delectable woman and she had begun to haunt his dreams.

Tanner wanted her, there was no denying that, and unless he was as deluded as a February flower, that smile was telling him Sara wanted him too. The smile widened as she reached him, and he realized he'd been staring at her legs.

"Good morning, Tanner, have you checked out?"

"Yes, what about you?"

"I'm good, and I just came from putting my bags in the car."

"Fine, then let's get to this meeting."

They stared at each other for a moment, then Sara headed for the side exit that led to the parking lot. Tanner was mesmerized by the sway of her hips, the way her calves flexed, and the bounce of her long, luxurious raven hair.

He cleared his throat and put his head on a swivel as his training and survival instincts had conditioned him to do. He had more enemies than he could remember and if he kept zoning out in public he might find himself lying in a puddle of his own blood.

It seemed that Sara Blake was harmful to his health whether friend or foe. Less than a minute later, he was staring again.

THE MEETING TOOK PLACE INSIDE ANOTHER HOTEL, IN A room on the fifteenth floor. They were there to talk with a woman named Sabella Barbieri, who was the assistant of former Interpol agent Jacques Durand. Durand was a contact Sara had made during a previous trip to California.

Durand, who was currently a true crime writer, seemed to be well-connected with current agents of Interpol, as well as other unnamed sources. Sara had asked him if he had any further information concerning Maurice Scallato, and Durand had come through. However, Durand had to fly to Europe to attend to another matter, but he had left behind his assistant to meet with Tanner and Sara.

Sabella Barbieri looked to be about forty-five, had a good figure and intelligent blue eyes. Those eyes widened with interest when she saw Tanner, as he and Sara entered her room, but they drifted away when they met the intensity of Tanner's gaze.

"You have very unusual eyes, Monsieur Tanner, and sexy as well."

"You seem to have all the usual parts, Sabella, but they're arranged very nicely," Tanner said.

Sabella let out a delicate laugh, then touched Tanner on the arm. "I think we could be friends."

Sara stepped closer to Tanner. "Friendship will have to wait; we're here on business, right?"

Sabella smiled at Sara even as her eyes looked her over with disdain showing in them. After looking away, Sabella produced a set of file folders from a slim black briefcase.

"The information you asked for concerning Maurice Scallato. It's not much, but I hope it helps you, Tanner."

"Tell Jacques that we thank him for his help," Sara said.

Sabella smiled, and this time it seemed genuine, although it was birthed by amusement. "Jacques speaks of you fondly, Miss Blake. I know it grieved him that he missed an opportunity to see you."

"I like Jacques as well, and I look forward to seeing him again someday."

Sabella moved in on Tanner and kissed him on the cheek. It did not go unnoticed by Sara that the woman was pressing herself against him.

"I look forward to meeting with you again, Tanner. Perhaps next time we'll meet alone. My contact numbers are in the files."

"Maybe we'll make that happen, Sabella."

"I would like that very much."

"Are we finished here?" Sara asked.

"Oui, and I wish you both luck."

On the elevator ride down to street level, Sara used a tissue to wipe Sabella's lipstick off Tanner's cheek.

"She was throwing herself at you, and she looks old enough to be your mother."

"She looked fine to me."

"Oh really? So, what, would you like me to wait in the hotel bar while you go back upstairs? She'd welcome you right into her bed, the slut."

"I think I'll stay by your side."

"And pass up a sure thing?"

Tanner turned to face Sara. "The uncertainty of what might happen with you is worth a hundred Sabella Barbieris."

With that said, Tanner turned back to face the doors, which opened onto the hotel lobby. No more words passed between them until they were in the car and back on the road. It was Sara who spoke.

"You can be certain of one thing when it comes to me, Tanner."

"And what would that be?"

"I'm a woman of strong emotion and I don't do anything halfway."

"I have noticed that about you."

"That goes for love as well. I don't know how to give half my heart away. It's all or nothing."

"I hear you, Sara."

"And?"

"And, you might have noticed that trust comes hard for me, and I haven't exactly been lucky in love."

"Maybe, but you have a way to go to match my track record. At least most of your ex-loves are still alive."

There was silence again, but this time Tanner broke it.

"I'm sorry."

"Sorry for what?"

Tanner pulled over to the side of the road, placed the car in park, then turned to her.

"I'm sorry I killed Brian Ames. It was work, not personal, but it hurts me now to know how much I hurt you."

Sara looked down at her hands, which were clenched together in her lap. "It took me a long time to admit to myself that Brian was no saint. He involved himself with the Conglomerate and reaped one of the penalties of that life. You killed him, yes, but I no longer hold you to blame for that. Like you said, it wasn't personal."

Tanner reached over and gently lifted her chin until their eyes met. "Thank you, Sara."

She nodded slightly, then picked up the files they received. "I guess I should read these."

Tanner placed the car back in drive and merged into traffic. As he drove along, he felt like he was leaving more than miles behind them, and that they had said goodbye to the shared animosity of their past.

What the future would bring, only time would tell.

2

ANGEL OF MERCY

Tanner drove as Sara perused the reports of the police investigation into the disappearance of John Doe. John Doe was the name given the survivor of an earthquake that had buried the man under a mudslide for days. Thanks to the science of Ear Print Analysis, Tanner was aware that John Doe was a Sicilian assassin named Maurice Scallato.

Scallato made a practice of hunting down and killing any assassin he deemed to be in his illustrious league. Tanner had attained such a reputation when he not only survived a Mexican cartel's best attempts to kill him, but wiped out the cartel leader, Alonso Alvarado.

Scallato had targeted Tanner for death, but Tanner survived, and instead of hiding, Tanner was on the hunt for Maurice Scallato.

Sara finished reading the initial police reports and stuffed them inside the large purse she carried.

"There's not much to tell since John Doe wasn't under arrest or suspected of committing a crime. The investigating officer worked missing person cases. She was looking into John Doe's disappearance because it was believed he needed more care to have a proper recovery."

"And did they put Homicide on the case once it was established that he was Maurice Scallato?"

"Actually, it was an FBI agent named Vince Callahan. He and his team conducted the interviews with the hospital personnel but came up empty. It's Callahan's opinion that Scallato has left the country."

"Is there anything useful in the personnel interviews?"

"I haven't read them yet; I'll do that next."

"Exactly what was wrong with Scallato?"

"Mostly dehydration, but he had also injured his—"

"—Right ankle," Tanner finished. "He had a slight limp in the hospital security video I saw of him."

"Yes, he hurt his ankle. But I watched that video ten times and never detected the limp."

"I watched it fifty times and will probably watch it again, the subconscious sometimes needs repetition to catch the subtleties."

Sara turned in her seat and stared at Tanner. "Is that something you've learned or something you were taught?"

"I was taught that by my mentor."

"Tanner Six?"

"Yes."

"I'd like to meet him."

"Why?"

"I'm dying to see if he's anything like you."

"He is, and he isn't."

"I'd still like to meet him."

"Maybe someday."

"Fine."

They drove along in silence for a moment as Sara studied the witness statements. When something struck her as interesting, she shared it with Tanner.

"I understand now why the sketches that were made from the recall of the hospital staff were so vague. After being trapped in the dark for such a long period, Scallato had a sensitivity to light and wore sunglasses. Add to that the full beard he had and there weren't many details of his face showing."

Tanner nodded his understanding and Sara read on. Twenty minutes later, she raised her head up from the paperwork.

"There was a nurse named Claire Newport caring for Scallato while he was at the hospital. In her FBI interview, she states several times how nice Scallato was and how she can't believe that he's capable of violence."

"It sounds as if she took a liking to Scallato," Tanner said.

"Yes, it does. And Tanner, we owe Jacques for all this. He did a good job of gathering intel for us. There are even pictures of the hospital staff included in this report, as well as pertinent background."

"Let me see the nurse's picture," Tanner said.

Sara held up the page for him to look at as he momentarily took his eyes off the road. It was a photo of nurse Claire Newport that was included in her hospital ID. It showed a thirtyish woman with blonde hair and brown eyes. She was somewhat pretty and wore a tentative smile.

"She was accused of stalking a doctor at the hospital where she was formerly employed, but a plea bargain was worked out. Apparently, her obsessive behavior toward the doctor was blamed on an addiction she had to a prescription drug called Triazolam. She received treatment for the addiction and six months of mandatory therapy, but she had to seek employment elsewhere. That happened three years ago."

"Hmm, I thought Scallato might have crawled into a

hole somewhere to hide until he was strong enough to travel, but this nurse could have seemed too good to pass up. Where does she live?"

Sara checked Claire Newport's info and looked for an address. "Ah, here it is. She lives in a town called Robbinsville that's close to where we're headed. Do you think it's worth checking out?"

"Why not? It's the only possible lead we have."

"I'll program her address into the GPS," Sara said.

"Do that, and also add the address for the hospital where she works. There's a good chance she's there and we can follow her once she leaves her job."

Sara had to lean over to access the buttons of the GPS that was set into the vehicle's dashboard, as she did so, her face moved close to Tanner and her blouse gapped open slightly. When she was done programming the device, Sara saw that Tanner was watching her.

"Were you checking me out just then?"

"I always keep at least one eye on you."

"Seriously? What Tanner, you still don't trust me?"

"I just like looking at you."

Sara's anger faded as she sat back in her seat. "Tanner."

"Yes?"

"You're not too hard on the eyes either."

Tanner laughed. "As I recall, you once said that you'd rather bed a dog than sleep with me."

"Did I really say that?"

"Yes."

"Well, you weren't exactly my favorite person back then."

"And now?"

"Let's just say that you've moved up considerably."

"Do I rank above canines?"

Sara laughed. "Yes, I would pick you over a dog."

"That may be the nicest thing you've ever said to me."

Sara laughed again, then, she took out her phone to check motels and hotels in the Robbinsville, California area. There was a chance they would have to stay overnight, and Sara wanted to know what accommodations the town offered.

When she came across the option on a hotel's website concerning room availability, she hesitated. How many rooms did they need, one for each of them… or just one? After a few seconds passed, in which her mind raced and her pulse sped up, Sara pressed the #2 key on her phone. As much as she was attracted to him, she wasn't ready to offer herself to Tanner, and despite their new-found friendship, Sara wondered if she ever would be.

"There are rooms available near Claire Newport's home."

"Yeah, make a reservation. I think I'll want to watch her for at least a day or two."

"*A* reservation, as in one?"

Tanner chuckled. "Relax, I wasn't hinting at anything. Make two reservations, one for you and one for me."

"I will… for now."

Tanner took his eyes from the road and studied Sara's face. "For now?"

"Yes, for now."

Tanner looked back at the road. When Sara glanced over at him, she saw that he was smiling.

3

DEMON OF DEATH

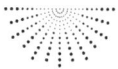

JACQUES DURAND'S REPORT INCLUDED INFORMATION ON Claire Newport's vehicle. Tanner spotted the car as he used binoculars to search the hospital's employee parking lot.

After an hour's wait, Claire Newport left the hospital by a rear door and waved to the parking lot attendant. Tanner placed his vehicle in gear and he and Sara followed the nurse.

"She looks better than that picture you showed me," Tanner said.

"She's wearing more makeup and has her hair arranged differently," Sara said. "That's a good sign. Perhaps it means that there's a new man in her life."

After Claire drove into the parking lot of a supermarket, Tanner parked and handed Sara the keys.

"I'm going to follow her and see what she buys. It may tell us if she's shopping for two."

"Even if there is someone in her life, it doesn't necessarily mean that it's Scallato," Sara said.

"Yeah, but let's hope it is."

～

Tanner entered the market and grabbed up a plastic basket from a stack near the entrance. As he moved along while keeping Claire Newport in sight, he added items to his basket to blend in. Claire had opted for a cart, and she seemed annoyed by the constant squeak that one of its wheels made. Tanner liked that squeak, it diverted her attention and made it less likely that she would spot him.

In any event, nurse Claire didn't seem nervous or watchful. However, she was adding a lot of items to her cart, including a can of shaving cream and a package of razors. Tanner joined a line of people waiting to pay, after Claire did the same at a different register. Tanner made it through his line first and joined Sara back in the parking lot. Sara had moved behind the steering wheel, and so Tanner took the passenger seat.

"Any smoking guns?" Sara asked. "Did she buy the latest copy of Assassins' magazine?"

Tanner smiled. "If the magazine existed, Scallato would be on the cover. We'll stick with her; she bought shaving cream and razors. Maybe Scallato is planning on shaving off his beard."

"Or Claire Newport is shaving her legs, but how much food did she buy?"

"More than she would eat, I'd guess, and several times she grabbed two of everything."

Tanner handed Sara the items he'd bought. There was a roll of duct tape, some first-aid supplies, and several candy bars.

Sara grinned when she saw the candy and tore open the wrapper of one. "These are my favorite; did you know that?"

"That's why I got them."

"Thanks, and why didn't you get those hard candies you sometimes eat?"

"They don't carry them here."

Sara broke off a piece of her candy bar and handed it to Tanner.

"We'll share then."

Tanner took the piece of candy and popped it into his mouth just as Claire Newport came out of the market. They followed Claire home but parked far down the street from her. Both Tanner and Sara used binoculars to watch her. Tanner studied the nurse carefully as she parked in her driveway, then she entered the house through a side door. There was no one in his line of sight, but he could see Claire's lips move, as if she were greeting someone.

"Did you see that?" Sara said. "I think she was talking to someone in the house."

"Yeah, and if it is Scallato, we have to be careful. I've been told by several people that he's as good as I am. If that's true, we can't make a mistake or we'll both wind up dead."

"We'll be careful, but it's not true that he's as good as you. You really are the best assassin that's ever lived. Scallato is going to find that out the hard way."

Tanner nodded. "Damn right."

They drove about the area. Tanner told Sara to stop when he saw that a house around the block from Claire Newport's was for sale. It was an old home and needed paint, and likely a new roof. They stepped from the car and climbed the stairs to stand on the home's front porch. After contacting a realtor, they had an appointment to look at the house that night.

Sara lowered her phone after talking to the real estate agent. "She sounded eager to show it and said that she lived just twenty minutes away."

Tanner looked at his watch. "It's late. Maybe the house is hard to move, and she doesn't want to miss an opportunity to show it."

Sara pulled up the listing on her phone. "It looks like it's set at a very good price for the area."

She clicked on the button for the virtual tour of the home and saw that there were only a few photos. They were enough to tell that the house had been neglected for a long time. All the appliances looked ancient and the walls were covered in faded wallpaper. The home's one saving grace was that it had a balcony that sat off the master bedroom on the second floor. It was a unique feature.

Tanner was looking at the phone over Sara's shoulder.

"I'd say it's a fixer-upper."

"That's an understatement. But the rear of this place is just to the left of the back of Claire Newport's house. Maybe there will be a vantage point we can use to look inside Claire's home."

"That's what I'm hoping," Tanner said.

ON THE OTHER SIDE OF THE BLOCK, CLAIRE NEWPORT sighed as Maurice Scallato ended their kiss. She then saw that their embrace left a smudge of dirt on her white nurse's uniform.

"How do you get so filthy just staying in the house?"

"I was in the basement straightening up," Scallato said. His voice carried a smooth Italian accent although he could speak English without one. However, Claire found the accent to be sexy, and for now he needed to keep her happy.

"Thank you for cleaning up down there, that basement was a mess, but I don't want you to overdo it."

Scallato took Claire in his arms again.

"I'm nearly at a hundred percent thanks to your care. Speaking of which, did you buy the shaving cream?"

"I did, and I can't wait to see what you look like without that scruffy beard."

Scallato smiled. As soon as Claire saw his face he would have to kill her. He pushed that necessity from his mind and turned it to more pleasant things, as he began unzipping Claire's uniform.

She took a step backwards. "I need a shower first; I'm grubby from work."

"We'll shower together while I ask you about your day."

Claire sighed. "I know the routine by heart. No, no one asked me any odd questions, and no, no strange cars are parked outside the house. I also saw no one looking at me in an odd way, and I saw no police cars parked nearby."

Scallato had unzipped the dress and it fell to the floor. "Good girl, now get naked."

Claire did as he said, then unzipped his jeans.

THE REAL ESTATE AGENT TURNED OUT TO BE A YOUNG Hispanic woman who took Tanner and Sara to be a married couple. They were using the surname of Myers, as Tanner carried ID in the name of Thomas Myers.

As they had planned beforehand, Sara kept the realtor occupied with questions about the home while Tanner roamed about. The attic proved to offer a great view of the

side of Claire Newport's home and her driveway, and
Tanner knew they had found a good observation post. He
finished replacing the fold-down stairs that he used to
access the attic, just as Sara and the real estate agent
started up the stairway from the first floor. When they
arrived on the second floor, Tanner was leaning over and
pretending to check out a damaged spindle on the
banister.

The young real estate agent smiled at Tanner and
asked a question. "As you can see, the home would need a
bit of work. Are you handy with tools, Mr. Myers?"

"Yes I am."

"Like a carpenter?"

"I'd be better classified as a mechanic," Tanner said.

AS THEY LEFT THE HOUSE, SARA TOLD THE AGENT THAT
they would think about the home and get back to her.
When they drove away, Tanner headed for the nearest
store where he could get the supplies he would need.

Returning to the home after midnight, Tanner entered
through the ground floor window he'd left unlocked earlier
and walked around to the back door to let Sara in. It took
two trips up the rickety fold-down attic steps, but by one
a.m., Tanner had the observation post set up.

A telephoto lens was pointed at Claire's house and a
scoped rifle was loaded and ready to use. There was a
cooler full of drinks and ice and, fortunately, the home had
running water and the bathrooms could be used. Tanner
had also purchased a pair of sleeping bags since Sara
insisted on helping to keep watch.

By two a.m. she was asleep in her sleeping bag with a
request to be awakened at six. When six a.m. came,

Tanner let her sleep on, but shook her gently as Claire Newport left her house at eight-thirty.

Sara blinked at the morning light, then checked her watch. "Oh, why didn't you wake me? You must be tired."

"I'll catch a few hours later."

Sara yawned, then combed through her hair with her hands. "I could use some coffee."

"So could I."

"I'll go get some from that coffee shop on the corner."

"No, drive a few blocks away. It's possible that Scallato is paying someone at the local store to keep an eye out for us."

"Really? How would he know about me?"

"He probably doesn't know about you, but if he did have a photo of you and passed around copies, he'd be on to us as soon as a call came in."

"It sounds unlikely that he would have a spy at a coffee shop."

"I once tracked down a target that way, and all it cost me was a hundred dollars paid to the clerk. Most people like coffee."

Sara stood and made a face. "I need to brush my teeth, and a shower would be great."

Tanner pointed at a large duffel bag. "There are towels and soap in that bag over there. You shower first while I keep an eye out for the real estate agent. Once we're done, we'll need to wipe the shower stall dry with a towel, just in case the house gets shown."

"All right, but how long are you planning to keep watch here?"

"I'll be going in there tonight if I can confirm Scallato's presence."

"You have a plan?"

"I do, but I'll need your help."

"You'll have it."

"Good, we'll put it in place after the nurse comes home. Scallato will be on the lookout for anything in his environment that's a departure from the norm. You're going to be that departure, but I'll need you to buy a few props too."

"What do you want me to do, knock on the door and pretend to be selling something?"

"No, disguise or not, Scallato might make you. If he did, he'd shoot you without hesitation."

"Then what do you want me to do?"

LATER THAT AFTERNOON, SARA STEPPED OUT ONTO THE balcony of the home they were staying in. Her face was obscured by a large plant she was carrying, and she was wearing a blonde wig and a floppy straw hat. She had her phone blasting music as she moved in and out of the house with more house plants, and soon the railing of the balcony was covered in greenery.

Her project took nearly ten minutes and she did her best to keep her face turned away from Claire Newport's house. When she came back inside and shut the patio door behind her, she sent Tanner a questioning look.

"It worked," Tanner said. "I saw a curtain move in an upstairs window, although I couldn't make out a face."

"That means someone else besides Claire Newport is staying in her home, and that just might be Scallato."

"Right, now we have to get ready for Scallato's reaction."

"Do you think he'll come here himself?"

"No, at this point he's still unsure if there's a threat. He'll send the nurse."

~

TWENTY MINUTES LATER, TANNER WAS PROVEN RIGHT AS Claire Newport deviated from her regular route home to drive down the block behind her house. Sara had removed the For-Sale sign and scattered toys on the lawn, including a tricycle.

As Tanner watched Claire's approach from an upstairs window, he called out to Sara.

"You're on."

Sara donned the blonde wig, pulled the shirttails of her blouse from where they were tucked, and put an angry expression on her face. As she stepped out onto the home's front porch, she tried not to look at Claire's car, which had slowed to study the house. Sara leaned back in the doorway and spoke as if she were chastising a child.

"We'll see how much talking back you do when your father gets home from work, young man, and—No! You stay right in that corner until I tell you differently."

Sara shut the door and muttered under her breath as she began picking up toys from the lawn. After hearing Claire's car drive off, she looked up to confirm it, then headed inside.

Tanner was waiting for her in the living room with a smile on his face. "You should have been an actress."

"I was, if you count high school plays, but do you think Scallato will check on us again?"

"No, and anyway, I'm going in after him tonight. If I wait much longer he may leave and it could take months to track him down again."

"Let me come with you; two guns are better than one."

"No, I'll need you to be my eyes as I approach the house. I plan to enter through a basement window, and while I'm down on my stomach climbing in, it will be good to know that you'll have my back."

"Does that mean you want me to use the rifle?"

"Are you confident enough with it?"

Sara grinned. "I am. I've been practicing back at our lake and I'm getting good if I say so myself. A two-hundred-yard shot will be easy for me."

"Good, now I'd better get some sleep; I've a busy night ahead of me."

"How do you plan to kill Scallato?"

Tanner smiled. "Any way I can."

4
WHAT'S IN A NAME?

AFTER CLAIRE CAME HOME FROM CHECKING OUT THE house where he'd seen Sara, Scallato asked her about what she observed.

"It looked normal enough. There's a woman and a little boy there now, but I overheard her say that the father should be home soon."

"You saw the boy?"

Claire looked surprised by her own answer. "No... I didn't, but there were toys on the lawn, and I saw her hollering back into the house at someone; it sounded as if she were talking to a child."

"What did the woman look like?"

"She was blonde."

"What about her face. I couldn't get a good look at her earlier while she was out on the balcony."

"I only caught a glimpse of her, but she was pretty."

"I thought she'd be. I didn't see her face, but she had a very good figure."

Claire frowned. "Were you checking her out with those binoculars of yours?"

"You sound jealous, don't be. I'm only worried that she might be a cop of some kind."

Scallato gave the situation some thought. All of it sounded normal, but it could also have been staged. He concluded he was being paranoid but decided to move up his departure by one day. Smiling at Claire, he cupped her face in his hands.

"I feel like my old self again, thanks to you."

"You're welcome, but now you need to clear your name so that we can lead a normal life."

"I will, but I want to celebrate. Do you still have wine here?"

"Yes, I have nearly a bottle left, do you want some with dinner?"

"I do," Scallato said.

He had crushed sleeping pills into a fine powder while Claire was at work and planned to slip it into her wine to drug her. He had no feelings for her, but also saw no reason that she should die while fearful. Once she was soundly drugged, and in a stupor, he would kill her painlessly.

He had acquired the pills from the house next door, which he had broken into on a day when he knew no one was at home. Scallato had recently broken into the homes on either side of Claire's house while looking for weapons or other valuables.

For his efforts, he had found the sleeping pills, an excellent knife, two gold coins, and five-hundred dollars in an envelope that was marked with the words, Emergency Cash Stash. The gold coins and the money might not be missed by their former owner for months, or even years, they had been hidden at the bottom of an old dusty box marked, Tax Returns, 1990 – 1995.

Scallato smiled. "Let's eat soon."

Claire gave him a shy look. "Could we shower first...
like yesterday?"

"Ah, I see you have another appetite you'd like to
appease, fine, first we'll make love, then we'll eat."

Claire hugged him as if she'd never let him go and
Scallato realized she had fallen in love with him. He
smiled. She was even dumber than he'd believed her to be.

TANNER LOWERED THE ATTIC STAIRS AND LISTENED
intently. All was quiet, but that had not been the case just
minutes earlier when the real estate agent had returned
with more prospective home buyers. The woman and the
young couple with her had noticed nothing out of place.
Fortunately, no one had been interested in checking out the
second floor or the attic. The wife had taken one look at
the outdated kitchen and asked to move on to the next
house.

"Are they gone?" Sara whispered.

"Yeah, and I doubt she'll be back tonight; it's late
now."

They left the attic and moved into the master bedroom.
Tanner was dressed all in black and wore a long-sleeved
pullover that had a modified hood. The hood covered not
only his head, but his face. It had eye-holes and a strap that
could be tucked under his chin to keep it in place. One
eye-hole was larger than the other to accommodate a night
vision monocle.

They had just finished wiping down the house when
the real estate agent had arrived. Sara's long hair was
tucked under a cap and she was wearing latex gloves. As
unlikely that it was that anyone would ever dust the home
for her prints, it paid to take precautions.

Tanner's hope was to go in unseen, kill swiftly, and exit silently. To accomplish those goals, he carried a gun with a sound suppressor. There was also a knife and the few items he thought he might need to break-in through the basement window.

Sara would keep watch from the darkened balcony with a rifle and a pair of night vision goggles. However, once Tanner entered the home, he was on his own.

Before leaving, Tanner went over the plan with Sara once more, but this time he added new instructions.

"One hour; if I don't return in an hour, take off and don't look back. It will mean that Scallato has killed me and he may wonder if I was staying at this house."

"But what if you get delayed or injured?"

"If I'm only delayed, you'll hear from me again. If I'm injured, Scallato will probably finish me off. But don't think 'What if?' Once that hour is up you get out of here."

Sara nodded, but Tanner could see in her eyes that she wasn't happy about following his instructions.

"Sara, if he's good enough to kill me he's good enough to kill you. I don't want you to die."

Sara reached up and touched him on the cheek while silently cursing the latex gloves she wore. They made the emotion behind the touch seem somehow sterile.

"I don't want you to die either. Go kill that bastard for having the audacity to believe he was ever in your league."

Tanner returned her touch as he laid a gloved hand gently on her cheek. "Let's take some down time after this... together."

Sara arched an eyebrow. "Together in what way?"

"I think that's up to you, Miss Blake."

Sara grinned. "I may surprise you, Mr. Tanner."

They lowered their hands at the same time and Tanner ran a quick check of his weapons before picking up the night vision monocle. As he opened the door of the master bedroom to leave the house, he hesitated. Sara saw a look in his eye that she'd never seen before and wondered what was going through his mind.

"Tanner, is something wrong?"

Another moment passed before he answered her. "Cody Parker, my name is Cody Parker. I figure after all we've been through together that you should at least know my real name."

Surprise filled Sara's face and she mouthed the name quietly as if wanting to see how it fit her mouth. Afterward, she grinned at Tanner.

"It's a pleasure to finally meet you, Mr. Parker."

Tanner met her gaze, grunted, and left the house to go and kill a man who was, from all accounts, every bit as deadly as he was.

Maurice Scallato stared at the rear of the home Tanner was exiting from, while sitting beside a window in Claire Newport's bedroom. Scallato was dressed in black as Tanner was, but he lacked night vision capability or even a proper gun.

The only weapon Claire had in the home was an old .357 magnum that had belonged to her father. It held only six rounds and was cumbersome. Fortunately, he did have a decent knife, and he had honed it to razor sharpness.

Behind him, Claire snored softly. The sleeping pill laced wine had done its job and she should be out for hours. Scallato had already decided to use the knife on her. If he made several delicate cuts in the right places she might sleep through it and bleed out by morning. If Claire had the misfortune to stir awake, he'd simply slit her throat open.

The woman with the plants had bothered Scallato even though he felt assured that it was nothing. Still, the woman was a change in the routine of the neighborhood, and he wasn't happy that her balcony overlooked his hideout. He'd been watching the home, and in particular, the balcony. If he was over there and studying Claire's house, he'd wait until nightfall and slip out onto that balcony for a better view.

He had just decided to end his observation of the home and kill Claire when he saw movement on the balcony. It was subtle, so very subtle, but someone had slipped out of the house and was pointing something through the spindles of the left railing.

A rifle barrel? Scallato thought, although he couldn't be certain. In any event, everything had just changed. *Tanner? Is it possible the man has tracked me down?*

Scallato left Claire alive as he headed for the basement. He would have to return later to torture her and find out if she had betrayed him, and if so, if he had others to watch out for. In any event, the person on the balcony had to die first, and oh, how he hoped it was Tanner up there.

Tanner's name had been mentioned recently whenever anyone in the know spoke of the world's greatest assassins. Scallato couldn't abide that. He was the best, always had been and always would be. Once he killed Tanner, that fact would be plain to see.

Scallato entered the basement and moved over to a back corner where an old washing machine sat. The appliance hadn't worked in years and should have been hauled away, but Scallato was grateful it hadn't been. It covered the hole that led to his tunnel. Claire's observation that Scallato was often dirty was correct, for while she was at the hospital, he spent his time digging an emergency exit. The work had gone slowly at first, but as the weeks passed, his strength returned. Scallato had found the digging and the hauling away of the dirt to be great exercise.

The tunnel was only wide enough to crawl through and had a length of just over a hundred feet. The other end of it would place him in a back corner of a neighbor's shed. From there, he could easily make his way to the other side of the block and to the house with the balcony.

Scallato crawled headfirst into the hole. Before going deeper in the tunnel, he hooked his right foot around a strap he had fastened to the washer. The strap was made from an old belt he had found in Claire's closet, and it helped him to pull the washing machine back in place over the hole, concealing his tunnel entrance.

With that done, Scallato crawled forward. A lesser man would have been psychologically scarred by the time Scallato had spent trapped beneath rubble in the aftermath of a recent earthquake. But Maurice Scallato was several notches above most men in guts and temperament. As he slithered through the tunnel, the thought of being trapped beneath the earth again never entered his mind. His thoughts were on the objective that lay ahead. He was going to find out who was on that balcony, then, he was going to kill them.

THE ONE-HOUR TIME LIMIT THAT TANNER HAD SPOKEN OF to Sara was needed to ensure it was safe to proceed into the house. Maurice Scallato had been living in the area for weeks and had plenty of time to enhance his security. He had done so, and Tanner came across two mirrors that had been attached strategically to telephone poles. If glimpsed at through a pair of binoculars from Claire Newport's windows, the mirrors would allow Scallato a view around corners. It was a trick Tanner had used in the past and it reminded him that Scallato was not to be taken lightly.

When he finally made it into the home's backyard, he looked up and saw Sara. She was not much more than a greenish outline in the monocular, but he was glad to see that she was all right. Using the house as an observation post had been a calculated risk, but it appeared to be working out.

Two steps later, Tanner detected a trip line and avoided it. The line was high enough off the ground so that a small animal wouldn't trigger it, and so thin that it was barely visible. If not for the night vision device he wore, Tanner was certain he would have missed seeing it. He smiled. Scallato was good, very good. It would be a pleasure to kill someone who was as hard to kill as he was. It made him understand Scallato's pattern of murdering anyone who he deemed competition. Most people died easily, but a fellow assassin was a true challenge.

Tanner moved toward the front of the home to avoid more tripwires, then lowered himself to the ground and crawled toward a basement window. It was time to enter the house.

SARA WATCHED TANNER'S ERRATIC MOVEMENTS ACROSS THE yard and understood that he was avoiding traps set by Scallato. That was both good and bad. Good, because it meant that the Sicilian assassin was confirmed as being inside, and bad, because it meant that the Sicilian assassin was confirmed as being inside.

Tanner would kill Scallato. Sara never doubted that outcome for an instant. However, she did fear that Scallato might not expire easily, and that would mean that Tanner could be gravely injured.

She shook her head slightly as she marveled at her feelings for Tanner. She had once hated the man with a white-hot passion and wanted only his death. Now, if he were to die, Sara knew it would devastate her, and she wondered what the future held for them.

Those were the thoughts dancing through her mind when Scallato came up behind her, placed his knife to her throat, and sliced into her.

5

WHAT LIGHT THROUGH YONDER WINDOW BREAKS

Right about the time that Scallato was emerging from his makeshift tunnel, Claire Newport awoke with an incredible urge to pee. She was woozy and assumed it was the wine, but it was the sleeping pills Scallato had mixed with her drink. Claire had consumed enough of the drug to keep the average person unconscious until noon, but she was not most people.

Claire had once been addicted to the drug, Triazolam, a sedative. The over the counter sleeping pills that Scallato used on her weren't enough to overcome the resistance to such drugs that Claire had acquired.

After stumbling to and from the bathroom, Claire realized that Scallato wasn't in bed. When she went to look for him, she couldn't find him anywhere, although all the doors and windows were still locked from the inside.

"Maurice? Where are you?"

Puzzled, Claire wandered around in her robe and slippers while still in a dazed state from the sleeping medication in her system. Then, she saw him from the back window in her kitchen. A light had come on high up and at the rear of that house she had visited earlier.

The light was bright enough to make out two individuals, one was Scallato, while the other was the woman she had seen earlier. From Claire's vantage point, it looked as if Scallato was hugging her from behind. Claire's eyes narrowed in rage as jealousy filled her heart. She grabbed her keys off the hook by the side door and headed for her car, determined to catch Scallato in the act of cheating on her.

~

SCALLATO CURSED LOUDLY AS THE LIGHT CAME ON AND HE saw spots before his eyes.

Sara had managed to turn on the flashlight she had hanging from a belt in the hope that it might warn Tanner of the danger. As for herself, she was certain she would soon be dead, as she believed her throat had been slit open. She was half-right, for although Scallato had cut her, his blade hadn't bitten deeply enough to end her life.

Scallato hissed. "Stupid bitch," and while keeping his knife at her throat, Scallato dragged her backwards into the house and tossed her on the floor of the empty master bedroom. Before Sara could react, he had removed the gun from the holster on her hip. The sniper rifle was still out on the balcony, but Scallato dared not risk going back for it. If Tanner had seen that light come on, he would be ready to shoot.

"You're working with Tanner?" Scallato asked Sara. She remained silent as she explored her wound with her fingers. Her knit hat had come loose, and her long dark hair framed a face that was full of relief.

Scallato spoke to Sara while examining her gun. The

gun was a modified Glock with a silencer attached. It was a much nicer weapon than the clumsy revolver Scallato had taken from Claire Newport's house. That weapon was tucked at the small of his back in his waistband.

"Talk to me, woman, or I'll kill you right now."

"Yes, I'm with Tanner, and he's going to kill you."

"I think not."

Scallato smiled as he pulled Sara up off the floor by her hair. That was a mistake, and she took his legs out from under him with a sweep kick. Scallato was on his back as Sara readied a foot to kick him in the testicles. However, her foot froze in midair when she saw that Scallato was pointing her own gun at her.

He sprang to his feet with a grunt and let loose a small chuckle. "I see you're not without skills, but if you strike me again, I will kill you."

Sara said nothing, but she didn't fight back as Scallato grabbed her by the collar and held her in front of him. He hustled her downstairs and pressed his back against the wall beside the kitchen doorway. That allowed him a view of the street out front, the stairs, and the rear door in the kitchen. If he were fired upon, Sara would likely be struck first, and visibility was poor in the darkened house.

"I hope Tanner has feelings for you, otherwise, you'll make a poor shield."

TANNER HAD BEEN ENTERING THE BASEMENT THROUGH A window as Claire was walking out her side door. When he heard her attempt to start her car, he thought it was Scallato trying to flee. In any event, the car wouldn't start, as Tanner had disabled it.

Moving with care, Tanner went upstairs and into the

living room. A look out the window showed the car door sitting open. Tanner moved outside, while thinking that Scallato was taking off on foot, but, to his surprise, Claire Newport was running along in bedroom slippers. Tanner watched her, and when she turned the nearby corner, he realized where she might be headed.

She must have awakened, found Scallato gone, and remembered his interest in the house on the other side of the block. Tanner took out his phone as he headed toward the rear of the home. Sara had to be warned.

SARA NIBBLED AT HER BOTTOM LIP AS SHE FELT HER PHONE vibrate. She wouldn't let herself be used as a pawn in Scallato's quest to kill Tanner, but she seemed helpless to change that. When she didn't answer the phone, Tanner would be certain to return to check on her.

"That's him, isn't it?" Scallato said. "Good, when you don't answer he'll grow curious, and once I kill him, you're dead too."

Scallato stared into the kitchen to eye the back door, as Sara saw movement outside. Someone was approaching the front of the house on foot. Scallato turned back around, then gestured at the stairs with the gun.

"My guess is that Tanner will climb up onto the balcony the way I did. What do you think?"

Sara pretended to look toward the stairs, but her gaze drifted to the front door. Scallato had been waiting for her eyes to betray her and he shifted their combined weight so that they were facing the front door. The sound of footsteps followed, faint, but audible, and Sara felt Scallato stiffen with anticipation.

"Get down Tanner!" Sara shouted.

Scallato tossed her aside and fired half a dozen silenced shots at the front door. One of the shots blew apart the lock while the others hit the front door in a cross pattern that should assure a strike. They did, and when the door swung open on its own, Claire Newport stood in the threshold on a pair of wobbly legs with the lower half of her right arm dripping blood. The pain of her wound had yet to reach her drugged brain and Claire fell to her knees soundlessly with a puzzled expression on her face.

"Damn you, woman!" Scallato bellowed, then he spun about looking for Tanner to appear. When he realized that Tanner was nowhere in sight, he figured to cut his losses and leave the scene.

Scallato aimed at Sara's forehead. "I hope your death grieves him."

The sound of running footsteps came from upstairs and Scallato shifted his gunsight that way. Sara used the distraction to roll into Scallato and knock him off balance. He nearly fell on top of her, but then managed to only go down on one knee.

SCALLATO FELT A TUGGING SENSATION AT HIS BACK AND realized what was happening. Sara had claimed the .357 he had tucked into his waistband. Still fearing that Tanner would appear at the top of the stairs, Scallato leapt sideways and landed near Claire. He held her up as a shield in front of him just as Tanner dived into the upstairs hallway.

SARA STOOD AND HELD THE BIG GUN IN BOTH HANDS BUT didn't fire for fear of hitting Claire, when she looked up, she saw Tanner taking aim with the sniper rifle. Scallato sent two slugs toward Tanner's position before leaping out through the open doorway. Claire, still oblivious to her wound, stood to follow after him. That was a mistake. The moment she walked through the door her head was blown apart from a shot fired by Scallato.

Sara gasped, then nearly shrieked as an arm snaked around her waist. It was Tanner, and he drove her down flat on the floor an instant before a string of bullets perforated the wall and passed through the spot where she'd been standing.

Sara raised her gun up to return fire, but Tanner stopped her.

"He's not where he fired from, and your rounds could travel into the houses across the street."

"What should we do?"

"We'll leave out the back and go to the nurse's house."

"What about Scallato?"

"He's gone. By my count, he has only three rounds left and there are two of us, with police on the way to the scene. His best bet is to go into hiding and wait for another chance at—" Tanner stopped talking as he noticed Sara's bloody neck. "How bad is that cut?"

"It stings like hell, but it's superficial."

"Another reason to kill him," Tanner said.

Sara was headed toward the rear exit, but Tanner told her to wait a moment. There was something he needed to do. The previous owners of the home had left their old curtains hanging on the windows, and Tanner tore a few of them down.

"Sara, were you bleeding when you were upstairs?"

"Um, yes, Scallato cut me on the balcony."

Tanner raced upstairs with Sara following and set one of the curtains on fire.

"What are you doing, Tanner?"

"Hopefully, a fire will erase all traces of your blood, and DNA."

After starting more fires in strategic places, they left the house cautiously through the back door. Once outside, they headed for the rear fence. They were going to the home of the newly deceased Claire Newport, an angel of mercy slain by a master of death.

6

LA CASA DI PAPÁ

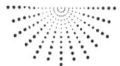

Scallato was furious at himself for having failed to kill Tanner and worried by the fact that the man had tracked him down. Worst of all, Tanner and the woman had seen his face, although he still wore the beard and was sporting a knit cap.

Tanner was good, that was certain, and Scallato understood that he'd have to engage the man again someday. After leaving the vacant home after the shootout, Scallato moved through the neighborhood stealthily, while looking for a car to steal.

When he came across a ten-speed bike left unchained on a porch, he settled for it and rode out of the area. Miles later, he found a car with the keys left inside that was in the parking lot of a bar. He drove that into Nevada, where he stole a second vehicle and headed for Las Vegas. The second car also had a cell phone plugged into a charger. Scallato used it to call a contact who could get him out of the country. It was the same person he had spared in an alleyway nearly two decades earlier.

"You survived Tanner? There aren't many who can say that."

"He's the only one who's ever survived me… him and the woman."

"Her name is Sara Blake. She's an ex-FBI agent and formidable in her own right. She also survived Tanner."

"And now they're lovers?"

"Possibly, or at the very least, allies."

"Meet me in Las Vegas; we need to talk in person."

"As you say, and I'll make those travel arrangements the usual way, but Maurice, Tanner won't stop coming for you."

"I know that, and I won't stop coming for him either, but I'll choose the when and the where."

"As you say, I only hope he allows you that luxury."

AFTER THE SHOOTOUT, TANNER AND SARA WENT TO THE home of Claire Newport. It took Tanner only a few minutes of searching to uncover the tunnel Scallato had dug by hand. As he went over the home, Sara kept watch, but Tanner believed Scallato was in the wind. He also thought that it would be hours before Claire Newport's body was identified, since she was dressed in only her robe and slippers.

Outside, there was a red glow at the rear of the house from the blaze Tanner had set, along with all the emergency vehicles that had responded to the vacant home. It gave the look of a false dawn on the horizon.

Tanner held up a black backpack. "Scallato was planning to return. He left this here filled with spare clothes by the opening to his tunnel."

Sara pointed at the backpack.

"I don't suppose there are any clues in there to tell us where he went."

"No, but my guess is he won't pop up again for a long while. I had my shot at him and I blew it. Now, he can just sit back and bide his time."

"But he won't get the chance to do that, will he?"

"He's now as much a target as any contract I've ever taken, and a Tanner doesn't fail. Scallato will learn that the hard way."

They left the town of Robbinsville by a circuitous route and switched vehicles at a branch of the car rental agency they used. It was doubtful that Scallato had time to conceal a tracker on their car, but still possible.

By mid-morning they had eaten and found a motel to crash in. To Tanner's surprise, when he left his room at five p.m., Sara was already up and had left a note for him in the car.

Meet me at the bar across the street.

Tanner did as the note said and found Sara politely turning down the advances of a salesman type in a good suit. The man was handsome, but the wrinkles around his eyes gave the lie to his dyed dark hair, and on his left hand was a turquoise pinkie ring.

When Sara told her admirer that her friend was joining her, the man took one look at Tanner's steely gaze and swallowed hard.

"It was nice to meet you," he told Sara, then hurried off.

"That was Jack Kauffman. He was the number two carpet salesman in the northwest last year," Sara said.

"Good for him," Tanner said.

After Tanner had a beer, they decided to order an early dinner and discuss their options. When Sara suggested that they contact Jacques Durand for additional help, Tanner agreed that it might be their best bet, since Durand seemed well connected.

"But Durand and his people won't help us track down Scallato for free; they'll want something in return."

"A hit?"

"Likely, and I'll do it if Durand can come up with real intel on Scallato's whereabouts."

"I think there's a good chance that Scallato will go home to Sicily," Sara said.

"So do I, but there are over five million people there, and for all we know, Scallato could be anywhere."

∾

TWO DAYS LATER. RAGUSO, SICILY, POPULATION: 2,300

MAURICE SCALLATO BREATHED IN THE SWEET AIR OF HIS homeland as he took in the sights and the sounds of the old fishing dock. Feeling eyes upon his back, Scallato turned to find a man staring at him.

It was the local priest. Scallato sent him a wave. In the town of Raguso, Scallato was known by the name of Maurice Rizzo. The priest, Father Rossetti, sent Scallato a smile and headed toward him. He was without doubt coming over to pester Scallato about attending church on Sunday, or perhaps to ask for a charitable donation.

When the priest was stopped by a pair of old women, Scallato left the area quickly. Raguso was small, and so Scallato reached the center of town in less than a mile. He had been gone longer than he'd intended, but the picturesque town looked no different.

That opinion changed when he saw a shopkeeper

hand over an envelope to a fat man Scallato had never seen before. The extortion of business owners was practically a tradition in Raguso, but Scallato noticed that the shopkeeper looked defeated. Perhaps there was someone new running the local mob and they were bleeding the merchants dry. That was not good business, nor was it good for the town. Scallato grew curious enough to follow the thug as he went along his collection route.

The fat man was soon joined by two partners. One was very tall and rough looking, while the other was short and somewhat handsome. Despite their differences, if Scallato had to guess, he'd say that they were brothers.

As the three men were headed inside the fish market, a woman was exiting holding a package of saltwater bass. She was a good-looking woman in her thirties. Two of the brothers, the fat one and the tall one, spoke to her while leering at her legs.

When the tall brute reached out to touch the woman's luxurious raven hair, she smacked him across the face with her bundle of fish. That made the men laugh, and after cursing at them, the woman went on her way.

Scallato had seen enough of the men and decided to follow the woman home. He enjoyed watching her walk, as her shapely hips swayed beneath her dress. She lived on the outskirts of town in a house that was larger than most in the area. It was secluded and peaceful, with woodland on three sides and a steep cliff at its rear that was over a hundred feet high.

Scallato knew that if the woman screamed, no one would hear her. After dropping his duffel bag behind a tree, he came up on the woman fast. She had been opening the door and Scallato grabbed her about the waist from behind, causing the packet of fish to fall to the floor. A spirited woman, she produced a blade even as she let out a cry of surprise.

Scallato disarmed her with ease while kicking the door shut with his foot. An instant later he had her bent over the kitchen table as his right hand held her struggling form and his left hand caressed her breasts.

The hate was visible in the woman's eyes as she turned her head to glare at him. The vehemence in her gaze softened immediately and a laugh escape her.

"Maurice, you animal."

"Is that any way to speak to your husband?"

Scallato loosened his grip and his wife, Maria, turned around to embrace him. After a long kiss, Maria took a step back to study him.

"Oh, look how thin you are, and there's a scar on your chin."

"I had a bit of difficulty due to an earthquake."

"An earthquake?"

"I survived. I will always survive."

Maria took her husband by the hand and moved toward the bedroom. "The children won't be home for another two hours."

"How is my son?"

"Antonio is fine, but he misses you, as does Anna, and yesterday was her birthday."

"Really? I hope you brought a gift for her."

"I bought her a few gifts, but having you home again will be the best present, Anna adores you."

"And how do you feel about me?"

Maria smiled as she began unzipping her dress. "You're about to find out."

7

A DEAL FOR A KILL

JACQUES DURAND SENT SARA A SMILE EVEN AS HIS EYES studied Tanner.

The ex-Interpol agent turned true crime writer was in his fifties, had wavy brown hair, and a pair of sleepy eyes. The eyes belied Durand's true nature. He was as sharp as they came.

Before the meeting, Tanner had asked Sara to describe Durand's character and Sara said she would have to classify the man as cool.

"He reminds me of you in that way, Tanner, he seems imperturbable."

"Maybe he knows something we don't."

"You don't think we should trust him?"

"Just don't let your guard down," Tanner had said.

THE MEETING TOOK PLACE IN AN UPSCALE BAR IN BERLIN, Germany, where Sara and Tanner had flown to meet up with Durand. Tanner had chosen the bar's location after visiting it earlier and determining several ways to escape if things went bad. The bar was in an old brick building, while the meeting took place in a back booth.

Before taking a seat, Durand had removed his suit jacket as a way of showing Tanner that he wasn't carrying a weapon. When Tanner mentioned the small gun hidden away on the inside of Durand's boot, the Frenchman's upper lip twitched.

"You have a keen eye, Tanner. The gun and holster are colored cobalt blue to match my socks. I've even had it missed during a frisk once."

"What sort of gun is it, a Beretta Nano?"

"Correct."

Never much of one for chitchat, Tanner got right down to business after their drinks came.

"I need a line on Maurice Scallato's whereabouts. Can you help me with that, Durand?"

"Possibly, but why don't we order something to eat and talk things over?"

"Either you can help, or you can't, which is it?"

Durand straightened his back and glared at Tanner. "I know you're an American, Tanner, but that's no reason to be so brusque." Durand smiled at Sara. "I enjoy Miss Blake's company and do not wish it to end too soon."

Tanner leaned forward and spoke in a low voice, so that his words wouldn't carry. Although there was a soft murmur in the bar and music played over a sound system, it was always best to discuss murder in whispers.

"If you have info on Scallato you'll want something for it. That something will be a hit on a difficult target. Tell me who you want dead and I'll kill them, but I'll want a hard lead on Scallato's whereabouts in return."

When Tanner leaned back in his seat, Durand made a sniffing sound. "You have no class, Tanner. I wonder if you're up to killing Maurice Scallato. Scallato is truly the best assassin that's ever lived."

Tanner slid out of the booth. "You're wasting my time."

Sara looked up at Tanner and then over at Durand. "Jacques, can you help us?"

Durand raised an eyebrow. "You've involved yourself in this, Sara? That could prove fatal if Scallato kills Tanner."

"I know that, which means I have nothing to worry about. Now please, let's talk business."

Durand gestured for Tanner to sit again. Tanner continued to stand, and Durand sneered at him before speaking. "I know people and still have many contacts in law enforcement circles. Perhaps something can be worked out."

"You're lying."

"About my contacts?"

"You're lying about who you are. You claim to be retired from Interpol and just a writer with some clout, but you're more than that."

Sara had been looking at Tanner, but her gaze turned to Durand. "Jacques, is Tanner right?"

Durand's face displayed nothing, but then, a smile played at the corners of his mouth.

"Maybe you're sharper than you look, Tanner. Yes, I am still active, but not with Interpol. The organization I head is, what you would call… unconventional."

"Which is why you're fighting fire with fire," Tanner said. "Or in this case, pitting hit man against hit man."

"Yes, and the winner will be eligible for future contracts, but I only hire the best."

"To face off against Scallato I have to find him first. Can you help me with that?"

"We don't know the whereabouts of Scallato, but we do know where he might someday show up."

"Explain that," Tanner said, as he once again took a seat.

"The whereabouts of Maurice Scallato's father, Carlo Scallato, has recently been discovered. The old man is in an Italian nursing home under an alias. It's believed that the younger Scallato will come to visit the old man someday."

"The nursing home is under surveillance?"

"Unfortunately, no, the people at the top refused to allocate the resources needed for full-time surveillance."

"So, Scallato could have come and gone from there already?"

"Yes, but if so, it is likely that he will return someday, no?"

Tanner frowned. "Why is the old man in the nursing home?"

"He suffers from dementia, which I believe is in its early stages."

"If his dementia isn't late-stage, then he may still be aware enough to give me a lead on his son."

Durand looked doubtful. "Why would the old bastard help you?"

"He likely won't, but if I can get him to talking, something may slip out."

"Possibly, so what do you say, do we have a deal?"

"It's a good lead, but Scallato might not show up for months."

Durand made a small shrugging motion.

"Or, he could be there when you arrive."

Tanner turned to look at Sara. "What do you think?"

"It's a long shot, but it's better than nothing."

Tanner looked down at the table for a moment as he

considered things. When he looked up, he stared at Durand.

"I want the name of that nursing home. Who do I have to kill to get it?"

THE TARGET WAS AN ALGERIAN TERRORIST NAMED MALEK Kalah.

Kalah was living in Berlin and was unofficially under the protection of Germany's Federal Intelligence Service. The Germans made a deal with Kalah, in which he secretly betrayed several fellow terrorists in exchange for his freedom. Malek Kalah rarely left his brick townhouse and was protected by four bodyguards.

Two attempts had been made on Kalah's life by Durand's people and both failed. It was rumored that he had a safe room that could withstand an assault by a tank. His bodyguards were well-trained and had killed both assassins before they ever reached their boss, Malek Kalah. The assassins sent to kill Kalah were considered to have been two of the best, and one had often been compared to the late elite assassin, Lars Gruber.

It was their failure that prompted Durand to approach Tanner by way of Sara. Durand's people had become aware that Scallato was out to kill Tanner to prove his superiority. In any event, the two appeared to be the best assassins on the planet, although Scallato would work for anyone who paid, regardless of the target.

Still, if Scallato triumphed over Tanner, Durand would offer him future contracts when the need arose. In Durand's trade, sometimes you had to work with a devil to get things done.

Tanner asked for and received details about the brick townhouse and the security set-up. He also had profiles of the four bodyguards and Kalah.

Sara was reading her copy of the reports about the bodyguards, while Tanner read a report about Kalah. When Sara finished reading about the guards, she wore a worried look.

"These aren't your average bodyguards, Tanner. They're a four-man team that's been together for nine years and have never lost a client. Before starting their security company, they met while working as mercenaries in Africa. While there, they successfully defeated the guardsmen of a warlord when the odds against them were twenty-to-one."

"The fact that they're a tightknit team is bad news for them; it means I can't leave any of them alive or they would seek revenge."

"Battling them head-on will alert Kalah and he'll hide in his safe room. Do you have a way to prevent that?"

Tanner held up the profile of Kalah he'd been reading. "Yeah, I think I might even know a way to lure him out of his building."

Malek Kalah and his mother had moved to the UK from Algeria when he was only thirteen. Young Malek began getting into trouble immediately. By the time he was fifteen he was running a street gang that specialized in snatch & grab robberies along with muggings of tourists.

Malek Kalah held hatred for the homeless, and his gang and he would often beat any vagrants they saw on the street. At nineteen, Kalah crossed the line into murder when he set a homeless man on fire.

He'd been wearing his gang colors and was caught on the CCTV cameras committing the vile act. His face hadn't been captured, but his distinct jacket was identified, and the cops brought him in for questioning.

Kalah's lawyer advised Kalah to say nothing and Kalah did just that. Once he was released on bail, Kalah talked one of the local kids into taking the fall for him. The other boy, an English punk named Johnny Whitman, had only been fifteen and wanted to prove that he had what it took to be a gang member. Although he was tried as an adult, Kalah's lawyer managed to get Whitman a lenient six-year sentence that would see him set free on his twenty-first birthday.

During Whitman's six-year sentence, Kalah had grown more sophisticated and opened a nightclub. He had also become radicalized and entered the drug trade.

Johnny Whitman, the boy who'd taken the fall for Kalah had grown sadder, but wiser, and thought that Kalah had used him. Innocent or not, Whitman had to finish out his sentence. While passing his best years away in prison, the boy had come to hate Kalah. However, Whitman made the mistake of talking too much. Kalah learned from an ex-con that Whitman was planning on seeking revenge as soon as he was released.

When that day arrived, Johnny Whitman took a bus into London with the intention of hunting down Kalah. Instead, he was accosted by three men and tossed into the rear of a van. The next thing Johnny Whitman knew, he had his hands bound behind his back and was having a hood placed over his head. Rough hands moved over his body as if he were being frisked, and then he felt something wet splash over him.

When the odor of gasoline reached Whitman's nose, he began bucking wildly upon the floor of the van to get free. His thrashing ended when a sap struck the back of his head. Kalah didn't have Whitman killed; he had other plans for him.

Whitman awoke in an alleyway next to the smoldering remains of a homeless man. His wrists were unbound, and although his head throbbed, he was still able to make it to his feet and stumble out of the alleyway.

The police picked him up less than an hour later as he sat on a park bench. His clothing stunk of gasoline and in his back pocket was an old Swiss army knife with initials carved into its handle. The knife was later identified by other homeless citizens as having been the property of the man who had been burned alive in the alleyway.

Whitman shouted his innocence while attempting to implicate Kalah. However, since he'd already served a sentence for a similar crime, and given the evidence against him, he was sent to a maximum-security prison. Whitman later died during a foolish escape attempt. When Kalah learned Whitman had died, he laughed and called the dead man a born loser.

"How will you use Kalah's hatred of homeless people against him?" Sara asked.

She and Tanner were eating at an outdoor café that seemed to be a favorite of the college crowd. Sara was eating a dish called Eintopf, a German stew, while Tanner was having Bratwurst with a double side of German sauerkraut. Both were drinking strong German beer with their meal. Tanner took notice that Sara was keeping up with him as they ordered their fourth round.

"I'm going to camp out in view of Kalah's building and pretend that I'm homeless. If I'm annoying enough, he might feel the need to confront me himself."

"Maybe, but what if he sends his guards out to harass you instead?"

Tanner smiled. "I've a plan in mind for that too."

Loud laughter erupted from a nearby table. It was followed by an exchange of German between two young couples.

"My German isn't good enough to keep up with them. What were they laughing at?" Sara asked Tanner, who was fluent in many languages.

"They were talking about a friend who fainted in the delivery room. It was a boy by the way, 7 pounds, 9 ounces."

Sara smiled, then asked a question. "Have you ever thought of having children?"

"My lifestyle isn't exactly of the domestic variety."

"Were any of the previous Tanner's father and son?"

"No, and it's amazing that the Scallatos were able to keep passing down the skills. Not everyone can kill, and far less can do it well and while under pressure."

"And will there be a Tanner Eight someday?"

"If I live long enough and find the right man to train, but what about you? Do you want children?"

Sara gave it some thought and nodded. "Yes, someday, I think I would like to have a daughter."

"Nadya had a daughter. She and Romeo named her Florentina, that was the name of Romeo's mother."

Sara slapped Tanner on the arm. "Why didn't you tell me she had the baby?"

"I just did, and I'm surprised you care so much."

"I like Nadya, and Romeo. Will you be going to see the baby?"

"I will, as soon as I deal with Scallato."

"Give them both my love, and bring back pictures, Uncle Tanner."

Tanner stared at Sara as a thought occurred to him. "When I go to visit them, why don't you come with me?"

"Are you serious?"

"Yeah, and it will also give you a chance to meet my mentor, Tanner Six."

Sara said nothing for a moment, but then she reached over and took Tanner's left hand, which was resting on the table.

"I'm glad we survived each other."

Tanner nodded in agreement, then wondered what the future would bring.

8

LIKE FATHER, LIKE SON

As he stood beside the breakfast table, Antonio Rizzo, who was actually Antonio Scallato, made a muscle with his right arm.

The thirteen-year-old was tall for his age and worked hard to get stronger. His father, Maurice Scallato, smiled with approval at his son's biceps. The boy had grown several inches since Scallato had last seen him and Scallato decided that Antonio was ready to move to the next level. That would entail additional training… as well as an introduction into manhood.

"You'll be as tall as I am someday, Antonio, but don't get too bulky, there are times you might need to fit into tight spaces."

"I know, Patri, but I wanted you to see that I'm still doing the exercises you taught me."

"That's good, but while I'm home we'll work on your shooting skills."

Scallato's wife, Maria, turned her head to look at her husband. She was standing at the kitchen counter and spreading honey on the croissants they would have for breakfast, along with cereal.

"We've been practicing with the rifle while you were gone. Antonio has gotten better at long distance shooting."

Scallato sent her a mock frown. "You've been teaching my son to shoot?"

"Of course, if we waited for you to do it, he'd barely know anything."

Scallato sighed. "I know I haven't been around much lately, but that will change soon."

"Soon? Does that mean you'll be leaving again?"

"Just a short trip to Italy to speak with a contact," Scallato said. He then looked over at his son. "I'll be leaving in a day or two and I'll take Antonio with me. We'll spend some time together."

After the family ate breakfast and the children went off to school, Scallato walked out to the large shed on the property. In his identity of Maurice Rizzo, Scallato professed to work as a carpenter. His absences were accounted for by claims that he traveled to America to do well-paying union work.

The inside of the shed looked like a carpentry shop. There were two table saws, a lathe, a drill, and other tools and assorted lumber, plus screws and nails. Hidden away within the walls and beneath the benches was an arsenal and thousands of rounds of ammunition. Despite the concealed weaponry, Scallato was a skilled carpenter, and the floor of the shop was covered in sawdust from a table he'd been working on.

Scallato's wife and son knew who he was, and that he was an assassin, but they had yet to clue in six-year-old Anna. The girl was smart, and had begun to ask questions, so she would be brought into the loop soon. If the child talked, or if the Scallato family became compromised in another way, they would have to flee their home and start over.

That had never happened to a Scallato. Keeping secrets was in the blood, as was the art of assassination. Young Antonio was being groomed to succeed his father, while his sister Anna would be told what a great honor and tradition she upheld by remaining silent. For her reward, Anna would never have to worry about money. And, knowing something that no one else knew came with its own perverse pleasure.

Maurice Scallato's two older sisters settled in the UK and receive a generous monthly check from accounts their father set up decades earlier. The downside is that they can never have normal contact with the rest of the family. That is of little consequence, since Maurice Scallato cares nothing about them, and his sisters never liked him.

MARIA KNOCKED ON THE DOOR OF THE SHED AT MID-morning and was let inside by Scallato, after he confirmed that she was alone by checking the camera feed on his phone.

He'd completed his table project and had been in the middle of cleaning his rifles and shotguns. They were laid out on a workbench.

"Who are those three fools I saw harassing you the other day?" Scallato asked his wife.

Anger filled Maria's eyes. "You saw that and did nothing?"

"Of course I did nothing. As Maurice Rizzo, the simple carpenter, I would have had to take a beating if I attempted to defend your honor in public. Otherwise, I would have had to reveal the fact that I had the skills to defeat three men. I will deal with them in private, as myself."

The ire left Maria's eyes as she nodded in understanding. After taking a seat on a wooden stool, she spoke. "Their last name is Martello, but I don't know any of their first names. Everyone just calls them the fat one, the tall one, and the short one. The fat one and the tall one are mean and stupid, it's the short one that is their leader."

"Did they kill old man Alleganti?"

"No, he just died, and you know his sons were worthless. Alleganti's sons were either run off or killed, but now the Martellos run the town."

Scallato thought about that and asked a question. "Did you write your brother about it?"

Maria made a face. "I did, he said that you would handle it. He doesn't want to get his hands dirty, but I bet you that he'll send some of his people here to take the Martellos' place once you kill them."

"Yes, that sounds like Bruno."

BRUNO ALLENDE WAS MARIA'S BROTHER. LIKE HIS FATHER before him, he worked for Emilio Degussa, who ran the mob in Genoa. The Scallato's and the Allende's had joined in marriage several times over the last two-hundred years, and Maria's marriage to Maurice Scallato had been an arranged one. Many years earlier, fourteen-year-old Maurice had balked at meeting his future bride, who was also fourteen. He was a Scallato, he reminded his father, and Scallato's did as they pleased.

"A wife will be good for you. She will help you to maintain a cover identity," Carlo Scallato told his son.

"What does she look like?"

"I don't know, but her mother was a handsome woman."

"Handsome?"

"It's an expression, it means she's good looking."

"Men are handsome, not women."

"You'll do as you're told, boy, now be quiet."

Young Maurice sulked the rest of the trip and wondered just how ugly this girl named Maria Allende would be. To his shock and delight, young Maria was not only beautiful, but looked old enough to pass for sixteen, as he himself did.

The shy girl blushed as Maurice took her hand, an act that upset their chaperones, who were two of Maria's great aunts. Maurice ignored the "Tut-tuts" of the old women and stared into Maria's blue eyes.

"I am Maurice Scallato."

"My name is Maria."

"You are very beautiful, Maria, and I'm told that you will be my wife someday."

Maria smiled as her shyness left her. She was an exceptional beauty and she knew it.

"Do you like what you see, Maurice?"

In answer, Maurice pulled Maria along by the hand and headed for his father's car. Maria hesitated only for a moment before jumping into the seat beside him, then the two of them drove off. It was scandalous behavior and caused a temporary rift between the two families. That rift healed when Maurice and Maria married at eighteen.

MARIA REASSEMBLED ONE OF THE RIFLES AS SHE SPOKE TO her husband.

"My brother isn't the reason you're going to Italy, is he?"

"No, Bruno and I are to have no direct contact, remember? Besides, I'm not going to be in Genoa. I'm going to Rome to speak to my pet cop."

"I don't like it when you deal with that coward."

"Why?"

"You can't trust a coward."

"I can, because that coward knows that to cross me would mean death."

"You won't be taking Antonio along, will you?"

"Of course not, woman, but the boy needs to see more of city life; he's nearly a man now."

"Your son or not, he's still a boy, Maurice."

Scallato said nothing to that, but maturing Antonio was a part of why they were taking the trip.

Maria left her stool and walked over to take Scallato in her arms.

"This man, Tanner, he still must be dealt with, yes?"

"Yes, and he has a woman with him that I intend to kill as well."

"A woman?"

"An American woman, likely a lover of Tanner's. I'm hoping that my pet cop will give me more details about her."

"Does that mean you'll be leaving soon to take care of Tanner and the woman?"

"There's no rush. Tanner can't find me here."

"Are you certain? The man seems to be capable of surprising you."

"He was lucky, Maria."

"And what if he's lucky again, hmm?"

Scallato sighed as he saw her point. "I'll deal with Tanner soon."

Maria kissed her husband. "No one is better than you, Maurice. Put Tanner in his grave."

Scallato smiled. "I'll make him suffer for worrying you."

Maria laid her head on her husband's chest. "And torture his woman too. I hate American women. They all think they're men."

Scallato began unbuttoning Maria's dress. "Let's see how much woman you are."

By the time Maria left the shed, her hair was filled with sawdust and she wore a wide smile.

THE FOUR MEN GUARDING MALEK KALAH DRESSED IN uniforms of a sort: black turtleneck, black slacks and boots, with tan corduroy jackets.

Two of the men wore their hair in crew cuts, while a third had dark hair of normal length, and the fourth man had long blond locks. Tanner told Sara that they would learn as much about the bodyguards as they could before the hit took place. Tanner particularly wanted to know about the blond man.

"Why him?" Sara asked.

"He'll be the easiest one to impersonate, and I may need to fool the others."

Sara smiled as she understood Tanner's meaning. "It's his hair, isn't it? If you wore a blond wig, it would not only help to conceal your face, but is also distinctive."

"That's right. And if I dress the same way as they do, they won't catch on for a few seconds."

Sara looked through the file they had on the men. It was a thin file that they received from Jacques Durand. "The blond man is your height, but he weighs nearly two-hundred pounds. You'll have to pad your clothing. He's also German."

"I need to know what he sounds like in case I have to speak."

Sara smiled. "I can take care of that."

ON THEIR THIRD DAY OF OBSERVING KALAH'S HOME, THE blond man left the building. He was a cigar smoker and there was a store just five blocks away, beside a bar. Kalah's food, as well as the bodyguards' food, was prepared by a chef who came to the building to cook three mornings a week. There was also a maid who visited once a week.

While the blond bodyguard walked, Sara drove past him in a rented van. She was waiting outside the bar as the bodyguard approached. Sara was dressed in a short black skirt and a blue leather jacket that matched her high heels. After looking the bodyguard over, she smiled at him, but then answered her ringing phone.

It was Tanner on the other line. He was perched on a rooftop in a shooter's blind. There was a low probability that the bodyguards were aware their boss, Malek Kalah, was the target of a new assassination plot, but Tanner wasn't taking chances. If the blond bodyguard grew suspicious of Sara and attempted to harm her, Tanner would shoot the man dead.

"He'll talk to you once he leaves the store," Tanner said.

"If I'm his type, maybe he likes redheads."

"He'll talk to you. That smile you gave him guaranteed it."

The blond bodyguard left the cigar store less than a

minute later while holding a small bag that contained his purchase.

Sara began to wonder if she were enticing enough to gain the guard's attention, when the man began walking back the way he'd come. However, after taking only a few steps, he looked over his shoulder to see if Sara was watching him. She was, and the German smiled and walked over to her. Sara answered his smile with one of her own, and as he stood before her, the blond man spoke to Sara in German.

"Du bist so schön, Fraulein."

Sara spoke enough German to understand him. He had said, "You are so beautiful, Fraulein," Still, she pretended ignorance and told him that she only spoke a little German.

He smiled and switched to a heavily accented English. His voice was deep, a vivid baritone.

"Ah, an American. I said that you are very pretty."

"Thank you," Sara said.

"What is your name?"

"I'm Diane," Sara lied. "And what is your name?"

The bodyguard moved a little closer. "I am Kurt, Diane, and I want to buy you a drink."

Sara made a show of looking at her watch. "My friend said she'll be late picking me up, so why not?"

THE HANDSOME BLOND BODYGUARD BOUGHT SARA A GLASS of wine and she told him she was married. Kurt seemed unfazed by her marital status and poured on his considerable charm. As Diane, Sara claimed to be in Germany to visit an old high school classmate but said that her husband had to stay back in Chicago to work.

Kurt said her husband was a fool to let her out of his sight. He left the bar only after Sara mentioned that she was staying at a nearby hotel, but that she often stopped in the bar or stood out front to wait for her friend to pick her up. Kurt said that he hoped to run into her again. Before leaving, Kurt asked a question.

"How long have you been married, Diane?"

"Three years."

Kurt smirked. "That is enough time to become bored with someone."

Sara didn't say she agreed, but she smiled.

After Kurt left, Sara shut off the recording device she wore.

SARA JOINED TANNER FOR DINNER LATER THAT NIGHT AT A restaurant inside their hotel. Tanner had been working with the recording Sara made of her conversation with the bodyguard, as he needed to be able to mimic the man if necessary.

"You'll definitely need to wear padding. Kurt is thicker in the chest and arms than you are. Also, Kurt's hair is a bit curlier than it appears in the photo of him we have. I'll need to find just the right wig."

"Kurt? Just how friendly did you get over drinks?"

"Friendly enough, how is your impersonation coming along?"

Tanner leaned across the table and stared into Sara's eyes. He then spoke to Sara in a perfect impersonation of Kurt's deep and German-accented voice.

"You are so beautiful, Fraulein."

Sara let out a small gasp of surprise. "That's perfect. You sound just like him."

"And I meant every word of it," Tanner said.

Sara stared back at him. "You're not the best-looking man I've ever seen, but you are so damn sexy."

"Are you saying you're ready to be more than friends?"

Sara broke eye contact, but she gave a small nod. "I'd like that very much."

"Not that I'm complaining, but you once hated me enough to kill me. Why the drastic change of heart?"

Sara shrugged. "I've come to know the real you, and I like what I see."

Tanner reached over, took Sara's hand, and caressed it in his own. "Why don't we go up to my room?"

"No."

"Ah, I see your game now; you're out to torture me."

Sara laughed. "I'm not, I promise. But I think we should wait until Scallato is dead, or we could have one very dangerous voyeur sneaking up on us."

Tanner released her hand and leaned back. "You're right, and I've already underestimated the bastard once, but I want to continue this conversation when it's safe to do so."

Sara grinned. "Absolutely."

"So, how else would you like to spend the evening?"

Sara grabbed a deck of cards out of her purse. "I play a mean game of Blackjack."

9

WALK LIKE A MAN

Maurice Scallato smiled as he watched his son's eyes glitter in surprise.

Antonio was standing in the doorway of an apartment and looking at the woman who had opened the door to greet them. Her name was Veronika. Veronika was Russian and a stunning redhead. She was also the mistress of Antonio's father.

After Veronika invited the pair inside, Antonio was shocked to see his father kiss Veronika. Antonio's stunned expression soon morphed into an angry look as his face reddened. The boy rushed from the apartment, but Scallato reached his son before he could make it back onto the elevator.

"Why are you running away, Antonio?"

The boy's anger was palpable. "You're cheating on my mother."

Scallato looked back down the hall, where Veronika stood in the doorway. "We'll be back in a few minutes."

Veronika's smile bordered on a laugh. "I'll be here.

And tell him about his present. That should quiet him down."

Scallato said nothing to that, he just ushered Antonio onto the elevator and hit the button for the ground floor.

∾

As Veronika moved back inside the apartment, a young blonde peeked out from behind the bathroom door. The girl was beautiful, petite, and dressed in a red bikini. Her name was Yana and like Veronika, she was Russian. When she saw that only Veronika remained, she came out and pointed at the apartment door.

"Tell me that wasn't my date."

"The boy is young, but you'll make a good teacher."

"I'm no damn, teacher, Veronika, and I don't screw children."

"You'll do as you're told, and you've been well paid to do so."

Yana's anger turned to sadness as she paced. "How old is the boy?"

"I don't know or care. All I know is that we're paying you to make him a man. And he better be a happy man when you're done with him."

"He should be with a girl his own age, or no girl at all, as young as he is."

"I don't know any whores that young, but don't worry, he'll like you. And if he's anything like his father, you'll like him too."

Yana crossed her arms over her chest. "You should have told me how young he was. I would have said no."

Veronika rushed over to Yana and pushed her backwards onto a sofa. Before Yana knew what was happening, Veronika held a knife near her left eye.

"You smile and treat that boy right or I'll blind you. You're a whore, Yana. You're not paid to think; you're paid to fuck."

Yana's eyes were locked on the tip of Veronika's blade as she answered.

"All right! Yes, yes, I will make him happier than he's ever been."

Veronika patted Yana on the cheek with the flat side of the knife. "I'm glad we understand each other."

DOWNSTAIRS, AT THE SIDE OF THE BUILDING, SCALLATO schooled his son on the ways of the world.

"I love your mother, Antonio, but I need more than one woman to satisfy me. As you get older, you'll discover that truth for yourself."

"It's still cheating," Antonio said.

Scallato shook his head. "Morals like that are for lesser men. We are Scallato's, son. We walk this world and do as we please."

Antonio pointed up in the direction of Veronika's apartment. "I bet my mother doesn't know about her."

"She doesn't, but she knows that I spend time with other women just like she knows that I kill for a living."

"Really?"

"Yes. Your mother is honored to be my wife, but she knows I'm a man of deep desires. She's also not foolish enough to think that she alone could satisfy me. All she cares about is that I don't embarrass her by flaunting other women in her face. I would never do that, which is why I only meet with Veronika away from our home."

Antonio leaned back against a wall as he thought things over. "This woman, Veronika? Do you love her?"

"Of course not. She pleasures me, and I pay for her apartment. It's a business transaction, nothing more or less."

Antonio gave that more thought, then had a question. "Why am I here?"

Scallato's grin was wide. "You're going to love this."

SCALLATO MET VERONIKA NEARLY A DECADE AGO, WHEN she was the fifteen-year-old daughter of a Russian who was an acquaintance of Scallato's. Scallato handled her father's problem by killing three men and left Veronika's life. The next time she saw Scallato, Veronika was nineteen and a college student. The two became lovers and she'd been Scallato's mistress ever since. Veronika longed to be more than a mistress, as she loved Scallato, but she knew he would never leave his wife, Maria.

Veronika's apartment was large, lushly furnished, and had a great view of the city of Rome. Antonio Scallato registered none of this. His eyes were occupied with taking in the loveliness of the blonde and beautiful Yana. She was seated on a sofa beside Veronika and was still wearing only the red bikini. Antonio stared at her body without shame and only ended his gazing when his father spoke to him.

"What do you think of Yana?"

Antonio looked into Yana's green eyes for the first time, but then quickly glanced away.

"She's nice," Antonio said, with a voice that had gained a bit of huskiness. He had kissed several girls from his town and had even felt the budding breasts of one through her blouse, but he had never become as aroused as he did when looking at Yana.

"She's yours, Antonio."

Antonio stared at his father. "What?"

"Yana, she is a gift from me to you. It is time you became a man and Yana will be your first woman."

Antonio smiled, but then caught himself as he looked over at Yana again.

"You mean that I can… I mean, that she'll let me… touch her?"

Scallato laughed. "You'll do more than touch her. She's yours, boy, and when we leave here, you'll be a man."

Sitting beside Yana, Veronika gave the young whore a small nudge to get her moving. Yana rose from the sofa, walked over to Antonio, and offered her hand.

"Come with me."

YANA SAW A SILLY GRIN TAKE OVER ANTONIO'S FACE AS HE rose from his seat. Despite his young age, he was still an inch taller than the petite Yana.

Yana had plastered a smile on her lips, but her eyes still held a touch of sadness. Antonio was tall and muscular, yes, but he still had the face of a boy. He also bore a resemblance to Yana's younger brother, who was ten-years-old. As she disappeared into Veronika's guest room with Antonio, Yana felt like a pervert. She vowed to herself that someday she would pay Veronika back for making her have sex with a child.

Once they were behind closed doors, Yana walked over to the bed and laid back upon it, she then called Antonio over and told him to lie beside her.

"You've never been with a girl before, have you?"

Antonio shook his head.

With a practiced move, Yana reached back and removed her bikini top, she then guided one of Antonio's hands onto her breasts. The boy's eyes widened with wonder as a soft moan escaped him.

Yana forced herself to keep smiling, but being with the boy felt so very wrong. After releasing a resigned sigh, Yana said the words that Veronika told her to say to the boy.

"Take your clothes off, Antonio, and let Yana make you a man."

Antonio sprang from the bed and stripped naked. When he rejoined her on the mattress, Yana had to fight the urge to cry.

1 0

BUMMER

TANNER DRESSED HIMSELF IN A BLACK TURTLENECK, BLACK slacks, and black boots, then donned a tan corduroy jacket. The jacket was bigger than needed and was well-padded at the shoulders, chest and back. The outfit was the same one that Kalah's bodyguards wore, but it was to be only the first layer in Tanner's disguise.

After checking his look in the mirror, Tanner removed some of the padding from the front and rear of the jacket. The change made the added bulk less noticeable up close and gave him a more natural look of greater size. Once satisfied, Tanner left his room.

In times past, Tanner would have merely placed a hair in the doorjamb as he closed it shut. If he found the hair missing or in a different spot upon his return, it would have let him know that someone had broken into his room. Those days were over, and now it took only a few dollars to buy a hidden camera that could be left in the room. The devices even had motion detectors that would alert your phone of an intruder's presence. And yet, Tanner still placed a hair inside the doorjamb. It was an extra layer of protection that took only seconds to apply, so why not?

After taking the elevator down to the hotel lobby, Tanner met Sara in the coffee shop and sat with her at a table. She looked him over with a keen eye as she took in the padded jacket.

"You're not quite as bulky as Kurt, but you'll be able to pass for him once you're wearing the blond wig."

Tanner took a sip of the coffee Sara passed to him, then nodded. "I only have to fool the man inside the house watching the camera above the door. Once they buzz me in, the ruse will be over."

Sara looked concerned. "Even with the element of surprise it will still be three against one, and they are deadly men."

"You're worried about me?"

"I have no doubts about you coming out on top; I'm only concerned that you might be injured."

"Don't be. Once I'm inside Kalah's home, they'll all be dead in less than ten seconds."

Sara stared at Tanner.

"What?" Tanner said.

"You, your confidence, if any other man talked like that I would swear it was bravado. You say such things as if they're facts."

"You don't like it?"

"I actually find it to be sexy."

"Why?"

"Because it's true, you'll kill them all, and despite their training, experience, and superior numbers... they don't stand a chance."

"And that's sexy?"

"Strangely enough, yes."

"You know what I find sexy?"

"What?"

"You Sara, and I want us to take that vacation together when this is over."

Sara grinned. "It's a date."

~

In Rome, Scallato had left Antonio alone in the hotel room while he met with the informant he called his, "pet cop." This was the same cop whom he let live on the day he killed his older brother, Bernardo, so that he could succeed his father as the next generation of Scallato assassins.

Scallato also had a younger half-brother named Dario, but Dario Scallato never had any interest in becoming an assassin. Maurice considered Dario a nonentity and had not spoken to him in many years.

The meeting with his pet cop took place inside another hotel room, and the two drank wine as they talked.

The two met rarely, but Scallato thought it appropriate given his failure at killing Tanner. His contact had proven invaluable over the years, and this day was no exception.

Scallato looked down at a photo of Sara Blake and nodded. "That's her, and you say that she is an ex-FBI agent?"

"They expelled her after she shot her own partner."

Scallato was a man who rarely showed surprise, but shock showed on his face as his contact explained the history between Tanner and Sara Blake.

"This is one hell of a woman. I feel better now about failing to have killed her. And she and Tanner are now lovers?"

"Likely, yes, which I find unfortunate."

Scallato tossed a hand in the air. "Women are fickle,

and no doubt Tanner is quite the man. If he were a lesser man I would have killed him easily."

"He won't stop looking for you."

"I know. Keep track of him. When I'm ready, I'll travel to where he is and kill him."

"And what about the woman?"

"I will kill her too."

The contact sighed. "Such a shame."

Scallato smiled. "My wife wishes me to torture her, this Sara Blake."

The contact frowned. "You have an interesting wife, Maurice."

"Where is Tanner now?"

"In Berlin. He's there to kill Malek Kalah."

"Ah, a worthy target, perhaps Kalah's bodyguards will kill Tanner for me. I understand they're exceptional."

The contact said nothing, but just stared at Scallato.

"Is there something on your mind?" Scallato asked.

"Just this, I think you take Tanner too lightly. Why not go to Germany and kill him now, while he's distracted with Kalah?"

Scallato made another dismissive hand gesture. "Tanner has been lucky, I'll grant you that, but he'll be just another in a long line of assassins who thought they were in my league. I will let Tanner wonder about me for a few weeks. Every odd sound at night will be me sneaking up on him, and every dark corner will bring fear. There is a psychological aspect to the art of assassination, and the constant fear about where I am and when I'll strike will wear the man down."

The contact held up a wineglass. "As you say, but I'll be glad when you kill him."

Scallato clinked glasses with his contact. "Tanner is dead already; he just doesn't know it yet."

∽

AFTER LEAVING THEIR HOTEL IN BERLIN, TANNER CLIMBED into the rear of a stolen van as Sara drove.

Tanner found the narrow European vehicle to be cramped compared to its wider American counterparts, but still managed to don his "bum" costume. The bulk of the costume was an old threadbare overcoat that had stains and tears showing. Its buttons were fastened using Velcro and the front of a shirt had been sown into it. The bottom half of the pant legs were from a ratty pair of jeans that were secured above Tanner's knees. These were also held in place with Velcro. To complete the outfit, Tanner wore a floppy hat that had a hole in its crown, while the tops of his black boots were hidden by the upper section of work boots that looked caked with old mud.

Tanner had spent an hour the night before practicing taking off the outfit. He was confident he could strip down to his bodyguard clothes in less than five seconds. Add to that an additional few seconds to secure the blond wig in place. The wig was hidden away in a pocket and had an elastic band that Tanner could use to hold it to his skull.

Within ten seconds he could transform himself from homeless man to trusted member of an elite security team. However, for it to work, he had to lure the blond German down on the street. Ideally, Kalah's hatred of the homeless would cause the man to deal with the "bum" himself. Tanner wasn't optimistic of that outcome since Kalah's security team was known to be topnotch. They would advise their charge to stay inside the protection of his home while they dealt with the bum, Tanner, themselves.

Being well trained, they would doubtless send out two men; Tanner hoped that the blond man would be one of those men.

"You sewed that costume together yourself, Tanner?"

"Yeah, it's a handy skill for an assassin, especially when it comes to stitching up your own wounds."

Sara made a face. "No wound talk, everything will go smoothly."

"Let's hope so, but this could take a few days. I may not get under Kalah's skin quickly enough, or he may not glance out his window at me."

"Oh, I hadn't even thought of that. So, what happens if they don't react?"

"Plan B."

"What's plan B?"

"A frontal attack on the guards."

"That sounds riskier."

"It's not, but it increases Kalah's chances of reaching his safe room before I can kill him."

"Let's hope the bum routine works."

MORE THAN A DAY WENT BY BEFORE KALAH RESPONDED TO Tanner's presence. Tanner littered, begged for money from people passing by, insulted a woman who told him to get a job, and avoided the police. When he was tired of playing the waiting game, Tanner upped the stakes by urinating on Kalah's doorstep.

He had just made it back across the street when two of the bodyguards came out and shouted for him to stop. Neither man was the blond German, and so Tanner attempted to evade the confrontation by running through an alleyway and climbing over a fence. When one of the security guards vaulted the fence like it wasn't there, Tanner had to decide on a course of action. He could kill the guards chasing him and then hope to take the other two by surprise, try to outrun the guards, or take a beating. While the beating was the least appealing of the three options, it did leave his cover intact.

If he were to outrun the bodyguards, the men would rightly suspect he wasn't homeless. Unless, that is, he was a homeless athlete in exceptional condition. Killing the guards was an appealing option after two days of playing pretend, but one of the two remaining guards could easily make him as an imposter. Tanner was counting on the blond wig to aid in his deception, without it, he bore little resemblance to the two guards that chased him.

And so, a beating it was to be. Tanner slowed as he neared the end of another alley and pretended to be winded. He looked back at an approaching guard with a fearful look and turned to put his hands up. When he spoke to the man in German, Tanner did so while pretending to gasp for breath.

"I'm… sorry. Don't hit me."

The guard kicked Tanner's feet out from under him and sent him sprawling onto his back. The other guard was behind them. He was straddling the fence and watching, but he seemed uninterested in joining the scuffle.

Tanner raised his hands in a pleading gesture and the first bodyguard kicked him in the ribs. The blow hurt, but its impact was lessened by the padding Tanner wore under his coat. That kick was followed by one aimed at Tanner's head. He nearly managed to avoid it, but the toe of the bodyguard's boot caught him on the bottom of his scruffy chin.

Tanner rolled over as if the blow had spun him, and as he did so, he freed a knife. He was willing to take a minor beating, especially given the protection of the padding he wore, but if the man got carried away, Tanner would kill him.

Another kick followed. It was a kick to the butt and it was accompanied by a warning that Tanner never return to the street where Kalah lived.

Tanner gushed out promises that he would never return, and the guard left him lying on the ground. Tanner watched the man move back over the fence with ease to join the other bodyguard, he then stood and assessed his injuries. They were all minor, but he supposed that he'd have a bruised chin for a few days.

As he left the alley, Sara pulled the van to the curb.

"Are you hurt?"

"The guard only tuned me up a little. I don't think his heart was in it."

"What's next? Try again tomorrow and hope that they send out the blond guard to chase you off?"

Tanner answered her as he removed his homeless costume. "I think I'll try a different tact, that is, if you're willing to help me."

"What do you need me to do?"

"Lure Kurt inside that bar again, but this time keep him there longer."

"I can do that, but what will you be doing?"

"I'll be killing his friends, along with Malek Kalah."

RITE OF PASSAGE

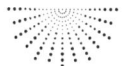

Scallato and his son Antonio returned from Italy to the relief of Maria.

Maria held her son out at arm's length and studied his face. "You look different, Antonio, more mature somehow. Did you enjoy being in the city?"

"Very much, Matri, and Patri showed me around."

"I'm glad you enjoyed yourself, but I'm happier to have you both home."

Scallato's daughter, Anna, was at school, and so only the three of them sat down at the kitchen table, where they sipped on wine. The kitchen was large and had new appliances and countertops. There was also a slanted skylight above the breakfast nook. Maria was an excellent cook who loved to bake. She spent much of her time in the well-lit room.

If anyone wondered how a carpenter had managed to afford one of the nicest houses in town, along with the surrounding acreage, Scallato made a vague mention about an inheritance. The story was never questioned, and on the surface, the family appeared to live simply.

"Antonio and I will be going into town, Maria."

"Why?"

"I want to get another look at the Martello brothers and check to see if a certain boat has docked. That boat will be smuggling in a supply of ammunition for me."

"Bring me back some things from the market, Antonio."

"No, Maria. Antonio's days of running errands are over. It's time we started treating him as a man."

Maria caressed Antonio's cheek. "But he's still so young, Maurice."

"Nonsense. I was assisting my father with contract kills at his age."

Maria stared at her husband while looking as if she wished to protest his decision to bring Antonio deeper into his world. The moment passed, and she nodded in resignation.

"My brother Bruno was also working with our father at that same age. Yes, it's time Antonio grew up."

"His will be an exceptional life and the name Scallato will continue to be feared and respected."

"Is that something those Martello brothers will learn soon?" Maria asked.

Scallato smiled. "You might as well send your brother a letter telling him to get his people here. The Martello brothers won't be a problem much longer."

"I'll demand a percentage of the protection money Bruno will get from the merchants," Maria said. "If you're going to take out the trash for him, we might as well profit by it."

Scallato tapped the side of his head. "Good thinking. Bruno and his people get the town and we make more money. It works out for everybody."

Antonio pointed out something. "It doesn't really work

out for everyone. The merchants will still be paying for protection, Patri, even if Uncle Bruno charges them less than the Martello brothers."

Scallato locked eyes with his son. "The merchants are the sheep we wolves feed on. If they had guts they wouldn't give up a cent. Never feel sorry for the sheep, Antonio; they reap the reward of their cowardice." Scallato stood and beckoned for Antonio to do the same. "Let's go find the Martello brothers. I want to see where they live."

"I heard in the market that they took over old man Alleganti's crumbling villa," Maria said.

"That's good. That villa has seen better days, but it is surrounded by stone walls that will keep anyone from seeing what happens there."

"I've also heard that there are dogs on the property, so be careful."

Scallato smiled at his wife. "The dogs will be the only things left alive after I've visited that villa."

A SHORT TIME LATER, SCALLATO AND ANTONIO WERE walking about the town. Antonio asked when he could see Yana again and was shocked by his father's answer.

"You may never see her again. But don't worry, there are a world of women out there. I'll tell Veronika to arrange another escort for you."

"We'll be going back to Rome soon?"

"No, but I'll be moving Veronika to a town nearby for a few months. I'll tell her to have a friend ready for you."

Antonio hesitated, but said the words that were on his mind. "Veronika is so beautiful… maybe she could be my friend?"

Scallato laughed. "You have good taste, but no, that one is mine. Still, I'll make sure you have a redhead next time too, how's that?"

Antonio nodded enthusiastically and Scallato laughed again. "I see you like being a man."

The local priest, Father Rossetti, smiled as he grew near and greeted Scallato, whom he knew as Maurice Rizzo.

"Maurice, it is good to see you, but when will I be seeing you in my church again?"

"Soon, Padre, but I've just returned home a few days ago."

"Do the Americans pay that well, son?"

"What do you mean?"

The priest patted Antonio on the head. "This boy here is at an age when he needs his father around. Perhaps you can find work closer to home, eh?"

Scallato felt his face redden, as the urge to beat the priest to a pulp had to be fought against. Who did the man think he was to involve himself in his life? As his anger faded, Scallato spoke with a phony smile on his lips.

"You're right, Padre, and I will be spending more time at home."

Father Rossetti's hand left Antonio and patted Scallato's shoulder. If he had patted Scallato on the head, Scallato would have slit the man's throat, and his identity of Maurice Rizzo be dammed.

"Good, good, Maurice, and don't forget to come to church with Maria. There are also a few things that could use the blessing of your carpentry skills."

"Yes, Padre."

After the priest left, Antonio had a question.

"Will God send us to hell for what we do, for killing people?"

"If there is such a place as heaven, Antonio, we don't belong there, and if hell exists, we will rule it. We are Scallatos, son, and we have only two truths. We will survive no matter what comes our way, and we are the greatest assassins the world has ever known. Morals, rules, and societal norms are for lesser men, for sheep like that priest. We are wolves, Antonio, ravening wolves."

Antonio repeated the phrase, "ravening wolves," and liked the way it tasted on his lips. He then startled as the three Martello brothers came into view. To the eyes of the young teen, all three men looked formidable, even the short one, who was about his height.

The other men in town scattered as the Martello brothers walked toward them and no one made eye contact, not even the priest, Father Rossetti. He had ducked inside a women's clothing store as the men approached him. Scallato also avoided them, as he guided Antonio several meters to the left and behind a wall. The Martello brothers would be handled, but not in full sight of the other townspeople.

After the three men passed by and disappeared into a tavern, Antonio looked up at his father.

"You can kill all three of them by yourself?"

"I could kill those three in my sleep, but I won't be the man who murders them."

"Then who will get rid of them?"

"You will, Antonio. You'll take a shotgun and blast them to bits."

"Me?"

"Yes son, that whore Yana made you a man, but killing the Martello brothers will make you a Scallato."

Antonio swallowed hard as he stared at the tavern the Martellos had disappeared into, he then looked up at his father.

"I can do it. I can kill them."

Scallato placed an arm across Antonio shoulders. "I know you can kill them. You are my son."

Antonio smiled at his father, but there was a nest of fear in the pit of his stomach.

THE FIFTH MAN

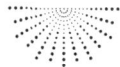

Sara checked her watch for the third time in ten minutes, then warded off the advances of yet another man. The bar she had shared a drink in with the bodyguard named Kurt was much busier than it had been on her previous visits.

It was Unity Day in Germany, a celebration of Germany's reunification, which took place in 1990.

There were no fireworks, parades, or raucous crowds, but many had the day off and were gathering with friends at the bar. Sara was sitting alone at a small table in a corner, but she knew she would have to give it up when the place became more crowded. In the meantime, several men had sent her drinks which she had declined. She had also warded off two blatant attempts to pick her up, one of which was made by a rude drunk.

"Are you alone?" the man had asked, as he weaved unsteadily on his feet.

"I have a friend nearby," Sara had said.

"This friend a man?"

"Yes."

97

The man stared at the table's other chair. "I don't see him."

"He's on his way."

"You want to come back to my place, American chicky? I have some good weed."

"No thank you, my friend should be here soon."

The man whispered something in German, before stumbling out the door.

Tanner was listening in to her conversations through a hidden microphone. When Sara called Tanner to ask him what the man had said, she grew angry.

"He called you a dyke."

"That bastard. If a woman turns him down that means she's gay? What a loser."

"I think our man may not show again, Sara."

"Let's give it a little more time before we call it quits."

"Fine, and I'll let you know if he shows."

Tanner called just nine minutes later, and Sara exited the bar as the blond bodyguard was leaving the cigar store.

Sara smiled at Kurt. "We meet again."

"So we do, and I see you're leaving the bar. Does that mean I can't buy you a drink?"

"I would love another drink," Sara said. They were the words she and Tanner agreed on earlier. That phrase meant it was all right for Tanner to attack Malek Kalah's home.

Assured that Sara would keep Kurt busy for a while, Tanner removed his earpiece and then disassembled his rifle. In less than two minutes, he was off the roof and inside the van. After putting on the blond wig that would make him look like Kurt, Tanner grabbed a bag off the front seat. The bag contained cigars and would help him create the illusion that he was Kurt coming back from the store.

Tanner had observed the German and could duplicate his easy but purposeful gait, while the padding in the jacket gave him the added bulk he needed. Tendrils of the blond wig swirled in the soft breeze and further obscured Tanner's face. The elastic band that held the wig to his head was tight, too tight really, but a little discomfort was better than risking the wig blowing away in a gust of wind.

As he came into range of the cameras outside the building, Tanner lit one of the cigars. Its smoke moved about him and supplied further camouflage. Once at the door, Tanner readied himself while also growing relaxed.

The next few seconds could spell success or failure. He had no way to know whether the guards used code words while coming and going. If such were the case, he would have to abort his attempt at killing Kalah and come up with yet another plan.

A buzzer sounded as Tanner neared the door. He believed he had fooled whoever was watching the camera, but as he opened the door, he saw that he was walking into a trap. With the door halfway open, Tanner spotted one of the guards with his back turned to him.

"Did you have a good walk, Kurt?" the man said in German.

Tanner barely registered the words, because his eyes had been drawn to the glass exterior of a grandfather clock. There was a reflection in the glass that displayed the area behind the door he had just opened. The other two bodyguards were there with silenced guns, just waiting for him to step through the threshold.

Tanner immediately understood that both he and Sara

had walked into traps, and he wondered if she were still alive.

∾

AFTER KURT OFFERED TO BUY HER ANOTHER DRINK, SARA was surprised when he suggested they try a bar he knew that was just around the corner. Sara smiled her agreement even as she went on alert. Tanner was nothing if not thorough, and he had insisted that they both become familiar with the layout of streets and alleyways within a two-mile circumference of Kalah's apartment. And while she wouldn't swear to it, Sara was certain there were no other bars or restaurants in the direction that Kurt was walking. The area was mostly factories that were closed due to the national holiday and there were no other pedestrians about.

As a distraction, Kurt began telling her a story from when he was a boy growing up in Düsseldorf. Sara pretended to listen as she folded her arms and gripped the area on her right forearm. Tanner had equipped her with a hidden blade. It was strapped to the inner part of her forearm, beneath the sleeves of her blouse and jacket. Sara released the clip that held it in place, if she straightened her arm the stainless steel knife would fall into her palm.

Sara's mind raced. Was Kurt trying to get her somewhere private or was he aware that she was part of a plan to kill Kalah? If he was aware that a hit was on, then that meant that Tanner was in grave danger.

"Kurt, where are we going?"

"It's just a little farther, Diane. That is your name, isn't it?"

Sara stopped walking, then felt two hands clamp onto her shoulders. After swiveling her head, she saw that the hands belonged to the man who had been in the bar. The one who had called her a dyke. Sara had thought he was drunk, but he was gazing at her now with a steady sober gaze.

He was the fifth man. An unknown member of the bodyguards who must have stayed in the immediate area of their location to sniff out anything that didn't seem right. Sara sitting at the bar for days at a time as she waited for Kurt's return must have made it onto his radar. No wonder they were so good at keeping their clients safe. They had an unknown advantage.

Kurt yanked her purse away, looked inside, and spotted Sara's gun. "I have her weapon."

"She has a partner too," the fifth man said. "Someone went walking back to the house dressed in our style and with a blond wig that made him resemble you. If I hadn't called and warned the others, he might have fooled them long enough to do great harm."

Kurt's lips formed into a smirk. "He's a dead man whoever he is. Now, what shall we do with this——" Kurt stopped talking as he saw Sara make a quick motion with her right hand. As she brought the blade up aiming for Kurt's throat, the bodyguard attempted to lean back out of harm's way. Instead, Sara's blade ripped open his left cheek and one nostril.

The hands gripping her shoulders released her and Sara sent a kick behind her. That caught the fifth man in the knee, and he staggered backwards, while reaching for a gun. Meanwhile, Sara had shoved her hand inside her purse to remove her weapon, but Kurt was gripping the purse too tight. She fired the gun off while it was still inside the purse, hitting Kurt in the chest, but he only grunted and kept struggling with her.

The man she'd kicked was bringing up his gun. Sara

tripped Kurt to place him in harm's way as the fifth man fired at her twice. One of the bullets struck Kurt in his already ruined face, just below his right eye, killing him.

Sara raised the hand that was still inside the purse and fired several hurried rounds at the fifth man. Sara's shots hit him in the shoulder area and damaged his collarbone. His weapon fell from his hand.

Their eyes met, and the fifth man pleaded with her for his life. He spoke the same frantic words, first in German, then in English.

"*Bitte töte mich nicht!* Please don't kill me!"

Sara remembered what Tanner had said about the bodyguards. That they were like a family, and if one were left alive, he would come after them and seek revenge.

"I don't have a choice," Sara said. She fired three rounds at his heart, then watched him die.

Sara's sunglasses and brown wig were sitting askew, and she had blood spattered on the back of her green jacket. The street had cleared when the shooting began, but in the distance, came the sound of a woman crying. Sara looked in that direction as she feared a wild shot had hit an innocent, but no, the woman was crying out of fear, not pain or grief. She probably thought the violence and gunfire were part of a terrorist attack.

Relieved that no bystanders had been hurt, Sara's FBI training kicked in and she forced herself to stay calm and think. Seven seconds later, she was pulling a set of keys out of the pocket of the dead man who had been in the bar. She reasoned that Kurt and the man must have been planning to take her somewhere, and she doubted they would have done it on foot.

As sirens wailed ever closer, Sara came across the vehicle that fit the keys. It was an old van much like the one she and Tanner had. In its rear was a set of handcuffs and a roll of duct tape.

Sara drove the van only eight blocks before abandoning it in an alleyway. Her wig, jacket, purse, and gun stayed inside the vehicle, which she had set on fire. After hailing a taxi two minutes later, she had it drop her off at a hotel. It was not the hotel she and Tanner were staying at, but she needed someplace to gather herself and think. It would also add another layer of protection against her being tracked down by the authorities.

As she sat in the lobby and watched tourists and business people come and go, Sara realized that she had only one course of action. She would return to their hotel and wait for Tanner to make contact. If he had walked into a trap, Tanner would assume she had done the same and wonder if she survived it or was forced to give up everything she knew. In any event, he would only make contact in person and resort to calling her if he had to. That was the protocol they had agreed on while planning Kalah's assassination.

Not once did Sara think Tanner wouldn't survive the trap set for him, no matter how tight a trap it was. No, Tanner would triumph, the other members of the bodyguards would be dead, and Malek Kalah would be one more successful hit.

Sara walked outside and hailed another cab to take her back to her hotel. When doubt about Tanner's survival tried to creep into her consciousness, she pushed it away. Tanner wasn't dead. The man was damn near indestructible. No one knew that better than she did.

If she could kill Kurt and that other man, then Tanner would easily defeat the odds against him. Sara sat back in her seat, and as the cab drove along she marveled at the twin emotions energizing her.

She had absolute faith she would see Tanner again, while being scared to death that he was injured, or worse. Then, a third emotion surfaced. It was hate, and it was directed at Maurice Scallato. The Sicilian was the cause of all of this because he couldn't be satisfied with knowing he might not be the best assassin in the world. To prove himself, he targeted his own kind and often killed without warning.

Killing Malek Kalah was just a stepping stone toward reaching Scallato, and she and Tanner were only facing danger because of him. Scallato had to die, and he would learn a lesson that many men before him had learned the hard way.

Quite simply, Tanner was death.

On the day he decided to go after Tanner, Scallato should have just placed his gun in his mouth and pulled the trigger. In the end, the result would be the same.

The cab driver spoke up from the front seat. He was an older man with a pleasant face who spoke German with a French accent.

"That's some smile you have there, Fräulein."

"Thank you."

"Whenever my daughters smile that way, it means they're thinking about a man."

"You're very perceptive."

"Not really; I just have five daughters. This man of yours, is it serious?"

"We, um… in a way; we're just beginning."

"In that case, I advise you to take things slow. There are more frogs than princes out there these days."

Sara gave a little laugh. "I once thought he was lower than a dog, but I was wrong."

"Oh, now that sounds like there's a story there."

"Enough to fill a book," Sara said.

They reached her hotel seconds later and Sara left the cab after giving the man a generous tip. She then took a seat inside the lobby where Tanner would spot her upon his return.

And he would return. Sara was certain of it.

13
NO ROOM IS SAFE ENOUGH

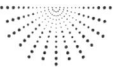

Tanner rammed his shoulder into the steel entrance door of Malek Kalah's townhouse, then dived to the floor while firing off several rounds. Two of his hurried shots tore into the throat of the man standing in the hallway. Tanner didn't know if he'd struck the man or not but assumed that the endless hours of training had borne fruit.

Given the panicked grunts he heard coming from behind him, Tanner guessed that he had done some damage to the man. That was good, because he had turned his back on him and was already flipping over to fire at the two behind the door.

Tanner's position on the entryway floor had caused the men to be in a crossfire position with their wounded companion. That created hesitation for just an instant as they adjusted their aim. Tanner used that precious time to fire first. He aimed at the jumble of legs he saw as the two men were crowded together between the door and a bookcase. Dual screams rewarded his efforts and Tanner rolled to his left and fired again. He was aiming for their heads and legs. If they had time to set up an ambush, they had time to don bulletproof vests.

One man fell to the floor with a pair of bloody kneecaps. He was the same man who had kicked Tanner while Tanner was dressed like a bum. The second man attempted to escape through the open doorway. His wounded calf slowed the man's efforts and Tanner shot him in the head.

As Tanner rolled away once more, bullets ricocheted off the spot he had just left. Tanner had been reloading as he rolled. As he came to a stop, he fired twice into the face of the man with the wounded kneecaps. That the man had the presence of mind to defend himself was impressive. The pain in his knees must have been monumental. That agony was over now, as Tanner's shots removed a chunk of his head.

After rolling once more and turning around, Tanner took aim at the first man he'd shot. There was no need to shoot him again. The man was seconds away from bleeding out from the wounds to his throat and his gun had skittered away when he dropped it.

Only several seconds had passed since Tanner stepped through the door, and the security team was either dead or dying. The carnage had been so swift and lethal that the cigar Tanner had dropped upon entering had yet to come to a rest. It was still rolling across the white marble floor of the entryway.

As he stood, movement from the corner of his eye caught Tanner's attention. It was Malek Kalah. He was holding a shotgun as he peeked around a corner.

"Did you get the bastard, Kurt?"

A small smile crept onto Tanner's lips. The disguise of the homeless man had done him no good, and the guards had been expecting him. However, they must have neglected to inform Kalah of the ruse he was playing. Tanner was still dressed like one of the bodyguards. Also, thanks to the tightness of the elastic holding it in place, the blond wig had stayed on.

"He's dead," Tanner said in a voice that was a spot-on impression of Kurt. "And you won't believe who it is. Come look."

Kalah was at the other end of a hallway. He took three steps in Tanner's direction, but then halted. The terrorist had grown up on the streets of Brixton, a crime-infested section of London. He had thrived there and ran his own gang. He had survived that environment by listening to his instincts. His instincts were screaming at him to run to the safe room and lock the door.

"Kurt, turn around and look at me… Kurt."

When Tanner realized Kalah had grown hesitant to come closer, he knew he had lost him. But when Kalah asked him to turn and face him, Tanner dropped to the floor. Kalah's shotgun boomed and steel pellets went screaming inches over Tanner's head.

Tanner returned fire as he jumped to his feet and saw that Kalah was already backing up toward the doorway. One of Tanner's hurried shots hit the door frame. It sent bits of wood splinters into Kalah's cheek, while Kalah's second shot shredded the wall on Tanner's left. Once around the corner, Kalah tossed aside the shotgun and ran full out toward the safe room.

Tanner heard the beep of an electronic keypad and the *whoosh!* of a sealed door flying open. Tanner came around the corner firing at the spot where he'd thought the sounds had come from and heard another electronic beep, one louder than the others.

Kalah had made it inside the safe room and hit the button which would close the door. Kalah's smile was wide as the door reversed, knowing that he was moments away from escaping death. Tanner fired a shot at the keypad outside the door. It blew apart the device; however, that had no effect on the door. Although Kalah was out of sight, Tanner stepped to the left, bent his knees slightly, then emptied his gun at the sliver of steel wall he could see. Afterward, the door shut and sealed itself with the finality of a bank vault, placing Kalah out of reach.

Tanner made one attempt to open the door, then turned to find a rear exit from the building. Once outside, he was startled by how close the sound of sirens seemed and wondered if the police weren't already out front.

He used a drain pipe along with toe holds in a brick wall to climb onto a nearby roof and was on the other side of the block in less than a minute.

At the rear of a restaurant, he started a fire in a dumpster that would consume the wig and the tan jacket. His slacks were splattered with the blood of his enemies, but the dark fabric hid the fact well.

Once on the street, Tanner bought a newspaper and tucked it under his arm. He also bought a bottle of beer. When he passed a store selling colorful clothes with the logo of the German National Football Team, he bought a cap and a T-shirt and put them on.

Seconds later, a police car drove by slowly. Tanner looked up from the sports page he was reading to find that the cops were staring at him. He took a sip from his bottle of beer and sent the cops a puzzled look.

The cop in the passenger seat shook his head and pointed across the street, where two men wearing leather jackets were walking along briskly. Tanner stayed on his course while the cops got out to talk to the two men. As soon as he made it around the corner, Tanner hurried his stride until he was back on the main drag. Once there, he hailed a taxi.

As Sara had done, he had the car drop him away from his hotel. After getting out of the cab, Tanner walked a block and hailed a second taxi. Ten minutes later, he was exiting the taxi two blocks from his hotel and began walking toward it.

Tanner spotted Sara sitting alone inside the lobby. The sheer joy he felt at seeing she was alive and well surprised him and he found he had trouble wiping the smile off his lips. He walked about the area for several minutes while looking for any sign that the hotel was being watched. When he found none, he used his room key to access the side door that led to a parking area, then, he approached Sara from behind.

"If we're being watched, run for the stairwell on the left."

Sara leapt up at the sound of his voice. Her smile matched the one that had been on his lips minutes earlier, and which reappeared as she went to him and hugged him.

"I knew you'd be all right."

"What about Kurt?"

Sara rested her head on Tanner's chest. "He's dead, and there was a fifth bodyguard, a floater that stayed out of sight."

Without thinking about it, Tanner stroked Sara's hair, then, he laid a gentle kiss on her forehead.

"Thank God you're as deadly as you are beautiful. I... I was worried."

Sara raised her head from Tanner's chest and they stared at each other, while still locked in an embrace. Whatever the moment might have led to, it was shattered by a buzzing sound, along with a vibration that they both felt. Sara separated herself from Tanner and removed a phone from her front pocket.

"It's a text from Jacques Durand. He wants to meet us as soon as possible."

"I can guess what the topic of conversation will be. Give him the location of one of the meeting sites we scoped out and tell him we'll meet in an hour. I need to shower and change clothes."

The phone buzzed again with another text. "He wants to know if Kalah is dead," Sara whispered, as people passed within feet of them inside the busy hotel lobby.

Tanner adjusted the ball cap lower, then nodded. "Kalah is dead, and the contract is fulfilled. Tell Durand I expect to receive the information he has on Scallato's whereabouts."

Sara typed, and Durand's reply came quickly.

"The meet is on in one hour," Sara said.

Tanner reached out and caressed her cheek. "Maybe we should have made him wait until morning."

Sara hugged him again, then looked up into his eyes. "I want all this behind us before we move forward. Can you understand that?"

"I can. Wondering if Scallato was sneaking up on us wouldn't exactly be an aphrodisiac."

Sara laughed, then, they walked over to step onto an arriving elevator, which they had to themselves.

"Tanner."

"Yeah?"

"I was worried about you too, even though I knew I didn't have to be."

"It's nice to know you care," Tanner said, as the elevator doors slammed shut.

14

WHY DO THEY ALWAYS ASSUME IT'S LUCK?

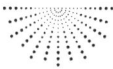

Tanner and Sara entered the bar, saw the angry expression on Jacques Durand's face, and wondered what had caused it.

Durand's expression softened as he greeted Sara, but it hardened again as he stared at Tanner. A waiter appeared and took their drink orders before anyone could speak about why they were there. Once the man left the table, Durand spoke to Tanner through teeth gritted in anger.

"You are a liar."

Tanner's face was impassive as he replied to Durand. "What is this lie you think I've told."

"Malek Kalah is alive and has himself locked inside that damn safe room of his. Once the Germans free him, he'll flee somewhere, and it may be years until he surfaces again."

"Malek Kalah is dead."

"You saw him die?"

"No, but I sent a series of rounds into the steel wall of that safe room. My angle was perfect and at least one of the ricocheting rounds would have hit him in the head, likely more than one."

Durand sat back in his seat and composed himself. When he spoke again, there was no anger in his tone. "You're telling me you think one of your wild shots may have killed Kalah with a lucky ricochet?"

"My shots weren't wild. They were precisely angled to rebound toward Kalah's position. I'm not a two-bit hit man, Durand. I am a highly trained professional killer and I've practiced such shots for more hours than most men spend on normal shooting. Call it a trick shot if you'd like, but there was no luck involved. It was skill."

Durand's phone was lying on the table, it buzzed just as the drinks arrived. Once the waiter was gone, Durand answered the call. Whoever was calling did most of the talking. Durand ended the call and stared at Tanner.

"My people say that agents of the German Federal Intelligence Service opened the safe and found Kalah dead. He had three head wounds and another round ripped open his throat."

"As I said earlier, Kalah is dead."

"I think you owe Tanner an apology, Jacques," Sara said.

"I think I do not, not for a string of lucky shots."

Tanner held out a hand. "You do owe me information."

Durand took a gulp from his glass before reaching into an inside pocket. When his hand came out, it held only a folded sheet of paper.

The paper contained the name of a nursing home in Genoa, Italy, along with the name of one of its patients, Mario Rossi.

"Mario Rossi is Carlo Scallato?"

"Yes, he is Maurice's father. Camp out at that nursing home and eventually Maurice will show up for a visit."

Tanner smirked at the sheet of paper. "Mario Rossi? Scallato isn't very creative when it comes to picking an alias. Mario Rossi is the Italian equivalent of John Smith."

"Perhaps, but that is the name he is there under. You'll find a file in the draft folder of the email account we agreed to use. That will supply you with photos of the facility and other pertinent information. And now, our deal is complete."

Tanner asked Durand for a pen. When the Frenchman produced one, Tanner scribbled three random sentences atop each other and the words already on the paper, making the original information unreadable. He then shredded it.

Durand emptied his drink and sent Sara a sad smile. "Do yourself a favor, Sara, and leave Tanner. His tricks won't help him once Scallato decides to eliminate him."

"Scallato is the one who will be eliminated, Jacques."

"As you say, but if you ever find yourself on the run, call me. I will offer you shelter."

"Thank you, but that won't be necessary."

Durand kissed her hand and then sent a glare and a grunt toward Tanner. He then left the bar.

"That shelter he offered you, I would bet it involves sharing his bed."

Sara grinned. "That sounded like jealousy."

"It wasn't, but Durand is jealous and believes we're sleeping together."

Tanner stood with his glass in his hand and gestured for Sara to follow him to a different table on the other side of the bar.

"Why did we move?"

"I'm testing a theory. I'm guessing that Durand is having us watched."

"Why would he do that?"

"He's willing to sell out Scallato for the price of a hit, perhaps he'll attempt to do the same with me."

Sara looked skeptical, but she sat and watched as people entered the bar. Without exception, their eyes would be drawn to the bar's hostess, a middle age woman with a wide smile. No one looked about as if they were searching for them.

After some time had passed, Sara made a comment. "No one seems to be paying us any attention. Maybe Durand can be trusted."

"Maybe, but Durand also knows where we're headed, since he gave us the address of that nursing home."

"You're thinking it's a trap?"

"I'm not sure, but I will be checking it out before I set foot in there."

"If it's not a trap, we could be on the verge of tracking down Scallato. I can't wait to see you whack that asshole."

Tanner raised an eyebrow. "Whack?"

"I'm from New York City; we sometimes say things like that."

"Youse do, don't youse?" Tanner said.

Sara stood and grabbed her purse. "Let's go back to our hotel; I want to soak in a tub and then I need some sleep."

"Sleep sounds like a good idea, but keep an eye out for cops. I doubt the police could track us down, but there's always the chance that Durand sold us out."

"You really don't trust him, do you?"

"No, and he is a cop himself."

"Yes, but not a traditional cop, and he's also a true crime writer."

"That's even more reason for him to turn us in; he might write a book about what happened today."

They stepped outside the bar. As Sara considered Tanner's words, she looked worried.

"What if Durand did decide to write about this battle between you and Scallato?"

"That wouldn't bother me, if he changed our names, you know, to protect the innocent."

Sara laughed. "You are many things, Tanner, but innocent isn't one of them."

Tanner grew quiet as they waited for a cab to come by. Sara studied his face, while wondering if something were wrong.

"What's on your mind?"

"I want to find Scallato, kill the bastard, and head back home."

"You will, but if he were easy to kill, he wouldn't have lasted as long as he has."

"Going to Genoa could be a trap, Sara. Maybe it's time you went back to America."

"Forget it, Tanner. I'm all in, or have you forgotten that Scallato tried to kill me too?"

"I haven't forgotten. I just want you to be safe."

"I will be, because you'll kill Scallato."

A cab appeared, and Tanner flagged it down. As they rode along, they saw that the streets were still full of people celebrating Unification Day, as many spent a night out at dinner, or with friends.

"Tanner, if Genoa turns out to be a trap and Durand can't be trusted, let me handle him."

"Why?"

"One, because you would kill him and bring down nothing but trouble upon yourself. But secondly, that would mean Durand used me to try to hurt you, and if that's true, he'll pay for that."

"I guess we have each other's back then."

Sara took his hand. "Yes, we do."

15

YOU WANT ME TO SHOOT WHAT?

ANTONIO FIRED OFF THREE MORE ROUNDS FROM THE shotgun he was holding and the ache in his shoulder increased. Scallato had been making the boy practice with the modified Mossberg for hours. Antonio was ready for a final test before night fell and their light was gone.

After telling Antonio to take a break, Scallato returned to the old pickup truck he'd used to drive them up into the hills. From the bed of the pickup, Scallato removed a cardboard box containing two puppies. The pups were a pair of Dogo Argentino, or Argentine Mastiffs. Once mature, they would weigh nearly a hundred pounds each.

Antonio smiled as his father released the dogs from the box, then laughed at their playful antics. Scallato had bought the pups from a woman who lived at the foot of the hills and Antonio assumed they were to be a gift for his sister, Anna, whose recent birthday their father had missed. When he learned the actual motive behind his father's purchase, Antonio was repulsed.

"You want me to kill them?"

"Why are you so surprised, Antonio, are we not

planning the murder of three men? What do the lives of a couple of dogs compare to that?"

"But Patri, these puppies are innocent."

"I'm training you to deliver death, Son; there are no innocents, only victims."

Scallato picked up the shotgun that Antonio had rested on a tree stump and thrust it at him. "Kill the dogs, Antonio. Do it now!"

Antonio held the rifle as he'd done all morning while shooting at wooden targets. When he stared down at the puppies playing at his feet, the gun felt as if it weighed a metric ton. After looking over at his father and seeing the expectant look on his face, Antonio took several steps backwards and took aim at the dogs.

A minute passed with the weight of an hour before Scallato took the gun from his son's hands and looked into his tear-stained eyes. After taking the boy by the arm, Scallato led him over to the truck and told him to get in. Antonio did so, then startled as his father walked back toward the puppies. He needn't have worried, as his father was only lifting the truck's tailgate back in place before returning to the driver's seat and starting the engine.

As they rolled down the hill, Antonio wondered if it might have been more humane to shoot the puppies anyway. They wouldn't survive for long on their own among the craggy hills.

"Why didn't you shoot?" Scallato asked. He received a shrug in return. The truck came to a hard stop and Scallato glared at his son. "You do not shrug at me, Antonio. When I ask you a question you answer me."

"I… I just couldn't do it. I couldn't."

Scallato let out a sigh. "My brother Bernardo was the same way, only they were kittens. Two days later, he killed the junkie who had snatched our sister's purse. You failed to kill the dogs, but you will not fail to kill the three Martello brothers."

"You still want me to kill them?"

"Yes, and you will find them much easier to kill than the pups."

"But, if I couldn't kill a dog... will I be able to kill a man?"

"You'd better be, unlike the pups, the men will kill you if you fail. I will help you gain entry into their home, but killing the Martello brothers is your task. If you're worthy of carrying on the Scallato tradition, you'll have nothing to worry about."

As his father placed the truck in gear and drove, Antonio turned his head and looked back at the shotgun that was now secured in its rack. Tomorrow it would be kill or be killed, but the thing he feared most was the disappointment he'd glimpsed in his father's eyes.

"I will kill the Martello brothers and make you proud, Patri. I swear it."

"That's my boy," Scallato said, and a smile returned to Antonio's lips.

After arriving back home, Scallato saw on the news that suspected terrorist Malek Kalah had been killed, along with his security team. Scallato retrieved one of the cheap cell phones he kept stashed away in his workshop and called his contact, his pet cop.

He had to leave a message, but he knew the contact would respond sooner rather than later. Despite the scant moonlight of the cloudy night, Scallato navigated through the trees in the hills above his home, as he waited for his call to be returned.

At the rear of the property was a cliff with a sheer drop of over a hundred feet. Below were boulders, many were small, but some were the size of a man.

Scallato left the cliff and strolled toward the front of the home. After leaning against a tree and looking down at the lighted windows of his house, it struck Scallato how like a dream the home appeared.

The two-story structure sat in the middle of its own land with no other homes in view. It was made of stone and hidden by the surrounding trees, while its earth tone blend of colors made it coalesce with the rocky hill behind it.

A rare whimsical thought came to Scallato, and he turned around and faced the trees. He could no longer see his home, and he thought that when he turned back around it would be gone, vanished. The realization that he would care little about the disappearance of his home and family both amused and pleased him. He was Maurice Scallato, the greatest assassin who had ever lived, or would ever live, and no one and nothing had claim to him.

His father had once called him a sociopath. That occurred when the elder Scallato finally realized that Maurice had killed his own brother, to take Bernardo's place in the family hierarchy. But no, Maurice had feelings, he knew he did. He was simply the master of them and not their slave, as were other men.

He turned around and saw his home was still there. That was good, he had invested a lot of time and much effort into establishing its cover identity. His wife was a good companion and his son would make a worthy successor. As far as his daughter, Anna, was concerned, Maurice held little affection for the child. She was a girl, and thus, of no benefit to him. The best he could hope for was that she would marry young and become someone else's burden.

The phone vibrated in his hand. He answered it, then waited for the other party to speak.

"Maurice?"

"I see that Tanner was successful in eliminating the target in Germany."

"He was, and I have news that will please you."

"Tell me."

"Tanner will be in Genoa soon, and I can give you his exact location."

"Which is?"

"He'll be at your father's nursing home. He thinks the old man will lead him right to you."

"That won't happen, and Tanner won't be fooled for long."

"Yes, so I suggest you fly to Genoa as soon as you can. This is a golden opportunity to rid yourself of that amateur."

"Amateur? Tanner is no amateur. He might even be second only to myself."

"Maybe, but when can I expect you? I'll be in Genoa tomorrow, and so will Tanner, most likely."

"I'll catch a late flight tomorrow. I have to deal with something here first."

"All right, but one thing, do you really need to kill Sara Blake?"

"Yes."

"But why?"

"You already know the reason. She was helping Tanner, for that, she dies."

A great sigh came over the telephone. "I understand."

"I knew you would," Scallato said, then ended the call.

⌇

BACK IN GERMANY, TANNER WAS SURPRISED TO GET A CALL from Sara, who he'd assumed was asleep in her suite across the hall from his own.

"When do you want to leave for Italy? I have to check the schedules."

"I'll hire a private jet."

"If you insist; I never pass on luxury, but I'll pay for our rooms."

"Rooms? You'd save money if you'd only get one."

Sara laughed. "Yes, rooms, at least until the threat of Scallato has passed."

Tanner released a soft moan. "I can't kill him quick enough."

"Agreed, and you may get the chance tomorrow."

"No, tomorrow we'll fly to Rome and stay there overnight."

"Why?"

"If Genoa is a trap, then, the ones springing it will be forced to wait a day and grow bored. People who are bored are also careless, and easier to spot."

"But what if it's not a trap and you miss an opportunity to kill Scallato?"

"It's a risk, yes, but a slight one. It's not very likely he would pick tomorrow to visit. The truth is, he may not visit his father for months."

"Months?"

"My longest hit took many weeks. That was weeks of me looking through a rifle scope and waiting for a sign of movement behind a window."

"Let's hope it won't come to that. Anyway, Rome it is. And I think I'll do some shopping while I'm there."

"So will I, I know a supplier there. I'll get us hooked

up." *Supplier* was Tanner's code word for gun dealer. While *getting hooked up* meant that they would acquire new weapons. Sara understood his meaning, as he had explained the phrases to her at an earlier time.

The sound of a yawn came over the phone.

"Hang up, Sara, and get some sleep, unless there's something else you'd rather do in bed?"

A giggle came over the line this time, and it was followed by one word. "Soon."

Tanner heard her click off and put his phone down. He smiled. Soon couldn't be soon enough.

16

PULL THE TRIGGER AND WATCH
THEM DIE

THE VILLA THAT THE MARTELLO BROTHERS LIVED IN WAS one of the oldest properties in town. It had been a showcase vacation home for an Italian mobster during the 1930's.

For most of its nearly hundred-year existence, the villa was well-maintained, but had been neglected since the mid-eighties by a series of short term owners. The grounds were the worst. They were overgrown with weeds and a fire had destroyed much of the olive orchard, what was left of the orchard had died of neglect. The main section of the three-story home was intact, but an earthquake had collapsed the roof of the west wing, while graffiti marked the walls of the east wing.

Still, despite having seen better days, the villa had a certain regal quality about it, and there was nothing wrong with it that a million or so euros couldn't fix.

An aspect of the villa that remained standing straight and tall was its stone walls and iron gates. They protected the villa from unwanted guests and were aided in their duty by a pair of pit bulls that roamed the courtyard.

Maurice Scallato had rendered the guard dogs useless by feeding them chunks of meat that had been laced with a sedative. Once the dogs began stumbling around, he climbed over the wall and moved silently toward the villa. A look through a lighted window revealed to him that the Martello brothers were at home. The tall one and the fat one were engrossed in a soccer game on TV, while the short one had headphones on and held his phone in his hand.

Scallato returned to the wall and called out softly to his son, who was waiting on the other side. After helping Antonio scale the wall, Scallato walked over to the dogs and nudged one of them with his foot. The hound didn't move, but he did release a foul odor as he expelled gas.

"Ugh, what did you feed them, Patri?"

"Never mind the smell and listen to me carefully. I will wait for you on the other side of this wall until I hear the shotgun blasts. Afterwards, you return here. Then, I will come inside and the two of us will load the bodies and dispose of them."

"Aren't you coming with me?"

"No, Antonio, these are your targets, not mine. Just enter the house through the rubble of the west wing and come up on them silently. If you catch them unawares, all you'll have to do is pull the trigger and watch them die."

Antonio swallowed so hard that the sound could be heard clearly.

His father took him by the shoulders and gazed at him solemnly. "Who are you?"

Antonio looked confused for a moment, but then understanding flashed across his young face. After straightening his back, he answered his father. "I am Antonio Scallato and a Scallato is a dealer of death."

Maurice turned his son sideways and pointed at the

lighted windows of the villa. "Go in there and claim your heritage. Kill those bastards and begin the legend of Antonio Scallato."

At the utterance of the word "legend," Antonio felt a fresh resolve come over him. Yes, he was a Scallato and the Scallato's had been feared and respected for over a century. A legend, he would be a legend just like his father. And all he had to do was sneak inside a building and tug on a trigger several times.

It will be easy. He told himself. *So very easy.*

The darkness swallowed him as he headed toward the ruined west wing of the building, as inside the villa, his intended targets were blissfully unaware of the fate that approached them.

WHILE MOST IN THE TOWN OF RAGUSO REFERRED TO THE Martello brothers as the fat one, the tall one, and the short one, they did have names.

The fat one was named Nerio and he was the youngest. The tall one was Romy. Romy had been of normal height until a growth spurt at nineteen added ten inches to him. The oldest brother and by far the smartest was Dante, who was called the short one. At five-foot-five, he was still the leader of the trio, and had been an only child until Romy came along when he was eight.

Dante was smart and crafty. He was far more intelligent than his two halfwit brothers. He also possessed a calm and dignified demeanor along with a sense of self-control.

While his brothers routinely approached women in the street and made lewd advances, Dante's approach to romance was subtler, although equally obscene. Dante made arrangements with the wives or daughters of the merchants they were strong-arming.

Dante's deal was simple. He got to sleep with the wife or daughter once every two weeks and the woman's husband or father paid a pittance in extortion as compared to the other merchants who were being bled dry.

Dante had made this offer to eighteen women he found desirable and seven had agreed to the arrangement. Five were wives while two were daughters. He wasn't a bad looking man, he thought, nor was he an insensitive lover, and women were far more practical than most men gave them credit for being. So, on average, Dante enjoyed the pleasures of a beautiful woman roughly every other day. Sometimes the timing was wrong, or the assignations had to be postponed to maintain discretion. Whenever a woman called and begged off a planned meeting, Dante was gracious and always agreed to the postponement.

None of the women ever asked him to release them from their obligation, not once they had lain with him and discovered that he was gentle and discreet. Dante even suspected that one or two of his paramours had true feelings toward him. He also knew of one who would gut him like a fish if she didn't fear reprisal.

In any event, Dante Martello had a virtual harem to pleasure him. Meanwhile, the brutish Nerio and the clueless Romy hadn't been laid in months, and their last "conquests" were a pair of forty-something hookers that they ran into down at the docks.

DANTE, NERIO, AND ROMY WERE ENJOYING A NIGHT IN, AS tomorrow they had to make their collection rounds. The

TV was on and Dante was listening to an old Giorgio Gabor album via a pair of earphones.

None of them heard the faint rustle of thick plastic that came from the hallway that led to the west wing, nor did they see the shadowy figure growing closer. They would have remained ignorant of Antonio Scallato's presence in their home had Dante's cat, Sonno, not let out a great hiss at first sight of the boy.

DANTE MARTELLO SAW HIS CAT STREAK OFF TOWARD THE kitchen and wondered what could make the lazy feline move with such haste. He pulled the earphones off his head while at the same time he saw his brothers jerk in their seats and stare at the hallway on the left.

There was a boy there, a rather tall boy, and he was holding a shotgun. The boy's breath was coming rapidly, and he was licking at his lips.

"Stay calm," Dante told his brothers before smiling at the boy. That the boy had come to kill them was plain to see, but so was the fear in his eyes. For once, Nerio and Romy were keeping their big mouths shut, which was good, because threats and foolish heroics weren't going to save them. This was the time for guile. Dante's smile widened as he shook his head. "Ah, I guess I lost the bet. I said you wouldn't have the guts to come here, but it looks like I was wrong."

The boy's brow wrinkled in confusion. "You… you knew I was coming here?" the boy said, and his voice traveled up and down in range due to puberty, or perhaps fear.

"I knew that was the plan, but I foolishly bet that you wouldn't be brave enough to break in. Now I know better, and I'm wiser too, but I'll still be twenty euros poorer after paying off my debt."

The boy blinked as he puzzled through Dante's words, and the barrel of the shotgun lowered several inches. From the corner of his left eye, Dante saw that Nerio had wrapped one of his large hands around an old glass vase that was perched on an end table.

"This was just a test?" the boy said.

Dante forced himself to laugh and hoped that it didn't sound phony. If the boy's doubt vanished, he would kill them.

"Of course, it's a test, that's why there are blank cartridges in the shotgun. You can tell them by the #2 engraved on the bottom of the shell."

The boy looked down at the shotgun in his hands. Dante wondered if he were about to break the gun open and study the shells. But no, when the boy raised his head again, there was anger in his eyes and Dante knew his deception had failed.

"You're trying to fool me," the boy said.

Dante shouted to his brother. "Throw it, Nerio!"

The glass vase rocketed across the room and impacted with the boy's chest. The thick glass was so heavy that it didn't break, and it caused the boy to take a step backwards. At the same time, the shotgun went off and blew chunks out of the floor. Already off balance due to the vase, the recoil from the shotgun blast caused the boy to stumble and he took one hand off the shotgun to steady himself.

That's when Romy threw the TV remote at the boy and hit him in the right eye with it. The shotgun fell to the floor. The boy had one hand on the wall to steady him, while the other had flown up instinctively to touch his now tender eye.

As big and fat as he was, Nerio still possessed speed, and he tackled the boy to the floor. Dante picked up the shotgun and told his brothers to back away from the boy. Once they were clear, Dante smiled down at the teen.

"I guess I win after all," he said, and fired the shotgun three times.

OUTSIDE THE VILLA, MAURICE SCALLATO FELT HIS BREAST swell with pride. His son had killed his first three men and would someday carry on the family tradition, ensuring that the name Scallato would continue to be feared and respected.

Maurice smiled. He would reward the boy by gifting him the shotgun he used to make the kills. He would also treat him to another woman. A nearby town had a whorehouse that specialized in exotic women and Antonio could take his pick. Maurice's smile grew wider. Hell, he would treat himself as well. It wasn't every day that a man's son proved himself worthy.

Scallato pulled himself up to gaze back over the wall. He expected to see Antonio running toward him across the weedy lawn with a big smile on his face, instead, he saw only the hounds he'd drugged, and the night was filled with silence.

NERIO MARTELLO POINTED AT THE SPACE ABOVE ANTONIO'S head.

"Why'd you shoot up the wall, Dante?"

"I had to. Someone else knows the boy was coming

here. That someone could be outside listening for the sound of shots."

Romy Martell pointed down at Antonio. "Look, the little asshole pissed his pants."

It was true. Antonio had urinated on himself when he was looking down the barrel of the shotgun. Until Dante raised the weapon and fired into the wall above his head, he thought he was about to die.

Dante handed Nerio the rifle, then left the room for a few moments. When he returned, he held a roll of duct tape. After kneeling beside Antonio, he instructed Romy to help him bind the boy's wrists together. Antonio struggled, but that ceased after Nerio punched him on the side of the head and nearly caused him to pass out.

"Not too hard, Nerio. We need him to walk," Dante said.

While Antonio was still dazed, Dante placed a wide strip of duct tape over his mouth. Panic entered the boy's eyes, but with his wrists taped together behind his back, there wasn't much he could do.

Then, they were on the move and heading for the rear of the villa. They kept a pair of ATVs in what used to be the estate's barn, and there was a trail back there that went on for miles.

Nerio complained. He wanted them to search the grounds to see if anyone else was around.

"Not in the dark," Dante whispered. "The dogs aren't around, haven't you noticed? Someone killed or disabled them, and I doubt it was this boy. But don't worry, before we're through with him, he'll tell us all we need to know. We'll round up his accomplices when it suits us."

"It must just be a bunch of boys," Romy offered. "No adult would have sent this kid here to kill us. That's funny, the boys in this town have more guts than the men."

"Maybe," Dante said. "But stay quiet and keep your guns ready, we may run into trouble."

Dante's warning proved to be unneeded as they reached the barn without incident, that is, after Nerio broke one of Antonio's toes. Antonio had attempted to escape the brute's grip by stamping on his foot. Nerio returned the favor by slamming the barrel of the shotgun down on the big toe of Antonio's left foot. The sneakers the boy wore offered no protection from the blow and his eyes grew teary from the pain, as a muffled howl had escaped him.

After grabbing a pair of shovels from the barn, they started the ATVs and took off with their lights on. The sound of the motors would travel some distance and there was no way to avoid that, but they would be going off-road, while anyone attempting to follow would likely only have a conventional vehicle.

If anyone else was involved, the boy would give up their names, after all, there were plenty of toes left to break.

A NIGHT OUT ON THE TOWN

In Rome, Sara had talked Tanner into going out for dinner, but then found that every decent restaurant was packed or required a reservation.

Tanner then surprised Sara by taking her to a club where the crowd was mostly of college age and the music was classic American country.

"You like this music?" Sara asked.

"I grew up in Texas."

"I grew up in Connecticut, so I never heard much country music."

"So what sort of music did you listen to, classical?"

"Hardly, I was a metal head, and oh, I so loved Bruce Springsteen and a band called The Bouncing Souls."

Space was tight in the club as well, and so they had to share a table with another couple. The man was Australian, while his wife was a native of Rome. They were both only twenty-two, newlyweds, and had recently graduated from college.

Sara declined the man's invitation to dance, since she knew none of the dance steps and wanted to sit with

Tanner while they were both relaxed for once. But to Sara's surprise, Tanner accepted an invitation to dance from the young wife.

Sara then sat spellbound as Tanner not only kept up with the woman, but danced as if he did it all the time. He returned to the table, as the woman's husband joined her on the dance floor. Sara slapped Tanner on the arm playfully.

"I didn't know you could dance."

"I grew up dancing to these old country songs; dancing was a good way to pick up girls when I was a kid."

"You could pick me up… if I wasn't already yours."

"Are you now?"

"You know I want to be with you."

The tables were small, and they were sitting close together. Tanner leaned toward Sara and they kissed. The kiss lasted several seconds, and when it ended, Sara sighed.

"Hmm, I knew you'd be a good kisser."

Tanner stared at her, then stood abruptly and tossed money onto the table. It was more than enough to pay for their tab and that of the couple they'd been sitting with. Afterward, Tanner took Sara by the hand and led her from the club. She followed him without speaking as he guided her across the street to where a taxi sat. As they climbed into the vehicle, Tanner gave the cabby the name of their hotel.

Tanner and Sara kissed all during the short ride. By the time they reached their destination, Tanner's hands were exploring beneath Sara's blouse.

She hadn't said a word since the club, had only moaned in pleasure, but as Tanner pulled her into his room, she spoke.

"We shouldn't… what about Scallato?"

Tanner shoved a heavy dresser in front of the door.

"Fuck Scallato!"

Sara laughed, but then grew quiet as she reached over and unbuttoned Tanner's shirt.

～

"WHO'S PAOLO?" DANTE MARTELLO SAID.

He was talking to Antonio, who was on the ground and holding his injured foot. The fat one, Nerio, had broken another of Antonio's toes and forced him to talk. They were high up in the rugged hills where a section of the land was more sandy soil than rock. It made for easier digging when a grave was needed. Dante was certain at least one grave would have to be dug, with more to follow once the boy talked.

"Paolo is my best friend," Antonio said. "His father runs the hotel in town. He bet me that I wouldn't have the guts to break into the villa and scare you. That's all this was, I was just trying to scare you."

"Um-hmm, and why would you want to scare us?"

"Because… because… your brothers! They're always hitting on my mother when she goes to town. I just wanted to scare them and make them stop."

"You're lying."

"No, I swear it's the truth."

Dante gazed impassively at Antonio for several seconds as he adjusted his position. He was leaning back against one of the ATV's, with the shotgun and shovels propped up beside him. The shotgun had been reloaded and was ready to be used.

Dante spoke to his brother. "Break another toe, Nerio, but this time on the other foot, the boy can't dig if he can't stand up."

139

Nerio, the fat one, approached Antonio again and the boy shouted something incoherent through sobs.

Dante held up a hand to stop Nerio, then asked Antonio a question.

"Are you ready to tell us the truth now?"

Antonio nodded and began talking rapidly. He told them he was the son of the world-famous assassin Maurice Scallato and that his father had given him orders to kill them. By the end of his confession, young Antonio was nearly babbling as he mentioned something about the puppies.

Dante looked down at the boy with irritation showing on his face. After reaching back to grab the shovel that was leaning beside the shotgun, he tossed the tool at Antonio.

"Start digging!"

"But I told you the truth."

"Dig!"

Antonio stood and gazed all about as if he were looking for something, or someone, but there was no one there. After picking up the shovel, he limped to his right and bit at the earth with the shovel's blade. And while he dug what he assumed would be his grave, he wept.

"THAT'S DEEP ENOUGH," DANTE SAID SOME TIME LATER. He was standing at the edge of a four-foot hole that Antonio had made.

Antonio gazed up at him with a tear-stained face. He was barely visible in the light from the crescent moon that hung overhead.

"I'll give you one last chance to save yourself," Dante lied. "Who else knows about this?"

"I told you the truth. Maurice Scallato is my father and he sent me to kill you."

"Every schoolboy in Europe knows about the Scallatos, and I have heard stories about the one named Maurice. If you were really the son of Maurice Scallato my brothers and I would all be dead men. Romy?"

"Yeah, Dante?" said the tall one.

"Pass me the shotgun; I'm tired of hearing this boy's lies."

"Where is it?"

"The shotgun? I left it leaning against the side of the ATV."

"It's not there."

"What do you mean it's not there? Nerio, did you move it?"

"No."

"I have it," said a cold voice from the darkness. An instant later, that darkness brightened three times in quick succession as the shotgun roared. Dante was the first to be struck, as steel pellets shredded his legs and he went tumbling down into the hole. Nerio, the fat one, had the left side of his head blown away, while his taller brother Romy took a blast to the chest and died before hitting the ground.

Antonio scrambled out of the hole by stepping on Dante's head and found himself lying at his father's feet. When he looked up at his father, Antonio saw an expression that turned his blood cold.

"Patri? I'm so sorry, Patri. I, I, they caught me."

Scallato ignored him, grabbed a shovel, and tossed it beside him. "Dig two more graves."

After Antonio picked himself up from the ground, Scallato straddled the hole and glared down at Dante.

Dante was hissing through gritted teeth, but he submerged the agony enough to call out to his brothers.

"Nerio? Romy?"

"They're dead," Scallato said.

Dante cried out in grief, then convulsed with a spasm from the pain of his damaged knees. He might never walk again, but he would live if he were to receive care. He was not going to live.

"Are you?" Dante asked.

"Am I what?"

"Him, Maurice Scallato?"

"I am."

A moment passed as Dante groaned while balling up his fists against the pain of his wounds, but then he spoke again. "I don't want to die. I can give you money."

"You'll die, and I'll find your money. I assume it's hidden somewhere inside the villa."

The look on Dante's face told Scallato he had guessed right. Scallato moved over to the ATV, grabbed the other shovel, and began filling in the hole. Dante's protests ended in a garbled sound after Scallato tossed dirt in his mouth.

Scallato looked over at his son and saw the shocked expression on his face.

"Keep digging, Antonio; maybe you're at least good enough to do that right."

Antonio went back to digging, while feeling lower than the dirt he shoveled.

18

THE MORNING AFTER THE NIGHT BEFORE

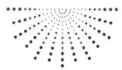

Sara awoke to find the sun lighting the windows, and the room had a golden glow from the color of the linen drapes. It matched the glow in her cheeks.

After turning her head, Sara saw that Tanner was no longer beside her, then, she smiled at her memories of the night just passed. Gradually, she became aware she wasn't alone, as she heard the repetitive movements coming from beyond the foot of the bed.

Sara sat up and leaned forward. Tanner was on the floor and doing pushups with an ease that was impressive. He wore only a pair of boxer shorts, and his hard, wiry muscles rippled. Sara watched him, and began keeping count, after more than a hundred repetitions, she saw Tanner stop, bring his knees up, and transition into a headstand.

Sara crawled to the end of the bed and saw Tanner smile at her upside down.

"Good morning," he said.

"If you've got that much energy, get back in bed."

Tanner slowly lowered his legs. Passed them between

his arms, then supported himself on just his fingertips. He still failed to exhibit any sign of strain or exertion.

"I hadn't worked out in a while; neglecting that could prove deadly in my profession."

"Last night wasn't enough of a workout for you?"

"It was the best night I've had in a long time."

Tanner stood, then leaned over and kissed Sara. She tried to pull him back into bed, but he resisted.

"I'm sweaty and need a shower."

She released him and nodded. "Okay."

As Tanner disappeared into the bathroom, Sara leaned back against the headboard and pulled the sheet up to cover herself. She sat there thinking as the sounds of the shower could be heard in the background.

She asked Tanner a question the moment he stepped back into the room. "What did last night mean to you?"

Tanner had been tightening a towel about his waist. He looked at her and asked his own question.

"Having regrets, are we?"

"No! And I'm sorry to ask that out of the blue, but I know you, Tanner. At one time, I even made a study of you. You've had more than your share of one-night stands."

Tanner sat on the edge of the bed and leaned over to kiss Sara. "You're not a one-night stand."

Sara made a face. "You must think I'm insecure, but this, us, it's not something I take lightly. We literally survived each other to get to this point in our relationship. I'd hate to think you don't really care about me."

"You want us to be exclusive? I have no problem with that."

"Really?"

"I won't cheat on you."

Sara said nothing else, but Tanner saw that something was on her mind.

"What? Speak up, Blake."

She touched him on the cheek. "No Blake, only Sara from now on. And, it's just that I'm wondering if this was too soon after Alexa."

"You're not a rebound love affair, Sara. Even Alexa knew I had feelings for you, although I denied it."

"I fought it too, and I was jealous of her. When she left you, I could no longer tell myself that I wasn't feeling what I was feeling."

"I caught the vibe, but I thought I was imagining it."

Sara moved the cover aside. "Get in here."

Tanner stood, dropped the towel, and climbed into bed. Moments later, they were making love again.

In Sicily, Maurice Scallato entered his workshop and slid aside a section of wall to reveal a hidden space. On a shelf, inside a small backpack, was what some would call a bug-out bag. The backpack contained a loaded gun, a box of spare ammo, a money clip with cash, a fake ID, a stun grenade, food, water, a compass, and a cell phone. This was his emergency equipment, and even his wife didn't know about it.

After checking to see that nothing was disturbed, Scallato slid the section of wall back in place. He then grabbed a cheap cell phone from a drawer that contained several. Each phone would be used once and then destroyed.

He left the workshop and walked up the hill behind it, to get better cell reception. The signal was weak, but the other party answered after nine rings.

"Hello?"

The voice sounded sleepy, but as always, sexy, it was the voice of his mistress, Veronika.

"It's me. Have you left Rome yet?"

"No."

"Good, I will be there soon."

"Are you bringing your son again? If so, I'll arrange another girl for him."

Scallato didn't answer. After a long silence, Veronika spoke.

"Maurice, is everything all right?"

"I need to see you. There is something I want to ask you and it is best if I do so in person."

"That sounds serious."

"It is serious, but nothing bad. I just have an offer to make you."

Scallato could hear her smile through the phone. "You know I'll never say no to you about anything."

"Yes, Veronika, and you are special to me."

"I love you, Maurice, you know that."

"I do."

"What about Antonio? Will he be coming?"

"No."

"Good, I want you all to myself."

"You'll have me soon, goodbye Veronika."

Scallato ended the call and sent a text off to his pet cop. The text informed his contact that Scallato would not be going to Genoa after all. As inviting an opportunity as the nursing home was, Scallato was wise enough not to face-off against Tanner when his mind was in turmoil over Antonio's failure.

With the text sent, Scallato removed the phone's SIM card, its Subscriber Identity Module. After breaking it in half, he set the SIM card on fire by using a lighter, then tossed the phone far into the trees.

As he walked down to his workshop, he saw Maria walking toward him. His wife had been in tears the night before, when she had seen her son's broken toes and wounded spirit. After Antonio told her what had happened, Maria had been furious with Maurice for endangering their son.

Scallato had ended the conversation by telling his wife to remember her place. Maria had bitten her tongue after seeing six-year-old Anna standing at the foot of the stairs and rubbing her eyes.

"What's wrong?" Anna had said. She was young, but even she sensed the tension in the room.

After putting Anna back to bed, Maria had Antonio keep the foot with the broken toes raised on a pillow and applied ice. Antonio's big toe had been crooked, but Maria straightened it and gave Antonio pain medication. Antonio also had a black eye from being hit with the TV remote that Romy Martello had thrown at him.

Maria had been raised in a family of criminals and was the wife of a world-class assassin. She knew a thing or two about healing and first aid. She had once removed a bullet from her husband's back with nothing more than a pair of tweezers and a bottle of rubbing alcohol.

Scallato had left the house after dropping Antonio there. He then spent the night searching the Martello brother's villa. He came away with over fifty-thousand euros, some gold, and a ledger that showed a record of protection payments.

He'd keep the money, but he would pass the record book over to the people his brother-in-law Bruno would be sending. Someone had to shear the sheep and it might as well be kept in the family.

Maria greeted him outside the house. She looked calmer than she'd been the night before, but still angry. Scallato didn't care about her anger. To him, wife or not, she was just a woman, and a man didn't run his life by catering to the emotional whims of women.

"Antonio says he feels better, but please go talk to him, Maurice."

"What would you like me to say to him, Maria?"

"For one thing you could tell him that you love him."

"Men don't say such things to other men."

"He's not a man, damn it! He's our little boy and you tried to rush him into manhood too soon. Give him another year, maybe even two, and then let him have another chance to prove himself."

"He had his chance and he failed. It was disgraceful."

"He's still your only son, Maurice, and he will be the one to carry the Scallato name forward."

Scallato took Maria in his arms. "We should have another child. With luck, it will be a boy."

Maria freed herself from his arms. "You're just giving up on Antonio, is that it? If you do that, you'll destroy him. That boy lives to make you proud."

"He's weak. It happens. Remember Dario, my younger brother? He was gutless too. But I'm still young enough to start over and train another son."

Maria shook her head. "I can't have any more children. The doctor said it would be very dangerous for me. Don't you recall how difficult Anna's delivery was?"

Scallato hung his head. "I'd forgotten the doctor's warning."

"You still have Antonio."

"Yes," Scallato said.

"Please go talk to him, Maurice. He's sick at heart thinking you don't love him anymore."

"I need to work out, then sleep. I'll talk to the boy later."

Maria started to protest, but then simply nodded. "Work out and rest, but you should eat first."

"I'm not hungry. Also, I will be flying back to Italy soon."

"To see your pet cop again?"

"Yes," Scallato said, although he was going there to see his lover, Veronika.

Maybe his wife couldn't give him more sons, but he knew a woman who could.

Scallato walked into his home and passed Antonio's room without giving him a thought. After the cowardice and incompetence he displayed the night before, Antonio was dead to him.

Scallato worked out in his home gym, showered, then afterwards, he lay down to sleep. His dreams were filled with visions of sons yet born.

19

CARLO SCALLATO

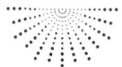

TANNER AND SARA ARRIVED IN GENOA, ITALY, IN THE LATE afternoon.

After checking into their hotel, they made their way to the nursing home where Scallato's father was living. An exhaustive examination of the area followed, until Tanner deemed it safe to enter the facility. Still, he told Sara to keep her eyes open and to stay ready.

They were both armed. Although lately, he infrequently took European contracts, Tanner still had a network in place that could provide him with arms, shelter, phony ID's, and medical care. The price of keeping such resources available was not cheap. Tanner was pleased to be getting some benefit from them.

Carlo Scallato was in the nursing home under the name of Mario Rossi. Tanner's ID identified him as Anthony Rossi, while Sara was his wife, Lorraine Rossi. The Rossi's were there visiting from America to see their Uncle Mario.

The young woman at the reception desk looked like a druggie and wore a skimpy outfit that revealed too much skin, given her surroundings. She spoke Italian, but it was of a dialect that Tanner had trouble understanding. When a nurse saw the difficulty he was having communicating, she stepped in to lend assistance.

The nurse's name was Ginevra Valli. She was in her early-forties and had an olive complexion along with long dark hair she kept tied up in a bun. As she led Tanner and Sara through the halls, she spoke over her shoulder, and she spoke in English.

"That girl at the desk is new. I am trying to get her replaced."

"Who hired her?" Tanner asked.

Ginevra frowned. "Our director, he claims she's his niece. She's the eighth niece he's had working here. One of them was black, while another was Asian. All of them were young and not very bright."

"It sounds like you might need a new director," Sara said.

"That will not happen. He is very rich. His family owns the nursing home and gave it to him as a plaything."

Ginevra stopped walking and sent them an apologetic smile. "I'm sorry. I shouldn't discuss such things with you. It's just that I get frustrated sometimes. This was once a very nice facility."

"And you're saying that's no longer the case?" Tanner asked.

Ginevra bit her bottom lip and Tanner could tell she was annoyed at herself for talking too much.

"I'll take you to see your uncle."

"Fine," Tanner said.

They passed several elderly patients who seemed to be just wandering the halls, while at a tall counter that resembled a nurses' station, several young women were gathered. Beyond them, there was a pair of double doors with an armed guard standing nearby.

The women, who looked more like hookers than nurses, were drinking from matching mugs that had the facility's logo on them. One of them, a young woman wearing gold hoop earrings and a too-tight top, stopped talking when she spotted Tanner. After her eyes roamed over him, she sent Tanner a smile. When the woman noticed that Sara was glaring at her, she looked away, as her friends broke out in laughter.

Ginevra escorted them to a large room where a pair of TVs blared away with what looked like an Italian soap opera. There were seven people in the room, all were men. They were in wheelchairs and seemed to be lost in their own worlds. Most displayed some form of compulsive behavior, like wringing their hands or tapping their knee. Tanner spotted Carlo Scallato and knew that he was looking at the legendary assassin, although he appeared to be much older than the picture that Durand had supplied. However, even in the grip of dementia and old age, Carlo Scallato stood out as someone special.

Tanner walked over, leaned down, and stared into the elder Scallato's eyes. The old man's eyes looked back at him with confusion and fear showing. That lasted only a second, then the eyes lost focus and wandered away.

"What's wrong with my uncle? He looks…odd. Is he on some sort of strong sedative?"

"He is on medication, yes, but everyone in this room suffers from dementia, Signore Rossi. I thought you knew."

"Yes, I did, but I was under the impression that he could still communicate."

"He'll speak, but it usually makes little sense. I'm sorry."

"Who comes to visit him?"

"You and your wife are the first ones, Signore. I had thought that he was alone in the world."

Through a doorway, Sara saw a row of beds lined up. She pointed at them. "Does our uncle sleep in there?"

"Yes," Ginevra said, but she wouldn't meet Sara's eyes.

"I was told my uncle had a private room," Tanner said.

Ginevra looked down at the floor. "You'll have to speak to the director about that."

"What's the man's name?"

"Signore Bianchi."

"Take me to him, Ginevra."

Ginevra gazed at Tanner and the words she was about to speak died in her throat. Tanner was angry, and it showed.

He didn't know Carlo Scallato, but Tanner knew that the man had been a legendary assassin. A fellow assassin deserved better than to be left to rot in a ward. He suspected that the nursing home's director was corrupt and taking advantage of Carlo. Tanner would put an end to that and get Carlo Scallato the care he needed. Once that was done, he would track down the man's son and kill him. In Tanner's mind, the two things had no connection. And while the sins of the father might be visited upon the son, Tanner didn't see any reason why that should work in reverse.

Ginevra led them to a corridor where the director's office was located. Signore Bianchi wasn't in, but he was expected at any moment. There were a pair of padded chairs across from the office door where they could wait for him. Tanner and Sara settled on the chairs' green vinyl covering.

Tanner was also aware that Jacques Durand had steered them toward what he must have known would be a dead end. That also angered him.

"Let me deal with Durand," Sara said.

"Why?"

"I'm going to tell him you're upset with him but that I know he had no way of knowing Carlo Scallato would be a useless lead. If Jacques believes I still trust him, he'll be easier to fool or trap later."

"It makes sense, and the man has a thing for you. He'll believe everything you say."

Sara took out her phone to play a game on it while they waited. She quickly grew bored with it, then fidgeted in her seat.

Tanner had been giving her sideways glances as he recalled their night together. Rather than cooling his desire for Sara, having been with her, the thought of having her again was becoming distracting.

"Can we go right back to our suite after we talk to Bianchi?" Sara asked.

"Yeah."

"Good."

"Why is that good?"

"Because, Mr. Tanner, all I can think about is getting you back into bed."

Tanner grinned. "Who'd of guessed we'd be so compatible?"

20

WHAT'S WITH ALL THE HOTTIES?

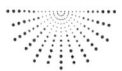

THE NURSING HOME DIRECTOR, SALVATORE BIANCHI, arrived back at the facility after having taken a three-hour lunch break. Bianchi was a handsome man in an expensive wool suit who was aging gracefully. He was tall and appeared to be in good shape.

Bianchi was in the company of a young woman who hadn't yet seen her twentieth birthday. After telling Tanner and Sara that he would be right with them, he kissed the girl goodbye and watched her ass as she walked away. Bianchi's eyes then traveled over Sara with a lecherous gaze.

Tanner snapped his fingers to gain Bianchi's attention. Bianchi looked insulted by the gesture and asked Tanner who he was. Once he knew he was there to inquire about a patient who was a relative, he opened the office, then excused himself and took out his phone.

The office was large for its type and richly decorated. The motif was Chinese, and Tanner noted that there were several paintings from a well-known Cantonese artist.

After ending the call, Bianchi settled behind his desk

and asked Tanner and Sara to take the two seats in front of it.

"You two are Americans?"

"Yes," Tanner said.

"You speak Italian well, which is good, my English is atrocious."

"What about your Chinese?"

Bianchi lit up with surprise and spoke to Tanner in Cantonese by asking him if he understood what he was saying. Tanner answered him in Cantonese and Bianchi was all smiles.

"It's wonderful to run into someone that can speak a Chinese language. I lived there for eight years when I was younger."

Tanner had been wondering who Bianchi had called before sitting behind his desk. The answer came when a pair of orderlies entered the room. The scrubs they wore were meant to be baggy and easy to move in, but they appeared a size too small. The men were both bodybuilder types and had full beards. They glared at Tanner menacingly before looking Sara over.

"Where were you?" Bianchi asked the men.

"We were parking the car, boss," the one on the left said, he was an inch taller than the other man, but looked no brighter.

"I want one of you with me at all times from now on."

"Yes sir," both men said.

Bianchi gestured toward the two men. "I've been threatened by irate family members in the past. Since then I find it best to have… witnesses present."

"You mean bodyguards," Tanner said.

Bianchi cleared his throat, then asked a question. "How can I help you?"

"My uncle Mario is in a ward. I understood that he was paying for a private room."

Bianchi shook his head. "You're mistaken. Signore Rossi is here on what we call our budget plan. I can show you the admittance paperwork."

"Do that," Tanner said.

Bianchi produced the form within a few minutes, and Tanner saw that Carlo Scallato had been assigned the lower-tier option. He also saw that a law firm was listed as the contact number for next of kin.

Tanner's respect for Maurice Scallato dipped in regard to the man as a person. What son doesn't see that his father gets the best of care? And Scallato had to be worth millions. When he looked over at Sara, he saw that she was thinking the same thing.

"I want him placed in a private room and I want to keep it just between us. My other relatives don't need to know about the change or that I'm paying for it."

Bianchi was shaking his head no before Tanner had even finished speaking. "There's nothing available, but I assure you that your uncle is getting the best of care."

"My uncle is wasting away here until he dies. I just want him to be comfortable while he does that."

"I can't help you, and you realize that you have no legal right to request anything, yes?"

Tanner stared at Bianchi, then turned his head to look at the two huge orderlies. The one on the right flexed while his arms were crossed over his massive chest.

After standing, Tanner offered Sara his hand.

"We'll speak again," Tanner said.

The two bodybuilders were blocking the door as they tried to stare Tanner down. Both men looked away after only a few seconds of taking in Tanner's intense eyes. The one on the left moved aside, and Tanner and Sara were back out in the corridor.

"Why would he have bodyguards?" Sara asked.

"That's what I was wondering."

"There also seem to be a lot of very young women around. And I can't be sure, but Bianchi's pupils appeared dilated."

"I'll look into it tomorrow; maybe it's all connected to Scallato somehow. I also want to meet with Durand."

Sara moved closer and kissed him. "Tomorrow. The rest of the day is all ours."

"Why don't we go back to the hotel?"

"That's a good idea."

As they were leaving the parking lot, Tanner spotted the nurse, Ginevra. She was seated alone at a picnic table and eating. When she saw Tanner, she waved and smiled. Tanner gave his horn a toot in reply. He made a mental note to talk with Ginevra again, as the nurse could be a good source of information. Something was going on inside the nursing home that had nothing to do with caring for the elderly, and Tanner planned to find out what it was. With luck, it would lead him right to Maurice Scallato.

IF AT FIRST YOU DON'T SUCCEED…

MAURICE SCALLATO ARRIVED IN ROME THE FOLLOWING morning and took a cab to the office of a private detective agency. The agency was of a high caliber and guaranteed results and confidentiality. Scallato was ushered into the office of an agency executive by a male secretary who asked him if he wanted anything to drink.

Scallato declined the offer while smoothing out a wrinkle in the tie he wore. A moment later, the man he'd come to see entered and sat behind the desk. His name was Reginald Thurgood the fourth.

After greetings were exchanged and the secretary left the room, Thurgood took a file from a locked drawer and passed it across to Scallato, whom he knew by another name.

Before opening the file, Scallato held it up. "Is there any bad news in here?"

Reginald Thurgood smiled. He was the son of an Englishman who had divorced his Italian mother when he was three-years-old. Despite his name and paternity, he looked like a Sicilian and had never learned the English language.

"You would have been informed, Signore. No, your lady has remained faithful, although she's constantly approached by men, but what beautiful woman isn't?"

Scallato studied the surveillance file that concerned Veronika. He usually browsed through the reports only once a year, since Thurgood had orders to contact him if Veronika was unfaithful. In truth, Scallato was amazed they were still together. He had never expected their relationship to last for years. He'd slept with many women during that time, including the late Claire Newport, and of course, his wife, none of them pleased him as Veronika did.

When he came across surveillance photos of himself and Antonio entering Veronika's building, he felt a pang of depression. That had been such a happy day for him, to have his son become a man. But Antonio lacked the killer instinct and had no guts. If the Scallato name was to carry on, Maurice knew he would have to have another son, or even better, two.

"That other information I asked for, were you able to acquire it on such short notice?"

Thurgood said yes and apologized for not remembering that they had other business. There was a slim red file on his desk. He passed it over to Scallato. It was a genealogy report on Veronika. It confirmed what she had told Scallato about herself over their years together. She was the only girl in a family of six children. Her five brothers had eight sons and only one daughter between them. Her mother had six brothers, and her grandmother had been one of only two daughters in a family of fourteen. Twins were also a frequent occurrence in the family, and every set born had been male.

Scallato finished with the files and passed them back across the desk.

"Destroy them."

"Yes, as usual. And do you require anything to be changed?"

"Not changed, ended. There is to be no more surveillance on her."

"Yes sir," Thurgood said. "but I do hope you'll use us again in the future."

"I will, but likely in a different capacity."

Scallato left the agency and headed off to see Veronika. She was about to get the deal of a lifetime.

THREE HUNDRED MILES AWAY IN GENOA, TANNER AND SARA were finishing a run. Neither of them had run in days, while both were habitual runners. The first lap had been taken at a languid speed for Tanner, who usually ran full out. When Sara saw that he was holding back, she told him he didn't have to stay at her pace. As a result, Tanner covered sixteen half-mile laps to Sara's nine.

When Tanner finally slowed his pace, then came up beside her, Sara saw that he showed only faint signs of exertion. Tanner's breathing was almost normal, although he was sweating profusely.

"If I ran that fast for that long I'd be puking," Sara said.

"You get used to it with training," Tanner said. He then pulled a water bottle off his hip and sucked down the contents.

Their hotel was near the park, so they walked back. Sara felt her phone vibrate and saw that she had a text from Durand.

"He wants to meet."

"Tell Durand that we'll get together at the airport bar. I want him to think we've given up on finding Scallato through his father."

"What if he asks where we're going?"

"We'll tell him we're going home."

"Do you think he'll believe that?"

"He will. Durand thinks I've gotten by on luck. He'll believe that when things got hard I just gave up."

Sara sent the text mentioning the airport, along with a time and place. Durand agreed to the meeting and she saw that they had four hours to kill.

"There's plenty of time before we have to meet Durand; why don't we explore the city?"

"Sounds good," Tanner said. "This is my first time in Genoa."

They showered together, with plans to get dressed and travel about like a pair of regular tourists. They should have bathed separately, as both became aroused, and they wound up back in bed, soapy, wet, and laughing like young lovers. By the time they left their hotel room, they had just enough time to get to the airport and meet Jacques Durand.

IN ROME, TWO OTHER LOVERS WERE LYING IN BED together. Scallato was with Veronika in her apartment and had just offered her the opportunity of having his children.

"Oh Maurice, of course I'll have your children, then I won't be so lonely while you're gone."

"I need sons, Veronika. Antonio is not worthy."

"Baby, I'm so sorry, but the sons I give you will make you proud."

"I understand that this is asking a lot. I will change our deal to reflect that financially. Also, I'll start looking for a house in Sicily for you, something secluded and with land."

Veronika straddled Scallato's hips, then lowered herself onto his chest.

"I don't want more money, but the house is a good idea."

"Why don't you want the money?"

"Because all I want is you. Instead of money, promise me you'll spend more time with me."

"Once you're pregnant and living in Sicily I'll be able to visit more often. My home holds little attraction for me these days."

"You could start over. You know, get a divorce and stay with me."

"Or, I could hire a whore like that Yana to have my sons and hire nannies to raise them."

Veronika's head jerked up. "No. I'm sorry. I wasn't trying to pressure you into anything."

Scallato sighed and caressed her cheek. "I know you wouldn't do that; I'm just in a foul mood."

"I can do something about that," Veronika said, as she slid down toward the foot of the bed and disappeared beneath the covers.

SOMETHING IS ROTTEN IN GENOA

TANNER SAW DURAND WATCHING THEM AS THEY LOADED luggage onto a cart. That was good. They wanted him to believe they were leaving Genoa.

Durand sent Sara a smile and disappeared into the airport bar, a well-decorated lounge with rich wood and deep red carpeting. Tanner and Sara joined Durand moments later and both ordered drinks.

"I'm disappointed in you, Jacques," Sara said. "You must have known that Carlo Scallato was in no condition to help anyone."

"No, Sara, I was unaware. But as the man's father, it was always a long shot that Carlo would have led you to Maurice Scallato's whereabouts, yes?"

"I don't like being played with, Durand," Tanner said.

"We had a deal, Tanner, and I kept my end of the bargain. I never promised results."

"I could kill you, Durand; that would be a result."

"No," Sara said. "Let's just put Europe behind us and go home."

Tanner gritted his teeth. "If only that damn nursing

home had worked out." Tanner looked back at Durand and saw that the Frenchman was taking in their act. He then waved a hand at Durand and stood. "Let's get out of here. I want to get back to the states. I'm sick of Europe, and if Scallato is stupid enough to come after me again, I'll kill him."

Sara stood and smiled at Durand. "I hope to see you again someday, Jacques."

"If you want that day to arrive, then leave Tanner, otherwise, Scallato may kill you too."

Tanner took Sara by the arm and spoke over his shoulder to Durand, as he headed for the exit. "Go to hell, Durand."

After leaving the bar, Tanner and Sara moved to a spot where they could view the bar's entrance. When Durand walked out, they followed him from a distance and saw him take a taxi.

"I think our deception worked," Sara said. "But I'm still not convinced that Jacques would betray us."

"We'll see. In the meantime, no one will be looking for us at the nursing home."

"What's next, the nurse?"

Tanner nodded. "Yeah, I think that nurse, Ginevra, knows what's going on in that nursing home, but is staying quiet about it to keep her job."

"And you're still hoping it will lead you to Scallato?"

"It's all I've got, Sara, and the man is linked to the place by his father's presence there."

"I agree, but I never thought that killing Scallato would be so difficult."

Tanner shook his head. "Locating him is difficult. Killing the man will be easy… and enjoyable."

GINEVRA'S SMILE WAS TENTATIVE AS SHE OPENED HER apartment door to find Tanner and Sara staring at her. Without waiting to be invited in, Tanner pushed past Ginevra and went off to check out the small apartment. He was surprised by the scant square footage and the sparseness of the furnishings, as he believed that the nurse was involved in something illegal that paid well.

Sara entered, then shut the door behind her as Tanner returned.

"There's no one else here," he said.

Ginevra looked from Tanner to Sara, then back at Tanner. There was anger in her expression, but her eyes held only fear. "Signore and Signora Rossi, why are you here?"

"I want to know what's going on in that nursing home you work at, and you're going to tell me."

Ginevra's breath caught in her throat, but then she pointed at the door. "Get out or I will call the *polizia*."

Ginevra's phone was on a coffee table. Tanner snatched it up and handed it to her.

"Call the cops. Maybe they can figure out what you and Bianchi have been up to."

Ginevra took the phone from Tanner's hand, then just held it, as she looked down at the floor.

"I am not involved with Bianchi's activities."

"That's a lie and we both know it. I believe you're being paid to keep silent; that makes you a part of it, whatever it is."

Ginevra looked up, and there were tears in her eyes.

Sara moved closer to her. "We're not here to hurt you. We just need to know the truth. Once we know what's happening, maybe we can help you."

"And what happens if I don't talk to you?"

"I'll find out some other way," Tanner said. "And if I have to do that, then you're on your own."

Ginevra considered Tanner's words as she wiped at tears. After inhaling a deep breath, she spoke.

"I do take money to stay silent. I have a younger sister who requires special care and it is very expensive. The government used to pay for it, but that ended."

Tanner softened his tone. "Tell us what's going on, Ginevra."

Ginevra gestured for them to sit on the sofa as she sat in a wing chair. "I'll tell you everything, and I apologize in advance."

"Apologize for what?" Tanner said.

Ginevra let out a sob. "For the way I've treated your uncle, Signore Rossi. I'm so sorry."

Sara reached over and gave Ginevra's hand a squeeze. "Just start at the beginning."

Ginevra did just that, as she recounted the changes that took place when Bianchi became the new head of the facility.

"At first, they were little things, although they were many in number. Everything the home used became of a cheaper quality, the food, the linen, everything. At the same time, we had many employees who were retiring, they were all replaced with young and inexperienced women. Since then, many more have quit, or found other jobs, and again, Bianchi hired very young women."

"Are these women qualified?" Sara asked.

"Their credentials say so, but I have my doubts about their authenticity."

"You said yesterday that Bianchi's family has money. I take it they own the nursing home?" Tanner asked.

"Yes, but he is what they call the black sheep, and his family never visits him. I think they put him in an old-age home because they believed it was one place where he wouldn't get into trouble."

"I think I can guess, but tell us what Bianchi did after hiring so many young women?"

Ginevra's eyes narrowed into slits as her face reddened in anger. "Yes, they are all whores. The east ward is off limits to the regular staff and has a new rear entrance. Cars come and go back there all day long."

"Who is Bianchi's partner?" Tanner asked.

Ginevra blinked in surprise. "How did you know he had a partner?"

"If the mob wasn't getting their cut, Bianchi's play zone wouldn't have lasted this long."

"The man's name is Bruno Allende. He is a mobster, yes, but he owns many other businesses, mainly bars and restaurants. He is the one who hired away so many of our people so that they could move the girls in."

"Why did they keep you?" Sara asked.

"They knew I needed money, and they still require some healthcare professionals to maintain the illusion that the nursing home is legitimate. The others who stayed, they are all like me and have need for money to help their families. If we talked, the mob would kill us, and even if the police protected us, then what would become of my sister?"

"I still don't understand why you're ashamed of the way you've treated my uncle," Tanner said. "It sounds like you're the only one looking out for him."

Ginevra began crying again. "Bruno makes Signore Bianchi some money with the whores, but Bruno gets most of it, so… Bianchi cut off the medications."

"The medication for the patients, including my uncle?"

"Yes. Your uncle's condition can't be cured, but it should be treated with drugs such as memantine or a cholinesterase inhibitor. They receive nothing but vitamins."

"Those drugs you mentioned, would they help my uncle enough so that he might be able to communicate with me?"

"Oh, yes, it is possible, but there are many factors involved."

Tanner glanced over at Sara and saw that she was as excited by the news as he was. Perhaps he would get to speak with Carlo Scallato after all.

"If I got you the drugs, could you administer them?"

"Sì, but I would need a doctor to recommend the dosage; there would also be lab work and blood tests involved."

Tanner stood and paced for a moment, then stopped and spoke to Sara. "Could Conrad Burke help us with this?"

"He has the resources, and he owes you his life."

"We'll contact him," Tanner said, then turned back to Ginevra. "We'll need your help, but when we're through, I think you'll no longer have to worry about Bianchi or the mob."

Ginevra stood. "How is that possible?"

Sara got to her feet. "Trust him. In the long run, we're your best hope."

Ginevra looked at Sara, then back at Tanner. "What do you need me to do?"

"We'll contact you soon with details. But tell me, can you get us in and out of the nursing home without being seen by Bianchi?"

"Yes, there's a side door we can use, and it leads to your uncle's ward."

"We'll be in touch," Tanner said.

A<small>FTER LEAVING THE APARTMENT</small>, S<small>ARA SENT OFF A TEXT</small> asking Conrad Burke to call her at his earliest convenience.

"If we can get Carlo talking about his son we'll have a lead," Tanner said.

"But Durand had a point," Sara said. "Carlo may not be willing to talk to us. Would you torture him?"

"No, but he may not have much love left for Scallato. Remember, he's the one that placed the old man in Bianchi's care."

"Maybe, but paternal love is strong."

Tanner arched an eyebrow. "Everything has its limits."

23

WELCOME BACK TO THE WORLD

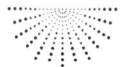

Conrad Burke came through with the assistance Tanner needed and Carlo Scallato began receiving the proper medication for his condition.

Tanner spent time with the man, but he saw no improvement the first week. When he wasn't with Carlo, his time was spent with Sara, as the two of them grew closer in their new intimacy. When Sara was alone, she shopped, something she hadn't done much of in years. Most of it was shipped home, but Tanner saw that her wardrobe was attaining a European flair.

He likewise was dressing like the natives, as he bought five new suits that fit him like a glove. These, he mixed and matched with casual shirts, sweaters, and a host of accessories such as watches and ties.

By their third week in Genoa, Tanner and Sara could pass as natives to the casual observer and were blending in quite well.

That was a necessity, for if they stood out their presence might be questioned by the wrong people. Tanner would deal with Bianchi, and Bruno Allende at a time of his own choosing, once he had gotten all he could from Carlo Scallato. Tanner maintained a rigid routine of checking for surveillance and any hint of Maurice Scallato. He felt as if he had underestimated the man in California. He did not intend to make that mistake again.

Tanner never thought of Scallato as his equal, because Tanner was certain he had no equals. The only man who came close was his mentor, Tanner Six. As the seventh Tanner, he was the best assassin in the world, not Maurice Scallato. Then again, a bullet in the head from a runner-up could kill you all the same.

When Carlo Scallato's treatment entered its fourth week, Tanner met Sara for dinner to update her on the elder Scallato's progress. They ate inside their room, since it made sense to limit their time in public. Whenever Sara did venture out, she wore a blonde wig and sunglasses.

After they'd consumed their meal, they sat out on the suite's balcony with a bottle of wine. As Sara lay back in his arms, Tanner gave her the good news.

"Carlo is talking more. Most of it is a confused jumble of events from the past, but the doctor says that we could see further improvement."

"That's great, and is the fresh air helping any?"

"Yeah, Ginevra makes sure that he gets outside for an hour when the weather is good, and I bought him a box of cigars and a bottle of Scotch whisky."

Sara laughed. "Why did you do that?"

"I don't know, wishful thinking maybe. I remember hearing that the old man liked his Scotch and cigars, Cuban cigars, of course. Maybe seeing them nearby will make him feel more like his old self."

"What about that new drug they were going to try?"

"He's been on it for only a few days; I guess we'll have to wait and see."

"I hate to follow your good news with bad news, but I received some today from Conrad Burke."

"What about?"

"Dan Matthews escaped. He was one of several prisoners that went on the run after a prison transport van was in an accident."

Tanner placed his wine glass upon the coffee table with a loud clunk. "That bastard sold me out to Alonso Alvarado. But wait, he also has a grudge against you, doesn't he?"

"Oh yes. I tracked him down in his island paradise in Panama and handed him over to the CIA. That was after I had him beaten to give up his money."

"What did Burke have to say about it?"

"He said if you wanted to thank him for the help you received, you could put a bullet in Matthews someday. Don't forget, he betrayed Burke too."

"Maybe I'll make Matthews a priority once Scallato is dead."

Sara sat up, turned around, then kissed Tanner. "Matthews can wait. I want to go visit Nadya and Romeo, and see the baby."

"Right, but you may get to meet Tanner Six too. Romeo and Nadya will be coming to the states soon."

"I thought they had come already?"

"That was cancelled when the baby developed an ear infection."

"Where does Tanner Six live?"

"His name is Spenser; he lives in Cody, Wyoming."

"He lives in a town that has your real name?"

"He says that's why he settled there."

"It sounds like he loves you."

"We're kind of like father and son, although he's only a few years older than I am."

"If he's so young, then why did he pass on the Tanner name to you?"

"He lost an eye and had to go through a long period of adjustment. Also, he knew I was ready."

Sara leaned back in his arms again and Tanner held her close.

"Do you have any plans to go back to New York?" Sara asked.

"Yeah, probably once we leave Spenser's place. Joe Pullo wrote and said he had some work for me, but that it could wait."

Sara laughed. "Imagine Pullo's face if he saw us now."

"I know. It amazes me that we're together. I can just imagine how Joe will react."

Sara tilted her head back so that she could look at Tanner. "I know, but we're good together, and I don't want it to end."

"We're just beginning," Tanner said, and kissed her.

TANNER ARRIVED AT THE NURSING HOME AND ENTERED through a side door with the use of a key. Ginevra was practically living at the home since Carlo Scallato began his treatment, and Tanner was surprised to see that the patients had been left alone. He calmed one man by picking up and handing him the pair of socks he liked to hold, as he noticed that Carlo was missing from the day room.

As he moved toward the ward where the beds were, Tanner saw an overturned wheelchair. Without having to give it conscious thought, his gun appeared in his hand. The wheelchair was near the last bed in the row, Carlo's bed, which was near the windows. As Tanner drew closer, he saw that one of the window panes was broken, and a cool breeze was drifting through the room.

Then, he saw a disturbing sight. Someone clad in pajamas was lying on the side of the bed, although only their lower legs, socks, and slippers could be seen. Tanner was moving to investigate when he realized his mistake. It was a trick, and one he had used more than once himself. There was no body, only a pair of pajama bottoms stuffed with a sheet from the bed, along with the slippers.

Tanner spun around with his gun at the ready and placed the barrel of it against the chest of his would-be attacker. It was Carlo Scallato. The old assassin was barefoot, wearing a pajama top and an adult diaper. In his right hand was a jagged piece of the window glass. He was holding the other end of the shard after having wrapped a pillowcase around it. The old man displayed no fear of Tanner's gun, but he appeared annoyed because his ruse hadn't worked. He looked Tanner up and down and asked a question in Italian.

"Chi diavolo sei?" which in English translated to "Who the hell are you?"

Tanner lowered the gun. "Welcome back to the world, Carlo Scallato."

24

THE GHOST

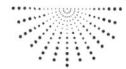

CARLO HAD FORCED HIS NURSE, GINEVRA, INTO A SUPPLY closet by threatening her with his makeshift knife. After Tanner freed her, she explained to Carlo about his dementia and that he was a patient of the nursing home. Despite having been threatened by Carlo, Ginevra still smiled at the old assassin as she helped him get back into bed.

"I don't even understand how you can walk," Ginevra told Carlo. "Most men in your condition would have needed weeks of physical therapy after having been bedridden for so long."

Carlo answered her in his craggy voice. "I'm not most men, and you're one good-looking woman."

Ginevra blushed, then leaned over and kissed Carlo on the cheek. After that, the old man went to sleep.

Tanner stayed beside the bed hoping to speak with him when he awoke, but when Carlo came around again, he was back to being confused and living in the past.

The doctor told Tanner that the new medication was experimental, but that Carlo's episode of normalcy should expand into longer periods of the same. It was another three days before the doctor's words proved true, and Tanner settled in a chair beside the old man, as Carlo sat up in bed.

"Have a nice reunion with your nephew, Signore Rizzo," Ginevra said. "I'll be back in a short time."

"It's a date," Carlo said.

When Ginevra was out of sight, Carlo threw a thumb after her. "Why is she calling me Rizzo and thinks that you're my nephew?"

Tanner explained it all to the old man, ending it by telling him that his name was Tanner.

"I knew a Tanner once. Are you one of those Tanner's?"

"You knew my mentor, Tanner Six; I'm Tanner Seven."

"Yeah, your mentor was so young when I knew him, but he beat me to the target, and I lost money on a bet we'd made too."

"Your son and I don't get along as well. We're trying to kill each other."

"You are a dead man then, Tanner. My son, Maurice, is the deadliest and most heartless killer who ever lived. He even killed his own brother."

"You knew that, and you still allowed him to follow in your footsteps?"

"I did, because I had no proof, but I knew. I knew the second I saw that ring on his finger."

"What ring?"

"It's a ring we all wear. It was made from the slug that killed my great-great-grandfather's first target. That was Gino Scallato, and he dug that slug out of a man who had raped and tortured two women."

"So, you're saying you never gave it to Maurice?"

The old man's face reddened. "I gave that ring to my oldest son, Bernardo. He died while making a hit. The next day, I saw that Maurice was wearing the ring, and I knew, oh yeah, I knew, but it was years before I could say the words."

"Tell me where I can find him, and I'll make him pay for killing his brother."

Carlo wagged a finger. "He is still my son. And anyway, I have no idea where he might be. The day I finally confronted him about killing Bernardo was the last day I saw him. I was in a hospital then with a broken back. I retired completely, and Maurice took over. Now he is *Il Fantasma*, The Ghost, and you Tanner, you will never kill him."

"I will kill him, Carlo. He's no ghost, he's just another assassin."

"The day you see him, Tanner, that's the day you die."

"We've already tangled once, but he got away."

"Are you serious? You survived a meeting with my son?"

"And he survived me, but he won't keep surviving me."

"I would make a bet with you, but dead men can't pay up. Anyway…I… the dog…the dog… the dog, somebody let the damn dog out."

Tanner was confused for a moment, but then realized that Carlo was slipping away into his dementia. He tried to bring him back, but the old man spoke to him as if he thought he was someone else, then, simply babbled.

Figuring that there was no longer any point in staying by his side, Tanner stood to leave. He was at the door when Carlo spoke again.

"I went away, didn't I?"

"Carlo?"

"Yeah, for now. Sit down, Tanner, and let me talk some sense into you."

"What's that mean?" Tanner asked, as he sat again.

"Maurice, he was never right, but he is a perfect killer. He's not one of those sickos that can't feel, no. I will never believe that, even though I accused him of that once. Still, he can turn off emotion and erase feelings at will. I've seen him do it. He loved Bernardo when he was a child, but ambition became more important."

"That happens to many men."

"Is it happening to you? If you were to kill *Il Fantasma*, you would be an instant legend in all of Europe."

"I don't care about that, but I don't run from a fight or hide from any man."

"Is this all you have, boy, this being a Tanner? Or is there something else in your life?"

Tanner thought that over and was surprised by the answer. The truth was that he wasn't sure. Being a Tanner had been everything, but Alexa had shown him that there was more to life. He had no plans to give it up, but he thought that maybe there could be something else as well. When he thought about that, Sara Blake came to mind.

"I have… someone."

"Then take that someone and hide, boy, or you will die."

In answer, Tanner shook his head.

Carlo shook his head as well, but it was in a sad slow motion.

"We Scallatos have a tradition, Tanner. Something we do to test the killer instinct of our sons. When Bernardo was fourteen, I handed him a shotgun and told him to kill three kittens I had put in a box. He couldn't do it. There was no disgrace, about half of us fail the test, but you see, a few months later, Bernardo told Maurice about it. I

184

arrived home from a fulfilling a contract a week later to find my wife in tears. Maurice had stolen the litter of five puppies from a neighbor's house."

"He killed them with a shotgun?" Tanner asked.

Something like shame passed across Carlo's face, then, he answered. "Maurice strangled them with his bare hands. He was only nine-years-old."

Tanner sat with the old man until Carlo fell asleep.

FOLLOW THE BOUNCING THUG

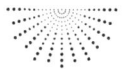

ALTHOUGH CARLO TURNED OUT TO BE NO HELP IN tracking down Maurice Scallato, Tanner still had a plan that might lead him to the Sicilian.

He and Sara followed the nursing home director, Bianchi, into a rough looking section of the city. The car Bianchi was riding in wasn't a limo, but it was as big as one and a luxury automobile. The two bodybuilder types were with Bianchi again and one of them was doing the driving. After turning down an alleyway, Bianchi picked up a short hooker who was standing among a group of taller women, and the car rode off.

Tanner followed, saw the car turn down a second alley, and realized that it was a designated spot.

"They'll park back there, and have the hooker do her thing," he told Sara. "Afterward, they'll leave. We should approach on foot, otherwise, they might take off."

They left their vehicle parked by a dumpster and began walking down the alley. The two goons were standing outside the car, and watched them approach, but made no move to reach for a weapon, nor did Tanner.

"What's your plan?" Sara whispered.

"I'll beat the hell out of them and grab up Bianchi."

"You're going to beat up those two giants?" Sara said, and Tanner smiled at the disbelief he heard in her voice.

"Yes, but stay back so I have plenty of room to work."

"All right, but why not use a gun to threaten them?"

"A gun will be too noisy. I'll only use it if I have to."

"Be careful, Tanner."

"I will."

As Tanner hoped they would, the bodyguards just watched as they approached. There was enough light in the alley to see that their hands were empty, and the two giants thought he and Sara posed no physical threat to them. As they came within yards of the men, one of the hulking figures took a step forward.

"Return the way you came. It's private back here."

"In a smelly alleyway?" Tanner said.

"Turn around or you'll be in for a world of hurt."

Sara stopped walking when she was ten feet away, but Tanner kept going. One of Bianchi's bodyguards folded his arms across his chest. He was wearing a sleeveless T-shirt and the sheer size of his biceps was impressive. The other guard held up a hand and then went to push Tanner backwards. That was his undoing.

Tanner grabbed the man's thumb with one hand and gripped his palm in the other, then yanked, dislocating the thumb. Even as the first hood was howling in pain, Tanner was using him as a brace to deliver a kick to the kneecap of the other one. The kick to the knee was followed by an elbow to the side of the second thug's head and the man was down and moaning.

The first thug pushed aside the pain of his thumb and reached for a gun he had at the small of his back. Tanner sent a foot flying into the man's groin. That doubled the thug over and he was fed a knee to the face. The blow was so hard that a tooth flew out of his mouth. After kicking the man's face, Tanner took his gun, then, he gave his buddy a kick in the face for good measure.

The back door of the car flew open and Tanner raised the gun.

"Don't shoot!" cried a small voice in Italian.

It was the hooker, and makeup or no makeup, Tanner could tell she was just a child of no more than twelve. Through the back window, Tanner could see Bianchi pulling up his pants. Tanner walked by the hooker and dragged Bianchi out of the car, to drop the man on his ass.

Bianchi was crying and whimpering as he begged for his life. Meanwhile, the hooker had pushed past Sara and said she didn't see anything.

Sara spoke to Tanner. "Shouldn't we go after her, help her somehow?"

Tanner shook his head. "Dragging her off the street won't help. She'd just be back out here tomorrow."

"I know you're right, but did you see her... she's a baby."

"A damaged baby, and men like Bianchi make exploiting her profitable."

Bianchi was still crying and begging for his life when they transferred him into the back of their car. Sara sat to his left while pointing the gun of his own bodyguard at him. Bianchi stopped crying long enough to realize that he had met his abductors before.

"I know you. I know both of you." He snapped his fingers as it came to him. "Rizzo, you're old man Rizzo's son, no wait, nephew, right?"

Tanner and Sara ignored him. Two minutes later, Tanner pulled into the parking lot of an abandoned factory. They had scouted out the place earlier and set it up for an interrogation.

Bianchi protested their intention to take him inside the building, but fear of the gun kept his feet moving. After entering the building through a door that was hanging open on one hinge, Tanner spun suddenly and buried a fist in Bianchi's stomach.

When the nursing home director's legs threatened to buckle, Tanner held him up and guided him over to a chair. The chair had zip ties attached to the arms and legs, and before Bianchi knew it, he was bound to the metal chair and helpless.

"A private room, right? You wanted your uncle to have a private room. Hell, you got it."

"This isn't about my uncle. You're going to tell us all about the whorehouse you're running at the nursing home."

Bianchi sank into the chair as if someone had let the air out of him. "Oh no, you're working for Degussa. Listen, none of this was my idea. It was all Bruno Allende."

"Who is Degussa?" Tanner said.

A little of the air returned and Bianchi raised his head. "You don't work for Degussa?"

"No, who is he?"

Bianchi smiled. "If you don't work for Degussa then I don't have to worry."

Tanner took out his gun and slammed the butt of it onto one of Bianchi's hands, then he did it again, and again. Tanner had intended to smash only one finger, but Bianchi's movements in the chair made him crush two digits.

After howling in pain and cursing in Italian, Bianchi looked at Tanner with tears in his eyes.

"Why did you do that?"

"To make you understand that you *do* have to worry about me. Now tell me who Degussa is."

"He's the head of the mob in Genoa, hell, maybe in all of Italy. He's also Bruno's boss."

"Why would Bruno Allende's boss come after you? You two are partners."

"Degussa doesn't know anything about the girls we have at my nursing home."

Sara stepped forward. "You're running drugs out of there too, aren't you?"

"At first, we just bought a little coke to keep the girls happy and numb, but then we thought, why not supply the customers too."

"Bianchi," Sara said. "Someone like Degussa would feed you to sharks if he ever found out what you were doing. Why would you do this? I thought you came from money."

Bianchi looked at Sara, but then shrugged. "It's the girls, so many damn girls and I can have them any time I like. The only thing better is the really young ones, like that one you chased off tonight."

A gun smashed into Bianchi's already mangled fingers. It was Sara, who also kicked Bianchi in the shin for good measure.

"Pervert! That girl was a child."

Bianchi was sucking in air between gasps of pain as Tanner stepped out of hearing range and gestured for Sara to follow. When she did so, he spoke to her in a whisper.

"I'm going to have to move fast on this. When we leave here, go back to the hotel while I track down Bruno Allende."

"I could help you."

"Not with this," Tanner said.

191

Sara began to protest, but then stopped herself. She wanted to be with Tanner, but knew the man was at heart, a loner. She would give him his space, even though she would have felt better about backing him up.

She kissed him. "You be careful."

"I will."

Sara looked over at Bianchi. "What about him?"

"He's going to tell me everything he knows about Bruno Allende and Degussa. After that, we'll gag him and leave him here."

"Just leave him like that?"

"He'll be fine. Either someone will find him tomorrow or we'll call the cops to release him, but I want him out of the way tonight."

They walked back over and saw that Bianchi had grown furious, yet sensible.

"I'll tell you anything you want to know, because once you find Bruno, he and his men will eat you alive."

"Like those two guys you had with you tonight, they work for Bruno too?"

"Bruno runs a big crew and soon he'll push that old man Degussa out and take over."

Tanner liked what he was hearing. The mob in Genoa was fractured and on the verge of a coup. That was good, he could use that to his advantage.

"Have you met a man named Maurice Scallato?"

Bianchi looked thoughtful. "The name doesn't sound familiar. Why, who is he?"

"Never mind, just tell me where I can find Bruno?" Tanner said.

It was going to be a long night.

26

FOLLOW THE BOUNCING THUG –
PART 2

BRUNO OWNED A "GENTLEMEN'S CLUB" THAT WAS CLOSED on Monday nights. That was when he played cards with a few of his men.

There were six guys playing cards, with a seventh man left to keep watch at the door. After observing the bar for half an hour, Tanner knew that the man on the door was a heavy smoker. The skinny hood had come outside twice to smoke, and as he did so, he left the door propped open with a chair, likely so he could hear if Bruno called for him.

The man was wearing a distinctive leather jacket. It was colorful and had the name of a rugby club in bold letters on the back and down the sleeves. Tanner thought of a way that might come in handy.

The night had grown cold, and while the passing traffic kept a steady flow, there was no one out walking in the area, and the surrounding businesses were all closed. Tanner approached the man as he was lighting up another cigarette. He blew on his hands to keep them warm and asked a question.

"Are you closed?"

"Yeah, every Monday night," the man said, and his rough voice told Tanner that he'd been a smoker his whole life.

"Damn, I wanted to look at some hot women," Tanner removed a cigarette from a pack he'd just bought, then pretended he didn't have a match. "Hey, give me a light, will you?"

The thug glared at him. "What am I, a doorman? Get the fuck out of here."

Tanner started to reply, then pointed into the club. "Who are those guys?"

The man turned his head to look and Tanner slammed a fist into his midsection. The smoker doubled over as his cigarette went flying out of his mouth. Tanner grabbed the man by his belt and collar, spun him around, and slammed the crown of his head against the brick wall surrounding the club's entrance.

Tanner stripped the leather jacket off the thug then gave him a quick frisk. Along with a wallet and a phone, he came up with a Berretta, a knife, a cigarette lighter, and cigarettes. As he frisked the unconscious thug, he kept an eye out for movement while listening for sounds coming from the club. He saw only cars going by and heard nothing else.

According to the ID in his wallet, the smoking man's name was Vito. Tanner searched Vito's phone and found its number, then memorized it.

When he bought the cigarettes, Tanner also acquired a cheap bottle of wine and a baseball cap. After dragging Vito near the gutter, Tanner thrust the cap on the man's head, poured wine over him, then placed the empty bottle in his limp hand. If a cop or pedestrian came along, they would take Vito for a drunk.

After putting the colorful leather jacket on, Tanner entered the club and locked the door. He was just in time to hear someone call for the smoker.

"Vito, bring in more beer."

Tanner growled in his throat to deepen his voice, then did a passable imitation of the smoker.

"I'm busy."

"Busy? Listen, you better get your ass back here with some beer damn quick if you know what's good for you."

"I'm on the phone with my girl."

"What girl? Are you cheating on my sister?"

Tanner winced at that. How was he to know that the smoker was married. The man had no ring on. Still, it was good bait, and at least one of the men from the back room would come out to give "Vito" hell.

After placing the smoker's phone inside a broom closet, Tanner leaned over the bar with his back turned and was careful to keep his reflection out of the mirror behind the bar. While he waited, he input the number of the smoker's phone into his own cell phone, but he didn't press the send button.

The sound of chair legs scraping over floorboards came from the back room; it was followed by the thumping of heavy footsteps.

"Vito?"

Tanner waited. He needed the man to get closer.

When a hand closed on his shoulder, Tanner reared back his elbow and caught the owner of the hand in the face. As the man stumbled backwards while holding his nose, Tanner hit him again, but this time he used a barstool. That sent the man sprawling, as the sound of multiple chairs scraping the floor came from the back room.

Tanner laid down beside the man he had just hit but

kept his face hidden from view. Beside him, the man moaned, but a quick look told Tanner that he was insensible and was out of the fight.

Five men came into the room and then stopped cold. Without seeing it, Tanner identified the next sound he heard, and knew it was the sound of multiple weapons clearing their respective holsters.

"Vito? Dom? Hey Dom, who hit you guys?" a voice said.

Then, an authoritative voice spoke, telling the men to spread out. However, Tanner had already pressed the send key on his phone, which caused the cell phone inside the closet to ring.

"Who's in there!"

It was the authoritative voice again, and Tanner guessed that he was hearing Bruno Allende.

"You might as well come out of the closet, dumbass, or else we'll light you up."

Tanner sat up and saw that five men had their backs to him and that their guns were pointed at the closet. "Drop the guns or I'll shoot Bruno first."

Two of the men jumped, while they all turned their heads to look at him. Tanner was holding a mini Uzi with a sound suppressor that was nearly as long as the gun. The aftermarket magazine inserted into it held fifty rounds. If Bruno and his men were stupid, they would all die fast, and quiet enough so that no one on the street would be any the wiser.

One of the men cursed in awe as he looked at the gun, while another put his hands up in the air.

"Who are you?" asked one of the men. He was the tallest, looked very fit, and seemed irritated. He had brown eyes, rugged looks, and an authoritative voice.

"I came here to talk, Bruno. But I'll be the only one

holding a gun while we do it. Put the other men in that closet."

Bruno gave a little laugh. "You put a phone in there and then called the number. Damn. I fell for that?"

"You'd be surprised how often it works, now deal with your men so we can talk."

"I'm not locking them in any damn closet," Bruno said. He then leaned over slowly and placed his gun on the floor. After his men followed suit, Tanner approached them.

"My name is Tanner. Have you heard of me?"

Bruno's eyelids flickered as he took a step backwards. "This is about Maurice?"

Tanner took note that Bruno was on a first-name basis with Scallato. Meanwhile, one of the other men realized who Tanner was, and he told the others, while mentioning the name, Alonso Alvarado. When the man finished speaking, the other men swallowed hard and looked more frightened. Apparently, Tanner's reputation had preceded him to Europe.

"I know you two are close, Bruno, so you're going to tell me where I can find Scallato."

"We're not close and I don't know where he is, but I can get a message to him."

"If I wanted to send him a message I could just kill you, Bruno. I want to know where I can find him."

"I don't know where he is, seriously. Think about it, why would he tell me where he lives?"

"Then send him a message from me. Tell him he needs to call me with a time and place to meet by tomorrow. If I don't hear from him, I'll come back here and kill you."

"Kill *me*? What did I do?"

"That's the message, now have one of your men give me a phone."

Bruno nudged the man on his right with an elbow. "Give the man your phone."

The hoodlum complied, but he passed it to Tanner as if he were feeding a mouse to a cobra.

"I'll expect to hear from Scallato at eight p.m. tomorrow."

"And if he doesn't call, you'll kill me?"

"Yeah, so you'd better make sure he calls."

"That's not right, Tanner. I didn't do anything to you."

"Just make sure you do something *for* me, or else."

Tanner backed up while keeping the men in sight. The thug on the floor that he had hit with a barstool pulled himself up to his hands and knees. He sent a string of Italian curses at Tanner.

Tanner thumbed the selector switch on the Uzi to single shot and pumped a slug into the man's head. After all, he had a reputation to uphold.

As he backed out onto the street, Tanner lowered his weapon and locked eyes with Bruno. The Italian mobster looked angry enough to kill him. Tanner was used to that look. It was an occupational hazard.

27

TICK TOCK

Before entering Bruno Allende's bar, Tanner had done a thorough recon of the area.

The silver Porsche 911 Turbo parked at the rear of the gentlemen's club was easy to peg as belonging to Bruno. Tanner had placed a tracking device on it.

The tracker he used had a feature that alerted you if the one you were monitoring came within a certain distance of your location. Tanner had set the tracker to beep out an alert at three miles. The device did just that the following morning as Tanner and Sara were stepping out into the hotel lobby. A quick look at his phone told Tanner that Bruno was closing in.

"Bruno has juice in this town. He tracked me down in just a few hours."

"It was the desk clerk over there," Sara said, while pointing with her eyes. "He looked nervous as we stepped off the elevator, and now he's on the phone."

"He's afraid we'll get away; let's alleviate his worries."

Tanner checked his pockets, made an "Aw man,"

expression, and pushed the button on the elevator so that it would take them back up to their floor.

As the doors closed, Sara looked at Tanner with questioning eyes. "What are you doing?"

"Luring them to our room. If we had driven away, the desk clerk would have given them the description of our car and we might be involved in a chase."

"But a firefight in a crowded hotel is better?"

"No, but we'll be long gone by the time they get here. Look at the screen, the car must be caught in morning traffic. They've hardly moved."

Sara studied the phone and saw a red dot on the map that gave a location south of the hotel. Bruno was still blocks away.

They stepped off the elevator at their floor and took the stairs down to the rear of the building, where the parking lot was. Tanner was carrying a bag full of supplies and necessary surveillance equipment. They had planned to spend the day watching Bruno, but Bruno was coming to them.

Tanner pointed to a gazebo that sat on a patch of grass. "We'll wait there."

"Wait for what?"

"Our ride. I'm going to steal Bruno's Porsche."

Sara laughed. "I should have known you'd have something clever up your sleeve."

"Expect the unexpected," Tanner said.

They watched the app on his phone and saw Bruno's progress. After the red dot reached their hotel, they heard a car braking to a stop. It came from the front of the building. Right after that, a white van came around the corner and parked near the rear exit. Six young men jumped out and went inside. They were all wearing baggy black hoodies, jeans, and sneakers.

Tanner and Sara strolled around to the front of the building and saw the Porsche 911 sitting there, with another white van parked behind it. There was no one in the Porsche, but the same desk clerk who had ratted them out was standing at the curb and keeping an eye on it. As he stood there, the man tossed a set of keys in the air, Tanner saw that the key fob had the Porsche logo on it.

Tanner sidled up on the man's right as Sara did the same on his left.

"That's a great looking car," Tanner said.

The man was nodding in agreement as he turned his head to look at Tanner. When he realized who he was looking at, the man turned white.

"Give me the keys," Tanner said.

The man's face crumbled as he handed over the keys. "Bruno will kill me."

"That's not my problem; give me your phone too."

Sara patted the man on the cheek as he gave Tanner his phone. "Just be glad that my boyfriend is in a good mood, or you'd already be dead."

"I don't feel good," the man said. He ran over and vomited into the gutter.

Bruno had a foot raised to kick in Tanner's hotel room door, but he stopped when his phone vibrated. He was wearing a hood that covered all but his chin from the sight of the hotel's cameras. After checking to see who was calling, he made a face of irritation.

"It's that desk clerk," Bruno whispered to his men, before moving down the hall and answering the call. "What do you want? I'm a little busy."

"I just wanted to tell you that you have a nice car,

although I'm partial to BMWs."

"What? Who is this? Oh, no, Tanner, is that you?"

"Tick tock, Bruno. If I don't hear from Scallato by eight tonight you're a dead man. Tick tock, that's the sound of your life slipping away."

"I can't get in contact with Maurice that quickly, but I'm meeting someone tonight who can."

"Who are you meeting?"

"Maurice says it's his pet cop."

"What time are you meeting?"

"I don't know. They have to fly in from somewhere."

"That's cutting it close, isn't it?"

Give me more time, Tanner."

"You mean I should give you more time to track me down again?"

"Yeah, this was stupid, I admit it, but now I know better. Give me another day, Tanner. I know I can get in touch with Maurice by then."

"You call him Maurice, does that mean you're friends?"

"Maurice doesn't have friends, but I've known him since we were young."

"You have until tomorrow night."

Bruno leaned back against the wall. "Good, but hey, don't hurt my car, okay?"

"I'll leave it near the train station."

"It is a sweet ride, isn't it?"

"You can't drive it in hell, Bruno. Tell Scallato to call."

Tanner dropped the phone into the center console, then looked over at Sara. "Did you refer to me as your boyfriend back at the hotel?"

"I did, and you are."

"Well, I'll be damned," Tanner said, and pointed the car toward the train station.

I KNEW IT!

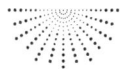

As he said he would, Tanner dumped the Porsche at the train station, but only after he was certain he could pick up another rental car there.

Bruno showed without delay and Sara used a new purchase, a pair of high-power binoculars with optional night vision capability. She could see Bruno sitting in the passenger seat of the Porsche while one of his men drove. He appeared to be occupied with something in his lap.

"I think he's writing… yes, I see a pen," Sara said.

"If he's smart, he's writing his will," Tanner said.

They followed Bruno's entourage for a few more blocks until they came to a halt near a street corner. One of the white vans had taken off, while the other stayed with Bruno.

"It's a letter," Sara said. "He just licked an envelope, and now his driver is headed for the mailbox on the corner. I'd love to know what's in that letter, and who it's addressed to."

Tanner looked around. There was a lot of foot traffic

and bike riders in the area. That would change once the shops closed in several hours.

"I'll come back later and break into the mailbox."

Sara lowered the binoculars. "But won't they have picked up the mail by then?"

Tanner chuckled. "I see you're not familiar with the Italian postal system."

"Slow?"

"It was glacial the last time I used it. I once mailed Spenser a letter from Rome and I was in Wyoming a month later when he received it."

Sara looked around and saw a police car drive by. "Tonight then, I've a feeling that letter is important."

TANNER HUNG BACK THE REST OF THE DAY AND FOLLOWED Bruno by using the app on his phone. The GPS tracker had a range of several miles, so he had the luxury of following the thug at a distance.

Whenever the tracker indicated that Bruno had come to a stop, Tanner got closer. Most of Bruno's day involved talking to his various underlings and making sure they knew he was keeping watch. Then, around noon, Bruno's car headed into a section of the city that the tourists never see. Tanner had to be careful then. He had to stay far enough back not to be seen, while keeping close enough to find out what Bruno was doing.

His car was a new vehicle. It stuck out nearly as much as Bruno's Porsche did in that area. Sara employed the binoculars again just in time to see the action. Bruno and his thugs had cornered some poor soul against an abandoned building and one of the men was beating him with a bat while two others held him.

"It looks like Bruno is a micro manager," Tanner said. "He likes to be there when the late payers get the message."

"Do you think they'll kill him?" Sara asked.

Tanner took the binoculars she passed him and zoomed in on the action. "It's just a major-league tune-up. A couple of cracked ribs and a messed-up face. They haven't touched his knees, so I guess Bruno wants to leave the man mobile. If the guy has to beg, borrow, or steal, I bet he comes up with Bruno's money after this."

"In any event, Bruno seems to be acting as if it's business as usual. Either he's not taking your threat seriously or he already has a plan in place to deal with you."

"Let's hope that plan includes meeting with Scallato."

When it was time for lunch, Tanner and Sara dined at a bistro that was on the other side of an avenue where Bruno was eating. The mobster liked a leisurely lunch. It was nearly four p.m. by the time he left the table in the company of a beautiful young blonde who had joined him at the restaurant.

That was when Bruno separated from his troops and went off with the woman alone to what was likely her apartment.

As they sat waiting for Bruno to emerge again, Tanner sighed. "I feel like we're filming a documentary. *A day in the life of an Italian thug.*"

Sara laughed. "What do you think he's doing up there?"

"Exactly what I'd like to be doing with you right now."

"You don't think he's living there, do you?"

"No, she's probably the girlfriend and he pays for the place. Bruno wears a wedding ring, there's a Mrs. Bruno somewhere."

Bruno emerged from the apartment just past seven and headed to a villa that had to be worth several million euros. Security was tight, and the property was walled-in.

"This must be where the boss lives, the man named Degussa," Tanner said. "Bruno must be checking in."

Several thugs could be seen coming and going while Bruno was inside. After he left the villa, Bruno drove to one of the bars he owned, where he passed a thick envelope to a young man wearing a suit.

"Did we just witness a bribery payment?" Sara asked.

"Probably, and the kid in the suit must work for a judge or a politician."

Sara laughed. "I wish we had filmed this day. Say what you will about Bruno, he's not boring."

Before leaving the bar, Bruno had drinks with a young woman who was not the same woman he'd met at lunch. She wore a tight skirt that barely covered her ass and her breasts were spilling out of the halter top that was visible beneath her open jacket. Bruno's car was parked on the side of the building in a narrow alleyway. There were people strolling by in front of the bar, but none traveled down the alley. The woman joined Bruno in his car and was soon burying her face in his lap.

"Our documentary will need to have an X rating now," Tanner said.

Sara made a face. "Out in public? What a pig, and that girl must be a hooker."

"She'll probably be working at the nursing home after this try-out."

When the act inside the car reached its inevitable conclusion, the girl got out of the Porsche, zipped up her jacket, popped a stick of gum in her mouth, and sashayed away. Bruno placed his car in gear and headed north.

THE PASSEGGIATA ANITA GARIBALDI A NERVI IS A SEASIDE promenade that looks out over a rocky coastline. It's located a short distance from the heart of Genoa and its wide walkway is a favorite of tourists and locals alike. It also has several great cafes nearby.

Tanner and Sara were sitting at a window in one of those cafes as they kept an eye on Bruno. Bruno stood at the rail on the walkway and kept checking his watch. He was meeting someone there, and that someone was late.

Both Tanner and Sara were in disguise, as a precaution. Tanner had a beard held on by spirit gum. The beard had wide streaks of gray in it that matched the gray of his shaggy wig. He also wore glasses. Sara had donned a wig of long dark red hair, sunglasses, and a baggy pant suit. At her feet were several shopping bags that marked her as a tourist.

The binoculars had been left in the car, but they both had cameras hanging around their necks. Using zoom lenses, they could see Bruno's companion when he arrived.

Sara sighed in disappointment. She was hoping Tanner was wrong about the man, but no, there he was.

"Jacques Durand," Sara said with sorrow in her voice.

Tanner's eyes narrowed, as he wished he were holding a rifle rather than a camera.

"Scallato's pet cop. And once I put a choke chain on him, he'll lead us straight to Scallato."

"Damn!" Sara said.

"What?"

"I liked Jacques."

"Sara, he's been using us, while working for a man who wants to kill us both."

"I know."

Tanner lowered the camera and took her hand. "I'll leave his fate to you. When we leave here, I'll steal a car and stay on Bruno while you stick with Durand, but be very careful. Scallato could be nearby."

"You'd let Jacques live, after knowing that he's conspiring to have you killed?"

"He can become *my* pet cop; I'll leave that to you."

"Thank you, Tanner, even now, knowing what I know, I don't want Jacques to die."

Tanner smiled. "I'm glad he's not a younger man; I might have competition for you."

They were still holding hands. Sara massaged the back of Tanner's hand with her thumb as she stared into his eyes. "There's not another man in your league."

Tanner patted his phony gray beard. "Not too bad for an old guy, hmm?"

BREAKING AND ENTERING

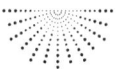

THE MAILBOX POPPED OPEN WITH A LOUD CLANKING NOISE and Tanner lowered the crowbar he'd used to break into it.

There was a couple walking along the street with their dog. Tanner ignored their stares and took the mail back to his stolen car, then drove several blocks away and parked.

There wasn't much mail, and Tanner was saved having to tear it all open when he saw Bruno's name on an envelope. The letter was addressed to a Signora Maria Rizzo and was being sent general delivery to a post office in the Sicilian town of Raguso.

Tanner tucked the letter in an inside pocket and left the vehicle with the other mail in his hand. He stuffed the letters and postcards in a different mailbox before finding another car to steal. He had to track down Bruno again and hoped that he hadn't lost him, but he felt it was more important to retrieve the letter.

After failing to get a ping from the app on his phone, Tanner parked his new stolen ride, an older model Peugeot, and opened the letter. He could speak Italian much better than he could read it, but Bruno's simple handwriting was easy to decipher.

MARIA,

There is a very dangerous man named Tanner who is looking for Maurice to kill him. Do not take this threat lightly! Your husband is deadly, but so is Tanner and I don't know if Maurice will survive. Take the kids and head to our sister's house in Palermo. If I don't join you there in a week, you'll know that Tanner killed me.

WITH LOVE, LITTLE FLOWER,
Bruno

TANNER WAS SHOCKED BY THE CONTENTS OF THE LETTER. He had never considered that Maurice Scallato could be married, much less have children. He had never known a high-level assassin who had a family life. As he had told Alexa many times, it just wasn't compatible with what he did.

Then, he suddenly felt foolish. Of course, Scallato had a wife and children, that's what the Scallatos were all about, handing down their legacy to another generation.

The Scallatos had been assassins for more than a century and were around before Tanner One had claimed his first contract. It was not only possible to raise a family while living such a life, but the Scallato's proved that it could be sustained for generations.

Tanner thought that Bruno's sister, Maria, must be an exceptional woman in many ways. She accepted the life her husband lived and kept the home fires burning during his long absences. In some respects, it must be like what a wife in the military had to do.

A wife and children? Tanner thought, then shook his head in wonder. Maybe an assassin didn't have to be alone forever, not if he found the right woman.

He renewed his search for Bruno and the app beeped when he came within range. As he closed in, Tanner chuckled. The signal was coming from a spot near his and Sara's hotel. Although their belongings were still there, they had made other arrangements for the night, just in case Bruno was stupid.

Tanner drove past the Porsche when he was half a mile away from the hotel. In thirty minutes, he identified several vehicles that held Bruno's men, as well as two vans packed with mercenaries. It was a small army, but if its commander died, the troops would disperse.

There was just one problem. Bruno was a thug, but he wasn't a low-level thug, not if he reported directly to a man like Degussa. Killing what the Americans called a "Made Man" could have Tanner embroiled in a war with the Italian mafia. That was not something he needed on top of his Scallato troubles.

Tanner sent Sara a text telling her to stay away from the hotel, then followed it by leaving the area himself. It was time he had a talk with Degussa. Tanner drove toward the villa he'd followed Bruno to earlier, and as he drove, his mind formulated a plan.

EMILIO DEGUSSA GROANED SOFTLY AS HE CLIMBED OUT OF bed and cursed his aged bladder for waking him up after only an hour's sleep. In the bed beside him lay a woman nearly seventy years younger than he, named Rosalia.

Emilio was old and kept the bedroom warm, so Rosalia always slept in the nude. Emilio stared at her tanned and perfect body, the long blonde hair flowing down her back, and felt not a twinge of lust. They had made love two days earlier, and lately, it sometimes took weeks for desire to return. He feared the day it would never return.

He sighed as he rose from the bed on creaking knees. What a stud he had been in his youth, often taking on three women a night. But those days were long gone, as were most of the women. He was eighty-eight and had outlived everyone he'd known growing up.

Before entering the bathroom, Emilio looked back at Rosalia. What a treasure the girl was. She loved him and cared for him. Why? Only heaven knew, and it wasn't an old man's imagination. Emilio had seen enough of the world to know how to read what was in a person's eyes. There was no guile in Rosalia, and she played no games. If she loved you, she loved you, and if she hated you—watch out! In that way, they were much alike, and Emilio wished he had met her when he was her age.

Most thought the girl a whore and nothing else, and yes, she had been a prostitute since the age of twelve, when her mother used her to get money. But Emilio had taken her off the streets when she killed her pimp to save another girl from being set on fire.

At any other time, a whore who killed her pimp would have been tortured to death as a lesson for others. And yet, one look at Rosalia and Emilio had been smitten. Sparing her and making her his mistress was a sign of weakness, Emilio knew that, but he hadn't the heart to have her killed.

He entered the master bathroom that was twice the size of most bedrooms and used the toilet on the right. The damn room had three toilets, two showers, and a hot tub.

Emilio had come up in a tiny apartment where he'd lived with his six brothers and four sisters. He'd had a mother, but no father, and so at the age of ten he ventured onto the streets to make a living, as his older brothers had done before him. The older brothers died during the second world war, but Emilio survived the war years and thrived after them.

He made that living by stealing, an activity he was exceptional at. By the time he was twenty-three, Emilio had bought his mother a house in the country.

After finishing his business at the toilet, Emilio moved over to the sink to wash his hands. The walk covered twenty feet and Emilio almost missed the days when his bathroom was about the size of a shoebox.

He splashed some water on his face as well, and when he raised his head from the sink, he saw Tanner standing beside him. Tanner was holding a gun in one hand and a towel in the other. It pleased Emilio to see that the gun was pointed toward the floor, while the towel was being offered.

"Who sent you?" Emilio asked as he took the towel to dry himself with.

"My name is Tanner and I'm here to talk."

Emilio sucked on his bottom lip as he processed the words, then a light came on in his old eyes.

"Tanner? The American assassin?"

"Yes."

"You're going to kill me?"

"No, like I said, I'm just here to talk."

"How did you make it past the guards, did you kill any of them?"

"I didn't have to. The perimeter guards are watching TV, while the gate guard is on his phone and smoking a cigarette."

The old man cursed aloud at his guards' incompetence.

"Emilio?" said a soft voice from the bedroom.

"That is Rosalia. Let me answer her or she'll grow concerned."

Tanner tossed his chin in the direction of the bedroom.

"Go to her and keep her from screaming and alerting the man outside the door."

Emilio let out a wheezing laugh. "Rosalia is not the screaming type."

After returning to the bedroom, Emilio held up a hand and pleaded with Rosalia. "Do not reach for the gun on the nightstand or this man will kill you."

Rosalia rose from the bed and went to Emilio. She was still naked and didn't care who saw her. She sneered at Tanner like a mountain lion defending her cub. "I will kill you if you hurt Emilio."

Tanner listened to her while staring at her body. The woman was an exceptional beauty. When Tanner looked away from her, he spoke to Emilio.

"I'm here to discuss Bruno Allende. I want your permission to kill him."

Rosalia's demeanor brightened as she smiled and relaxed. "I like this man, Emilio; he talks sense. I've told you many times that pig Bruno Allende can't be trusted."

"Quiet, Rosalia, and put on a robe before this man decides he wants to do more than talk."

Rosalia walked over to stand before Tanner, she looked up into his eyes and then took a step backwards.

"Ooohh, this man has power, but he's not evil. He would never force a woman… nor need to."

Emilio sighed, grabbed a pink robe from the foot of the bed, and handed it to Rosalia.

She kissed him on the cheek, put the robe on, and walked to a seating area to the left of the balcony entrance.

Tanner put away the gun and walked over with Emilio, who sat beside Rosalia in a love seat. As Tanner settled across from them in a chair, Rosalia took Emilio's hand and leaned against him, as she studied Tanner.

"Why do you want to kill Bruno Allende?" Emilio asked.

Tanner explained that Bruno had a whorehouse located in a nursing home and that he also suspected he was running drugs out of there. He could tell that this was all news to Emilio, who had grown angry as the story progressed.

"I'd kill him myself, except for one thing," Emilio said.

"What's that?" Tanner asked.

"Bruno is the brother-in-law of Maurice Scallato. If Scallato comes out on top, he will kill me."

"What makes you think I won't kill you?"

"You might, but not without a reason. If you were that type of man both Bruno and I would be dead right now." Emilio gave Rosalia's hand a squeeze. "What do you think?"

"Tanner will kill Scallato," Rosalia said, and said it with a certainty that brooked no disagreement.

Emilio rose with effort from the love seat and paced a bit. After placing his hands on the back of the seat, he sent Tanner a single nod.

"Bruno Allende is yours. Do you need help finding him?"

"No, he's probably still camped outside my hotel with his men waiting to ambush me."

"Not his men, Tanner, my men."

"When I take Bruno, I may have to kill some of *your* men. I'll try to keep the numbers down to a minimum."

"There's a rumor that you once single-handedly killed twenty men. Is that true?"

Tanner stood. "Don't believe everything you hear, but there is one man I will kill, and his name is Maurice Scallato."

"Call me if you need assistance," Emilio said, and recited a phone number.

"Why would you help me kill Scallato?"

"He and Bruno Allende are family. His death would make me feel safer."

Tanner walked toward the balcony. "I'll leave the way I came in. And oh, Degussa?"

"Yes?"

"If you hear that I've been killed don't believe it until you hear I died twice. I may need to fake out Scallato."

Emilio laughed. "Tanner versus Scallato, I wish I could sell tickets."

Tanner looked at Rosalia and she sent him a wink, then, he disappeared into the darkness from which he came.

LOOK BEHIND YOU

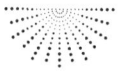

WHILE TANNER FOLLOWED BRUNO AND TALKED TO EMILIO Degussa, Sara had followed Jacques Durand.

Sara was disheartened by the discovery that Durand had been working for Scallato all along. She liked the man, despite his obvious dislike for Tanner. And perhaps it was ego, but Sara thought Durand's animosity toward Tanner was spawned by jealousy over her.

Durand wanted her, although she was at least twenty years younger than he was, and she couldn't say that she wasn't attracted to him as well. But not anymore, not if he were trying to kill Tanner, and was likely unconcerned for her welfare.

Sara had been so lost in thought that when her phone vibrated, it startled her, and a cry escaped her lips. After stopping at a light, she saw it was a text from Jacques Durand. He said he knew that she was still in Genoa and asked if he could meet with her, preferably alone.

When Sara typed back a reply inquiring when and where, Durand gave her the address of a hotel along with a room number. Then, Sara agreed to meet with him. Now that she knew where Durand was headed, Sara could take the time to send Tanner a message and tell him what was going on.

Be careful! Came his texted reply, along with the info that he was about to abduct Bruno and get information from him. Sara typed back, *You be careful!* Then, *Give them hell!*

When she drove again, she sped some, and reached the hotel in time to see Durand park his car. Sara abandoned her vehicle in one of the dozen empty handicap spots by the front door and walked into the lobby.

She was still wearing the disguise she'd had on earlier and looked twenty years older. She had brought one of the shopping bags in with her and pretended to be rummaging inside it as Durand joined her by the elevator. When a talkative young couple came over and joined them, Sara was glad. Jacques Durand had been an Interpol agent, and from all accounts, an exceptional one. She wasn't certain her disguise would fool him if he were to give her his undivided attention.

When they reached the floor that Durand's room was on, Sara stepped off the elevator and went left while Durand went right. After turning her head and seeing Durand disappear around a corner, Sara walked back past the elevator, peeked around the corner, and saw no one.

Thinking that Durand's room must be one of the first ones along the corridor, Sara moved down the hall while checking numbers. She was looking for room 758, and soon realized that it must have been in the direction she had been heading after leaving the elevator. But if that were true, then how had Durand disappeared so quickly?

No, she must have remembered the room number wrong. Sara had taken out her phone to double-check the room number when she felt something hard press against her back. It was followed by a voice speaking in French-accented English.

"You remembered the number correctly, Sara, and I would know you even if you had donned a burka."

Sara turned her head to find Jacques Durand smiling at her. She wondered if he would still be smiling when he handed her over to Scallato.

TANNER CLAMPED A GLOVED HAND OVER THE MOUTH OF A young thug while jamming an eight-inch knife between the man's ribs from behind, then twisting the blade. The man's youthfulness gave him strength and endurance. Tanner had to stab the punk three more times and keep a tight hold over the screaming mouth that gnashed at his gloved hand. Two minutes passed before the man's legs gave out and Tanner had to angle him away from a row of metal trash cans. If those were kicked, the noise would bring the others running.

When it was finally over, Tanner dragged him behind a dumpster, and had to flex his hand to dissipate the tension in it. Tanner was taking the long and now bloody black coat off the thug when he spotted the tattoo on the man's neck. It was a Fasces symbol, which displayed an axe in the middle of a bundle of rods. It was an ancient symbol meant to signify strength in unity. It was most notably used as a symbol in the twentieth century for the Italian fascists, led by Benito Mussolini. The Fascist Party ruled the former Kingdom of Italy from 1922 to 1943.

There were still pockets of believers of Fascism in the modern world, but they were few and far between. Tanner wondered if the twenty-something thug had been a true believer or just thought the tattoo looked cool. Whatever the reason, he would wear it forever.

A tweed cap went with the coat as well as a Walther PPK with a walnut grip. The gun was fully loaded and in excellent condition, and possibly had collectible value. Tanner thought the neck tattoo a poor choice no matter the reason behind it, but the kid had style when it came to clothes and weapons.

He trudged back with his head down and the cap pulled low. Both hands were thrust inside the pockets of the coat, with the Walther jammed into the right pocket, and the blade in the left.

One of the two other thugs who were hanging out with Bruno laughed as Tanner approached. They were leaning back against their car, which was parked behind Bruno's Porsche. From what little Tanner could see of Bruno, it appeared that he was on the phone and having a serious conversation, since there was a lot of hand waving going on.

The laughing punk made a comment. "Angelo, I thought you had gone off to take a leak, but you were gone so long it must have turned into a dump."

The other man laughed along, then added. "What's the matter, boy? Are you worried about going up against a guy like Tanner? Don't be. He's just another man, and they all die easy."

Tanner raised his chin off his chest to reveal his face. "Actually, Angelo died harder than most."

The man opened his mouth in shock and Tanner shoved his blade into it with so much force that the tip was protruding from the back of the man's neck. The Walther followed. It was pressed against the forehead of the other man and he froze from the contact. The first man was gagging on the knife, which Tanner still gripped with his arm held out straight and rigid. The man was grabbing Tanner's wrist with both hands, but the strength in the fingers was ebbing rapidly. When the hands fell away, the knees buckled, as the man's spine had been severely damaged, if not severed. He lay on his right side at Tanner's feet, moaning softly, as blood flowed around the knife. Tanner turned his attention to the other man, who had been wise enough to stay calm.

"Make too much noise and you'll join your buddy in the morgue."

The man's eyes flicked downward. "He's not dead," he whispered.

Tanner gave the knife handle a kick and the man on the ground fell over onto his back. The moaning soon stopped, as did the man's breathing.

The other man was vibrating with fury, but he kept his hands still and stared into Tanner's eyes. He was no kid, and close to fifty.

Tanner ignored the hateful glare. He had work to do. With the gun keeping the man compliant, Tanner searched him. He found a gun, a wallet, but no keys.

"Where are the car keys?" he whispered.

"In the car," the man hissed, then asked. "Is that Angelo's gun, the kid with the neck tattoo?"

"Yeah."

The man's eyes crossed at an upward angle as he took in the gun.

"I thought so, and you're Tanner?"

"Yeah."

"So I'm a dead man no matter what, is that it?"

"I just want Bruno over there. Who is he talking on the phone with?"

"A guy named Bianchi. Some bums found him tied up in a warehouse an hour ago."

Tanner almost smiled, he had thought Bianchi would have been found much earlier.

"What's your name," Tanner said.

"Giovanni."

"Do yourself a favor, Giovanni. Go to old man Degussa and tell him you just found out that Bruno was cheating him by running his own whorehouse out of Bianchi's nursing home."

"You're letting me live?"

"If I never see you again."

"You won't."

"Start walking away, nice and easy."

Giovanni did as ordered, but he soon transitioned to running.

Tanner shrugged out of Angelo's bloody coat, tossed away the tweed cap, but kept the gun. After removing the keys from Giovanni's ride, he threw them up on a roof.

In the Porsche, Bruno was so involved with his conversation with Bianchi that he never noticed Tanner until the assassin climbed into the car beside him. Bruno looked over at him, looked away, then let out a shriek of fright as he looked back again. Tanner smashed the Walther onto the crown of Bruno's head and the man slumped down in his seat, dazed, and with his eyes fluttering.

Tanner winced. It was a pity to employ such a first-rate gun on a third-rate head. Tanner used a zip tie to bind Bruno's wrists together behind his back, followed by a second one to secure his left ankle to the base of the seat.

A voice came from the phone. It was Bianchi. Tanner found the right buttons to transfer the call to the car's Bluetooth and spoke to Bianchi as he drove away.

"Tanner? That you?"

"That's right."

"Is Bruno dead?"

"If I were you, I'd worry about myself."

"I'll do what you want. I, I didn't know who you really were."

"I like your attitude. Now listen carefully, Bianchi, this is what I want you to do."

SHOOT ME NOW!

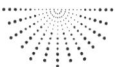

Sara silently cursed her carelessness. She assumed she was about to be taken hostage, or perhaps even killed, by Jacques Durand.

"You might as well shoot me now, Jacques."

"Shoot you?"

"With the gun you have pressed against my back."

"Turn around," Durand said, as the "gun" withdrew.

When Sara turned, she saw that Durand was holding a bottle of liquor.

"Wine?"

Durand made a noise of derision. "Not wine, champagne, remember, I am French."

"What's going on? Why did you sneak up on me?"

"You're the one wearing a disguise, mademoiselle."

Down the hallway, the elevator chimed its arrival and several people stepped out.

Durand took off down the corridor. "Let's talk in my suite."

Sara followed, confused by Durand's demeanor. While she followed, she moved a small gun covertly into a front pocket on her pants. It was a pistol that Tanner had given her. She hoped she wouldn't need to use it.

Durand unlocked the door and went immediately to the phone to call room service. Once he had them on the line, he asked that caviar and a set of champagne flutes be brought to the room. After hanging up, he turned to Sara and gave her an apologetic look.

"They say it will be twenty minutes. I should have remembered to bring flutes."

Sara removed her wig and glasses, then placed them on the coffee table. The room was a suite that opened onto a sitting area, but down a hallway, she could see the corner of a large bed.

"Why the champagne, Jacques?"

"To celebrate, of course. But tell me, Sara, why did you and Tanner make me believe you had left Europe? I learned today that you had been here all along."

Sara ignored the question and asked her own. "What is it we're celebrating with the champagne?"

"I have an informant who will lead Scallato into a trap. Once Tanner kills Scallato, you'll no longer be in danger."

"And who is this informant?"

"Bruno Allende."

"I know of him."

"I'm sure you do; Tanner has threatened to kill him by tomorrow night if he doesn't get in contact with Scallato."

"He told you that?"

"Bruno and I met earlier tonight."

Again, Durand confused her, this time by admitting he knew Bruno. Perhaps he had realized they'd been seen together and come up with a plausible explanation.

"So why is Bruno willing to give up Scallato by leading him into an ambush?"

Durand shrugged grandly as both shoulders practically reached his ears.

"The man fears Tanner. Personally, I'd be more concerned with Scallato. But even Tanner will be able to kill Scallato once we spring our trap."

Sara removed more of her disguise as she shed the jacket of her pant suit.

Durand sat on the sofa and asked Sara to join him there.

"I'd rather stand, but tell me, what is this trap you're talking about?"

"It's simple. Scallato trusts Bruno, so when Bruno tells him that they need to meet in a certain place at an agreed upon time, the Sicilian will go there."

"Okay, but what's the reason he'll give Scallato for the meeting?"

"He'll convince Scallato that he can set up Tanner, but that they need to work out the details. If Scallato looks into it, he'll know that Tanner and Bruno have already clashed and that Bruno wants Tanner dead too. When Scallato shows up to talk with Bruno, Tanner will be hidden nearby in a sniper's nest and kill Scallato. Scallato has no reason to think Bruno would betray him. They've been friends since childhood."

"It might work, but if Scallato grows suspicious and starts hunting for Tanner at the meeting site, it could turn into a shootout at the O.K. corral."

Durand raised an eyebrow. "I don't understand the reference."

"I'm just saying that if Scallato is nearly as good as Tanner he may smell a trap, then Tanner may lose the advantage."

"Tanner will still have time to set up at the site, while Scallato will be given only hours to prepare. If he conceals himself wisely and perhaps rigs a few booby traps, Scallato will be at a huge disadvantage."

"That's true, and where is this site located?"

"Bruno will call me tomorrow with the details. He has to find the perfect place, somewhere secluded."

Sara nodded as she studied Durand. He was so convincing, and even had a reason for meeting with Bruno.

"Do you hate Tanner, Jacques?"

Durand considered the question, then held up two fingers close together. "Perhaps a little."

"Why?"

"You two are lovers, yes?"

"Yes, but only recently."

"Then let's call it envy."

"Do you hate him enough to betray us?"

Durand studied her face for a moment, then spoke, as he bent over to tie his shoe.

"What are you saying, Sara?"

"Tanner thinks you betrayed us, but I'm not sure what to think."

"Let me help you to decide," Durand said.

He straightened up from fiddling with his shoelace and held the gun he kept in his ankle holster.

Inside the front pocket of her pants, Sara's finger tightened on the trigger of her gun.

BRUNO REGAINED HIS SENSES AFTER TANNER ENDED THE call with Bianchi. Bruno moaned loudly, then tried to see his reflection in the glass of the passenger side door.

"What did you do, Tanner, shoot me in the head?"

"Don't give me any ideas."

"You're going to kill me?"

"No, as of right now, we're partners."

"Partners?"

Bruno had shouted the word in surprise while sitting up straighter. That simple movement made him moan again from the pain in his head.

"You're going to help me kill Scallato."

"I don't trust you, Tanner. Even if you somehow killed Maurice, you would just turn around and kill me."

"Not if you do everything I say."

"Fine, then free my hands, partner."

"What were you and Durand talking about tonight?"

"You saw that? She said you would."

"Who's *she*?"

"Never mind."

Tanner had reached his destination. It was the rear of a shopping center that was closed for the day and had a section being renovated. He parked the Porsche behind a tall stack of wallboard and cut the engine. An instant later, he had a gun pressed hard against Bruno's side.

"I'm beginning to think you're stupid, Bruno. I don't partner up with stupid people. This 'she' you mentioned, who is it?"

"Sabella Barbieri, she's Durand's assistant and Maurice's pet cop."

"Pet cop? Sabella was a cop?"

"Yeah, that's why Maurice turned her."

"And Durand?"

"He's being used by Sabella. Whatever she learns by working with Durand goes right back to Maurice, same thing when she was with Interpol."

"You're telling me that Durand is innocent of trying to set me up?"

"Yeah, we had him thinking that he was helping you. He wants Maurice dead too. The funny thing is, Durand wants Maurice dead because of Sabella. Durand thinks she hates Maurice."

Tanner took out his phone. "Shut up while I make a call."

"You'll let me live, right?"

"Shut up!"

Tanner's call went through but was picked up by voice mail.

"Sara, call me back. It's urgent."

"Sara? Is that the woman you were with at the hotel? That desk clerk says she's hot."

Tanner turned his head and glared at Bruno.

"I'm shutting up," Bruno said.

SARA EASED HER FINGER OFF THE TRIGGER OF HER concealed gun as she realized what Durand had done. He wasn't pointing his gun at her; he'd been offering it to her. Sara reached over and took it, even as she felt her phone vibrate.

"Why did you give up your gun, Jacques?"

"To prove that I mean you no harm, nor would I try to have Tanner killed. Why would you think that?"

Sara showed Durand the gun she had in her pocket. "I almost shot you."

Her phone stopped buzzing and Sara took it out of her back pocket, where she had placed it to make room for the hidden gun.

"That was Tanner calling," she explained to Durand. Sara listened to the voice mail and then called Tanner's phone, when he answered, Sara only wanted to know one thing. "Are you all right?"

"I'm good. What about you?"

"I'm fine, but just a little confused about who to trust."

"Have you met with Durand yet?"

"I'm doing that right now."

"He's clean, Sara; don't hurt him."

"I could have used this call sooner."

"What happened?"

"Nothing serious," Sara said, then she told Tanner that they were in Durand's suite.

"You two stay put and I'll be right there, with a guest in tow. I have Bruno with me."

"Alive or dead?"

"Bruno's alive, and he'll remain that way if he stays smart."

"Hurry up, I miss you."

"Same here, and one more thing, Durand's assistant, Sabella Barbieri, she's Scallato's pet cop, not Durand."

"I knew there was a reason I didn't like her."

"I'm on my way, and hungry, tell Durand to order up some food. It could be a long night."

"There's champagne here and caviar on the way."

"I meant real food."

Sara laughed. Then thought how good it was to have someone in her life again. The weeks they'd spent together in Genoa had made the new phase of their relationship more real than its start, which was born of a mutual attraction. She and Tanner were lovers, yes, and perhaps not yet in love, but there was feeling and emotion between them, and they both knew the other felt it.

"Tanner."

"Yeah?"

"I'll tell you later, when we're alone."

"Sara, you don't need to tell me."

She smiled into the phone. "No, I don't."

"I'll be there in less than ten minutes, and oh, along with the food, order some aspirin for Bruno."

Sara ended the call and saw that Durand had a questioning look.

"Is Tanner coming here?"

"Yes, and he's bringing along Bruno Allende."

Durand studied her face as Sara handed him back his gun.

"There's more. I can tell by your expression."

"Jacques, how well do you know Sabella Barbieri?"

THE FIRST ONE TO DIE WINS

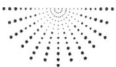

Inside Jacques Durand's small hotel suite, Tanner sat beside Sara in a love seat, while Bruno sat to their left in a chair. Upon arriving, Durand had cuffed one of Bruno's wrists while attaching the other end of the cuff to the small chandelier that hung above the coffee table. It resulted in Bruno having to sit up straight on the edge of his seat.

That allowed Tanner and Sara to have a private word with Durand in the bedroom. Once they returned to the suite's seating area, Tanner had Durand free Bruno, with the admonition that Bruno not do anything stupid.

Jacques Durand then paced the room as he talked about his assistant, Sabella Barbieri, a longtime friend whom he had just discovered had been betraying him for years.

"This doesn't make sense. Sabella hates Maurice Scallato. His brother, Bernardo Scallato, shot her in both legs while making a hit on an informant she was meeting. That's one of the reasons I'd prefer to work with Tanner rather than Scallato."

"How serious were Sabella's wounds?" Tanner asked.

233

"She was out for nearly a year before returning to work and could have easily retired or taken a desk job. Instead, Sabella came back to work."

"When did all that happen, say about nineteen years ago?" Tanner said.

"How did you know?"

"Carlo Scallato told me that he believes Maurice killed his brother Bernardo."

"I thought Carlo Scallato was unable to communicate?"

"He's getting better treatment and now has periods of lucidness, but I'm told they won't last."

"He might be lucid, but he's wrong. Bernardo Scallato was killed by an Interpol agent named Lance Robear. Robear and Sabella were lovers and he followed her to the meeting with her informant. When Bernardo shot Sabella, Lance must have snuck up on him and shot him. It's believed that Lance was later killed by Maurice Scallato, which is one reason why Sabella despises the man."

"What evidence is there that Robear killed Bernardo?"

"We found the gun that killed Bernardo in Robear's apartment. Afterward, we assumed that Maurice Scallato had killed him in revenge, although we had no proof."

"Or, it was planted by Scallato, and Robear and Sabella were never lovers. Carlo knows his son and he's convinced that Scallato killed his own brother. Sabella and Scallato then made Robear take the heat for Bernardo's murder."

Durand looked down at the floor, when he looked up, he made a face of disgust. "It was odd at the time, Sabella claiming that she and Robear were lovers. I had thought she hated the man for getting a promotion she deserved."

"And after he died, and she returned to work from her injuries, what then?"

"Her career took off, and she was soon supervising protection detail for visiting dignitaries."

"A perfect job for the pet cop of an international hit man," Sara said. "There is no end to the information she could feed him. She had firsthand knowledge of the personnel of those she protected. She could also create a hole in the security whenever Scallato needed one."

Durand nodded, sat in a chair, then popped up again when the room service cart arrived. After passing the food around, Durand began pacing again.

"Sabella and I met during our academy years. We were both so young and so eager to prove that we could make it as cops. Neither of us came from families that had money or influence, but we had ambition."

"Was Sabella much younger than you?" Tanner asked.

He was eating steak and eggs, while Sara had only soup. Durand had declined food, as learning of his friend's betrayal had killed his appetite. The champagne was forgotten; there was nothing to celebrate now.

"Much younger? No," Durand said. "Sabella is only a year younger than I am, but yes, she has aged very well."

Sara nudged Tanner with an elbow. "I told you she was old enough to be your mother."

"What's this?" Durand said, and Sara explained.

"When we met Sabella in California she threw herself at Tanner, the conniving slut."

"Ah yes, Sabella rarely dates men her own age."

"Were you two ever lovers, Durand?"

"What's that got to do with anything, Tanner?"

"I want to know how loyal you are to her."

"Any allegiance I felt toward the woman died when I learned that she's been aiding Scallato… but yes, we were lovers once. Our affair ended after we were assigned to different areas, many years ago."

Bruno spoke up with a mouthful of French fries. "Since it was just a matter of time before she got kicked out of Interpol for mandatory retirement, Maurice told her to hook up with somebody who still had connections. She was all set to join some ritzy private security firm in Paris, but then you called and made her an offer, Durand."

Durand sent Bruno a sour look. "I was trying to help out an old friend. She was still vital and full of knowledge. I knew she wouldn't be happy in retirement."

Bruno laughed. "She'd be dead in retirement. Once Maurice has no use for her, he'll kill her."

"Why?" Sara asked.

Bruno shrugged. "That's Maurice. He doesn't like loose ends, and after being with Maurice for so long, Sabella might know some things that maybe she shouldn't."

"Like the fact that he's married and has children?" Tanner said.

Bruno nearly gagged on the soda he'd been sipping. When he spoke to Tanner, the color was draining from his face. "How do you know about that?"

Tanner brought out the letter Bruno had written his sister, Maria, then passed it over to Sara.

"I broke into the mailbox and took that. Your sister married the wrong man, Bruno."

Bruno ran his hands through his hair in agitation, then placed his palms together in supplication, as if he were about to pray.

"I'm begging you, Tanner, don't hurt my sister. I'll do whatever you want."

"Relax, the only one I plan to harm is Scallato."

Bruno shook his head. "You're lying. You'll kill my nephew too. He's a Scallato and Maurice is already training him to be a hit man. You'll kill him just so you won't have to look over your shoulder."

"How old is the kid?" Tanner said.

Bruno was breathing heavily, as if he had just stopped running. Tanner was surprised by the moistness he glimpsed in the man's eyes.

"Antonio is only thirteen. And again, I'm begging you, please don't hurt him."

"I won't kill the boy, Bruno, but I'll kill his father, and you're going to help me do that. Afterward, you can take your sister and the kids and relocate somewhere."

"Maybe I'll bring them here."

"That's not a good idea. You're burned in this city. Emilio Degussa knows about that whorehouse you've been running out of the nursing home. He's not very happy that you've been cutting into his business and planning to push him out."

Bruno slammed a fist onto his knee. "Damn it! How did Degussa find out?"

"I told him. So, you see, you should help us Kill Scallato. It's your only chance. If Scallato comes out on top, he'll still know that you talked to us and would track you down and kill you."

"How would Maurice know that we talked?"

Clicking sounds came from Bruno's left. When he looked that way, he saw that Durand was taking photos of the three of them. After a moment, Durand showed them a picture on his phone.

"You look very cozy eating a meal with Tanner, Bruno. Perhaps I should share these photos with Sabella, I'm sure she would then forward them to Scallato."

"Damn it, Tanner! You got me by the balls. All right, no more games, what do you want me to do?"

"Tell us the plan, the real plan. What is Scallato's game?"

"It's not complicated. Maurice and Sabella are in Rome. They'll spend tonight and tomorrow setting up a place for an ambush. You can be sure it will have a great line of sight leading to it, and that Maurice will know six ways to escape from it. Once they're ready, they call me, I call Durand here, and then he would have clued you in. The thing is, I would have said that Maurice was just meeting me there to talk. When you went there before the meeting to set up a sniper's nest, you would have walked right into a trap."

"Do you know where the place is?" Sara asked.

"No, only that it's in Rome. They'll tell me tomorrow in time to meet that deadline you gave me. But since you'll have to travel, the meeting will need to be arranged for the following day."

Tanner folded his arms and leaned back as he thought things over. "Trap or not, it's too good to pass up. But even if I survive the ambush, Scallato would leave the scene. Like you said, Bruno, he'll know six ways to escape."

"So how do we outsmart him?" Sara asked.

Tanner looked at Durand, Bruno, and then Sara.

"I say we give the man what he wants and let him kill me."

Durand chuckled. "I like that plan, Tanner, yet somehow, I doubt you're serious."

"We make Scallato *think* that he killed me. Once he believes I'm dead, he'll relax and return to his life in Sicily. That's when I move in for the kill."

"No!" Bruno said. "My sister and her kids will be there."

"No, they won't be, because Uncle Bruno will get them

out of the house with some sort of ruse. You can do that, can't you?"

"Yeah, I guess, but I don't really know where they live in Raguso. That's why I sent that letter to general delivery. Maria and the kids always meet me in town when I visit, so I can't help you find the house. I've never been to it."

Tanner gave a little laugh. "Scallato doesn't trust easily, does he? How long have you known him?"

"Since I was sixteen and he was fourteen, and no, Maurice is not the trusting sort."

"We'll work it out, Bruno. What name is he going by in Raguso?"

"Maurice Rizzo, and Maria says Maurice pretends to be a carpenter."

"Someone in town will know where I can find Rizzo the carpenter. Does your sister go to church?"

"She's a good Catholic girl, so yes."

"Then I'll talk to the town's priest; he's bound to know where they live."

"How will you fake your death?" Sara asked.

"With help from Durand here."

Durand sat across from them in a chair. "What do you need from me?"

"A few things, with the biggest being a body, a fresh cadaver. Is that possible?"

Durand laughed. "I have connections all over Europe, Tanner, very good connections, but they have limits and I... wait. Maybe there is a way."

"Yeah?"

"Do you know what a body farm is?"

Tanner nodded. "It's a place where they do research on how the human body decomposes."

"Correct, and I receive updates from the facilities here in Europe. Just yesterday came a memo about a new corpse being added to the body farm that is located outside Rome."

"That might work, but what if it's a woman's body, or too old, or the wrong size?"

Durand held up a finger, as if to say, "Hold on a second." He moved down the hallway and into the bedroom, then made a small sound of triumph. When he came back into the room, he was holding a crumbled newspaper.

"I feared the maid had thrown this out, but fortunately, I found it still sitting on the dresser. Look at the man in this photo. He is to be the newest cadaver."

Tanner saw a photo of a man in his thirties with long dark hair and a beard. The article said his name was Nicholas Nardo. Nardo swallowed poison after the police showed up at his house to arrest him as a suspect in a string of strangulation murders. Objects belonging to the victims were found in his home. His only relative, a brother, decided to donate Nardo's corpse to the body farm, in the hope that his troubled brother would, in his words, "Be more useful in death than he was in life."

Durand had been fiddling with his phone while Tanner read the article, which was written in Italian. Although some words were unfamiliar to him, Tanner understood enough to explain the article to Sara.

As Tanner passed the newspaper over to Bruno, Durand held up his phone, so that Tanner and Sara could see the screen.

"There's a story here that says Nicholas Nardo passed away at 9:41 p.m., which means his body will be shipped to the body farm outside Rome tomorrow. There's scant security there, but there are cameras. Still, the body will just be lying out in the open. What do you two think?"

"Once we cut Nardo's hair and shave off the beard, he

might pass for Tanner at a distance," Sara said. "But he'd have to suffer a head wound or severe facial injuries to make it work."

Durand nodded in agreement, then sent Tanner an inquiring look. "What do you think?"

"I think Bruno and I will take a trip to that body farm tomorrow night."

Bruno had been reading, but his head shot up at Tanner's words. "Me? I'm no body snatcher."

Sara took her gun out and pointed it at Bruno. "I can think of a fresher corpse to use. Do you know what I mean, Bruno?"

Bruno tossed the newspaper onto the coffee table and slumped in his seat. "Tanner, where'd you find a woman this tough?"

"We met while she was trying to kill me, and she damn near did it too."

Bruno tapped himself between the eyes with the fingers of his right hand clamped together, it was an Italian gesture that suggested the person they were talking with was insane. He looked over at Durand.

"These Americans, they are crazy, no?"

Durand smiled as he looked at Sara. "Crazy, but very beautiful."

Sara smiled back at him. "Aw, I'm so glad I didn't kill you."

33

IT'S TIME TO PAY UP

Nurse Ginevra Valli arrived for work at the nursing home and was surprised to see the home's director, Salvatore Bianchi, already there.

It was 6:56 a.m. and Ginevra had never seen Bianchi arrive for work earlier than ten. The man did not look well either. He was gaunt, had shadows under his eyes, and wore a wrinkled suit. There was a cast on the fingers of his right hand and Ginevra wondered if he'd caught them in a car door. She had done that as a teenager and knew the pain was agony.

"Signore Bianchi, is something wrong?"

Bianchi swallowed hard and Ginevra noticed that his good hand, the left one, was shaking. The hand was holding several envelopes. Ginevra grew fearful that she was about to be fired or shipped off to another of the businesses owned by the man's family.

"Ah, nurse, I'm told that Signore Rossi's nephew has been spending much time with his uncle."

"Yes sir."

"I'm also told that you two are friendly."

"Yes sir, he is a nice man."

Bianchi made a strangled cry in his throat that was meant to be a laugh of derision. He stared at Ginevra.

"You are serious? You think Signore Rossi's nephew is a nice man?"

"He treats me well. Have you had words with him?"

Bianchi looked down at his mangled hand. "Yes, we have had words, but never mind that, here."

Bianchi thrust the small stack of envelopes at Ginevra. She sat the canvas bag on the floor that held her lunch, a book, and a new batch of medication for Carlo Scallato. With her hands free, Ginevra scanned through the envelopes and noted the names on them, one of which was her own. They were the names of all the people who kept the nursing home running.

"What is this?"

"Bonuses," Bianchi said, and spat it out as if the word tasted like acid. "A year's pay for each of you under your new salaries, which are double the old salaries."

Ginevra tore open the envelope with her name on it and gasped. The check was made out for more money than she'd ever had before, and to have her salary doubled as well. It was a miracle. Then, she saw the contract. It had only a few sentences and offered her a position with the nursing home for as long as she wanted it. It also stated that her salary would increase each year. All she had to do was sign at the bottom.

Ginevra held up the check and the contract. "Why? I mean, thank you."

"Don't thank me, thank your friend."

"My friend? You mean Signore Rossi's nephew?"

"Yes, and the area in the back that was being used for… other things, will be reopened as a ward for the

Alzheimer and dementia patients. They'll each have their own room."

Ginevra's smile lit up the lobby and she laughed aloud. The smile faded when she saw the angry look on Bianchi's face.

"I'm sorry, sir. I was just happy."

Bianchi's expression changed in an instant, to one of fear. "Oh, I'm not mad at you, nurse, no, and you'll tell your friend that you and I get along, right?"

"Yes sir, I think we'll be getting along just fine from now on."

"I won't be running things here anymore. The former director has agreed to return. Your friend said that he didn't care what I did but that I'd better do it somewhere else."

Ginevra avoided cheering by biting on her bottom lip, then sent Bianchi a nod. "You'll be missed, sir," she said, but couldn't quite pull it off, as a giggle escaped.

BIANCHI SPENT THE MORNING DISMANTLING HIS OFFICE AND packing away his Chinese artwork and other belongings. When he had everything sitting in the hallway ready to be picked up by a parcel service, he walked toward the rear of the nursing home.

There was no security guarding the entrance to what had been a very profitable whorehouse. Bruno had given the order to end it shortly before Tanner kidnapped Bruno. Bianchi wondered whether Bruno was still alive, or even in one piece.

Bianchi left the nursing home while cursing Tanner under his breath, but then saw something that made him smile. It was his bodyguards. They were back, if looking a bit worse for wear since they both had bruised faces. But perhaps Bruno Allende had bested that bastard Tanner after all, and things could return to normal.

Bianchi walked toward the two behemoths while grinning like a fool. When they came even with him, each man grabbed an arm.

"What are you doing? Let go of me or I'll tell Bruno about this."

"Bruno's done," the taller man said, the one with the bandaged thumb. "And we don't work for you anymore."

They practically dragged Bianchi over to a limo as he protested and asked what was going on. There were two vehicles parked at the side of the building. One was a van, while the other was the limo. The limo looked new.

The man inside the limo didn't appear to be new in the least, he looked like he should be a patient of the nursing home. However, sitting beside him was a young woman who was not only young, but very beautiful, and... somewhat familiar, although Bianchi couldn't come up with a name.

Bianchi was seated across from the odd pairing of young and old while sandwiched between the two behemoths. He'd been ordering the two thugs around only a few days ago. He had a feeling they were now taking orders from the old man.

"Signore Bianchi, I am Emilio Degussa. I believe you owe me quite a bit of money."

"Degussa? Oh, no, no, that was all Bruno Allende's idea. He forced me to bring hookers here and sell drugs. He threatened to kill me if I didn't cooperate. I would never have done so otherwise."

"The hookers were all Bruno's idea?"

"Yes sir, and may I say I was disgusted by the vile creatures. I don't know how... any... man... could ever..."

Bianchi stared at Rosalia as he finally remembered not only her name, but where he knew her from.

"What's wrong, Salvatore?" Rosalia said. "You look like you've seen a ghost."

"Rosalia? It, it, it is good to see you, and my, don't you look all grown, I mean… oh God."

Rosalia spoke to Emilio. "Salvatore here raped me when I was twelve, after my mother decided that renting me out to men was easier than working. I think he was the fourth man to rape me, maybe the fifth. After the first two my mind went numb. Salvatore became a regular."

Emilio Degussa took Rosalia's hand and gave it a squeeze of comfort. While doing so, his face reddened noticeably. There was silence in the limo for nearly a minute, that is, if you didn't count the rapid breathing that Bianchi was making through his open mouth.

"Signore Bianchi, I have good news for you," Emilio said. "You no longer have to pay me a single euro."

Bianchi tried to speak, but it came out as a gargled cry.

"You do not have to pay me, because you will not be alive long enough to do so."

Emilio nodded at the two behemoths flanking Bianchi. One of them clamped a hand over Bianchi's face. The huge hand covered Bianchi's nose and mouth, therefore cutting off his air supply. The last thing Bianchi ever saw were the moist eyes of Rosalia. They were no longer the eyes of the child he'd raped, and they held no pity for him.

BIANCHI'S STRUGGLES WERE USELESS AS THE TWO MEN HELD him and blocked his feet from kicking. After it was obvious that Bianchi had passed out, Emilio asked Rosalia a question.

"Should he never wake up, or would you like his death to be more painful?"

"Just kill him," Rosalia whispered.

The big man whose hand was clamped over Bianchi's face complied and Bianchi deflated minutes later, like a balloon that had suffered a puncture.

"Get him out of here before he soils himself," Emilio said.

The body was removed from the limo and dragged over to the side door on the van. It was kept upright enough so as not to draw attention, had anyone been around to notice.

Rosalia grabbed a tissue and wiped at her eyes. "I could have lived the rest of my life without ever seeing him again."

"You will now," Emilio said.

Rosalia leaned against him and Emilio told the driver to take them home.

34

PET COP GETS A NEW LEASH

SABELLA BARBIERI AND MAURICE SCALLATO STOOD together inside an old storage shed and stared out a grimy window at the surrounding landscape. They were on the outskirts of Rome near the convergence of three roadways, where a rail yard kept supplies and piles of broken equipment. The rail yard itself was on the left with a fourth roadway beyond that, allowing several ways to exit the area.

It was just after seven a.m. and they had been scrutinizing the field and its surrounding area for hours. The sun was battling its way past dissipating clouds on the horizon as sunrise neared, and Sabella couldn't wait to feel its rays. She was freezing. She had taken Scallato to a site in the city just before midnight to explore the area and make plans for the ambush of Tanner.

She had the building all picked out and Scallato had been there before. He'd made a hit on a Mexican cartel member when the man had been vacationing in Rome. That was only two years earlier and nothing in the building had changed.

She assumed they would be there an hour at the most, and then return in the morning to implement whatever traps or routes of escape Scallato might come up with. That was why she was wearing only a sweater over her blouse, and why she had brought no snacks with her.

But no, Scallato spent the early part of the night moving from one position to another around the building. Most of that time he just listened for sounds of movement as he watched the area through a pair of night vision goggles.

Sabella was angry. She had helped Scallato since the day he spared her life and yet he still didn't trust her. She assured him that there was no way for Tanner to know where they were, but he ignored her. His own brother-in-law, Bruno Allende, was in on the ambush of Tanner, and Bruno had every reason to want Tanner dead. Tanner had threatened to kill Bruno and would do so if Scallato didn't kill Tanner first.

Sabella had pointed that out to Scallato, but he ignored her and kept watch. The man trusted no one, was as paranoid as they came, and must be part robot. They had been out in the cold night air for nearly five hours at that point and Scallato hadn't drank or eaten anything, nor had he urinated.

She was grateful that she had grabbed a coffee on the way to meet Scallato, or else she would have also been without any liquid. But, of course, the coffee was long gone. She had swallowed down the cold dregs of it around three-thirty a.m. after returning to her car to follow Scallato to the railway yard, and now her mouth was dry.

On the way to the rail yard, they had passed an all-night eatery that catered to the crews working overnight in the train station. The aroma of the food and coffee wafting in the air was heaven as she drove by, and when the wind blew just right, she could still smell it.

Sabella was thirsty, hungry, cold, tired, had a headache, and her feet hurt from standing around most of the night. When Scallato removed the night vision goggles and exited the shed, Sabella assumed that they were done doing recon on the area. She figured now that it was morning, they would at least visit the little café down the block and have something to eat. Once fed and warmed, with a fresh coffee in her hand, Sabella would be ready to continue.

That's why, when Scallato casually made the comment that they would give it another hour or two while exploring the other side of the rail yard, Sabella forgot who she was talking to and exploded at him.

"For fuck's sake, Maurice. If Tanner was nearby don't you think he would have shot at us by now? I want to go get something to eat. I'm cold, tired, and I'm thirsty."

Scallato didn't react until she had stopped talking. When Sabella had finished, he turned his head and stared at her. She had seen that look once before. It had been early in their "partnership." On that occasion, Sabella had attempted to set a time limit on how long she had to be an informant for the hit man. She had been fearful of being exposed when she had risked her career to get a look at classified files. The thought of spending her life behind bars had emboldened her then to press for an end date to her servitude. She had learned the hard way that there was no time limit and that she was to do as she was told or die. The broken arm she'd suffered due to Scallato's anger was blamed on clumsiness while going down a staircase.

As she gazed into Scallato's cold eyes, Sabella wondered what part of her body was about to be broken this time. She shrank back in the expectation of pain.

"Who are you?" Scallato asked, and the calmness in his voice was as unnerving as if he'd screamed the question.

"I am… Sabella?"

"No. You are my pet cop, my dog. When I call, you come, when I say sit, you sit, and when I say stay, you stay. Get down on your knees."

Sabella blinked in surprise as she wondered what Scallato had in mind. During their years together he had never demanded sex, although early on, she feared that he would rape her.

She lowered herself onto her knees, slowly, and the frigid soil of the field outside the shed accentuated the cold, making her shiver. As she settled before him, Sabella realized her face was only inches from Scallato's crotch.

"Now get on your hands."

Relief of a sort swept over Sabella. At least he wasn't going to unzip and demand that she… do that to him. When she was down on her hands and knees, Scallato repeated his question.

"Who are you?"

Sabella fought back tears spawned by feelings of degradation and disgrace. "I… I am your dog."

"Yes, you are. Now rise before you attract the attention of one of the day workers arriving."

Sabella rose and had to wipe away a tear, then another one, before gaining control. She said not another word over the next three hours unless Scallato first asked her a question.

She fantasized about killing Scallato as she did every so often, but that's all it was, a fantasy. Even if she somehow killed him, Scallato had told her that Bruno had orders to murder her. If she failed in the attempt, she would die, and Scallato had promised her that her sisters and brother would die as well.

Not for the first time, Sabella Barbieri wished she had let Scallato kill her in that alley nineteen years earlier. Life would have been short, but she would have died a hero and left behind a legacy of service.

Scallato was correct. She was a dog, one covered in fleas and filthy with mange. She had spent nearly twenty years stroking the man's considerable ego. Telling him how great he was, agreeing with every word he said, doing anything he told her to do. Basically, she had eaten shit and smiled while she did so.

After returning to her hotel, Sabella stopped in the coffee shop and devoured a large breakfast while downing three cups of coffee. Once in her room, she soaked in a hot bath while playing with a gun.

The game was called, Should I, or shouldn't I? It was played by sticking a loaded weapon in your mouth and waiting to see if you had enough guts to pull the trigger. Sabella had played it occasionally over the years, and as always, she lost, as the gun was pulled from her mouth unfired.

Sabella Barbieri climbed from the tub, dried off, and got into bed. A few strands of her hair had come loose from the bun she had tied her long locks into. They smelled faintly of the perfumed water she had bathed in; they also made her pillow wet.

She didn't bother getting up to dry her hair or change the pillowcase. She often dozed off on a pillow damp from tears. It was how dogs went to sleep.

35

OVERKILL MEANS THEY'RE DEAD, RIGHT?

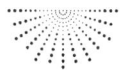

Bruno received the location of the ambush at six p.m., which meant that Tanner would have little time to prepare.

As a precaution, they wouldn't fly directly into Leonardo da Vinci International Airport, but would land at a nearby airfield and drive into the city from there. Once they reached Rome, they would return the rental and use two vehicles that Durand had arranged for them. One of the vehicles would be a van that would take Tanner within walking distance of where he and Bruno were to stage their meeting.

To Bruno's relief, Durand had his people handle the acquiring of the corpse they would need. It would be loaded inside a crate that was in the van and resembled a wooden casket.

As they stood by the van, Tanner and Sara kissed goodbye, as Durand and Bruno pretended not to look.

Sara caressed Tanner's cheek. "You're deliberately walking into a trap."

"It's the best plan I can think of, because once Scallato believes I'm dead, he'll be off-guard when we confront him at home."

"I still don't like it. There are a million things that can go wrong, such as Bruno."

"Bruno will be fine. That's one thing I'm not worried about."

"Be careful anyway, and I'll be waiting for you."

They kissed once more, then, Tanner tossed Bruno the keys to the van.

"You drive, and do just like we planned."

"I got it, Tanner. But I hope the stiff in the back of the van doesn't stink."

"The box is sealed; you won't smell anything."

After saying that, Tanner looked at Durand, who sent him a nod of assurance.

Once he was seated beside Bruno, Tanner asked for details about where he would be dropped off.

"There's a great spot about a mile away from the building. You'll have cover all the way there that will put you right behind the area where Maurice will be."

"What sort of cover, trees?"

Bruno smiled. "Better than that, they're freight cars; the building is near a train yard."

BRUNO WAS DRIVING ALONG A HIGHWAY, THE VIA DEI Monte Tiburtini, when he slowed and pulled off onto a gravel road that led down to the train yards. As he did so, Tanner rose and moved between the seats to enter the rear of the van.

"I want to check on this body before you drop me off."

"Good idea," Bruno said, then added, "Hey, Tanner?"

"Yeah?"

"Maurice is smarter than you'll ever be."

"Why do you say that?"

"He never stops thinking, that's why, and he plans for anything that can go wrong."

Tanner seemed to be giving little attention to Bruno as he unlocked the sealed crate, but he still spoke to him over his shoulder.

"Do you have something to say, Bruno?"

"Yeah, see, Maurice and I have code words worked out and what you call, um, protocols. When I didn't send the right message in my reply last night, he knew something was up."

Tanner turned to face Bruno as his hand went to his gun. "Scallato won't be at that building, will he?"

The van crested a small hill as Bruno shifted the vehicle into neutral. After turning off the ignition and removing the key, he opened the door.

"Goodbye, Tanner!"

Bruno attempted to step from the van, but he went tumbling away instead. The van had practically come to a stop on the hill, but the ground there was uneven and covered in sand. As Tanner watched Bruno hobble away behind a stack of wooden railroad ties, the van picked up speed. The vehicle moved down the hill and came to a stop sitting in the middle of an open field.

When it began, the gunfire seemed as if it would go on forever, but in truth, it lasted only a matter of seconds.

FROM A VANTAGE POINT HUNDREDS OF METERS AWAY, hidden behind a stack of metal drums, Maurice Scallato fired 600 rounds of 7.62 NATO ammo at the van containing Tanner. The M134 Minigun spat death from a rotation of six barrels at over three-thousand rounds a minute.

The van's top section was nearly separated from its bottom as hundreds of rounds stitched across its middle. Scallato calmly reloaded the Minigun as fire spread beneath the wrecked van. When the gun was ready, Scallato fired more death until over a thousand rounds had shredded the van. He allowed himself a laugh, as he was certain that Tanner was dead at last.

"Go!" Scallato shouted to Sabella, who was driving the Jeep they were in. She wore a hoodie pulled up along with a pair of large sunglasses. On the seat beside her, her purse held bottles of water and vitamin bars. But food was the last thing on her mind. She had just helped Scallato to commit murder. That made her a witness, and she wondered if she would be his next victim.

As the Jeep bounced over rough terrain, while headed toward a highway several hundred yards away, the thing in the field that had been a van, blazed. Gasoline from its perforated tank had encountered dangling wires, and fire engulfed the vehicle.

Several men from the train yard came running, and there was one who carried a fire extinguisher. He might as well have been brandishing a thimble of water, as his efforts were useless. The van burned and burned.

36

YOU CAN'T FIX STUPID

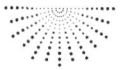

AFTER WATCHING THE JEEP SPEED AWAY, DURAND RACED HIS car down into the rail yard. He skidded to a stop a hundred feet from the blaze, then bolted from the car and sprinted to his left. As he ran, he was shouting orders into a phone.

Sara was confused by Durand's behavior as she got out of the car, but only peripherally, as her eyes took in the inferno before her.

"Tanner?" she whispered, then startled in fright, as a thunderous sound eclipsed the crackling of the fire.

It was Durand. He was behind the wheel of a massive dump truck that was carrying a load of sand. He maneuvered the behemoth of a vehicle near the van. After a slight hesitation as he figured out the controls, the rear of the dump truck tilted, and sand began pouring out. The sand doused the blaze, while submerging the bottom of the van.

Sara pushed past the stunned rail workers. She was still unable to get inside the van because of the intense heat coming off what was left of the metal frame. However, she could see inside, and said a prayer of thanks when she spotted the van's contents.

There was something intact inside the van. It had been concealed by the wooden crate, but the wood had been ripped apart by the Minigun and partially burned by the fire. The object was metal, shaped like a coffin, and constructed of inch-thick steel. Hundreds of pock marks marred its surface, but no rounds had penetrated it. Its padded interior was the only thing that kept Tanner from being seared by the metal.

When the top unsealed with a popping sound and Tanner sat up inside the box gasping for air, Sara let out a scream of joy, but then, she saw his expression. They locked eyes for only an instant before his lids began to close, and he passed out.

Several vehicles approached, with one of them being an ambulance, while another was a fire engine. When a man stepped out of the lead vehicle, he flashed a badge and told everyone to back up. The railway workers did as ordered, while Sara and Durand stayed near the van, which was still smoldering.

Sara called Tanner's name, but he didn't respond.

The man with the badge spoke to Durand. "Sir, is that our asset in there?"

"It is, and we have to get him out of there. I think he's suffering from heat exposure."

"Step back!" came a voice from behind them, and there appeared a policeman with a device called the jaws of life. It was a hydraulic tool that spread and cut metal and was normally used to free victims from car wrecks.

It opened a space in the van and two firemen stepped up through it wearing protective gear and carefully lifted Tanner from the metal box. The gathered crowd grew silent as one of the fireman laid a hand on Tanner's chest, but a cheer rose up as the man spoke.

"He's breathing!"

The men laid him on a gurney and Tanner was rushed into the rear of the ambulance. When he stirred awake from the oxygen mask being placed on his face, the first sight he saw was Sara. The joy in her eyes at seeing he was well was something Tanner would always remember. It dimmed other memories, memories of the times she gazed at him with hate and murderous intent.

Tanner removed the mask despite the paramedic's admonitions to keep it on. He also declined an IV, but asked for water. He received it, along with a salt tablet, and drank heartily. His clothes were drenched in his own sweat and his damp hair hung in his eyes. Tanner removed the shirt and the slight exertion left him dizzy. Sara spoke to him, but he pointed at his ears and told her he couldn't understand her, because his ears were ringing. Sara understood, the hundreds of rounds slamming into that metal box must have sounded thunderous.

Durand took the paramedic's place as Tanner finished his third cup of water, and to Tanner's surprise, Durand looked pleased to see him sitting up.

"Can you hear me, Tanner?" Durand said loudly.

"Yeah, my hearing is coming back."

"In case you're wondering what hit you, it was a Minigun. I'd say you survived a barrage of more than a thousand rounds."

"Thanks to you and your contacts, Durand. If I had been behind anything less than an inch of steel I think I would qualify as Swiss cheese right now."

"You can thank Bruno as well. If he hadn't fallen for our story about grabbing a corpse from a body farm, he would have wondered what was really in the crate."

"I expected Scallato to hammer the van with a sniper rifle. Using a Minigun was overkill; he really wanted me dead."

"The man doesn't lack resources," Durand said. "That gun cost as much as a house."

"Who dumped the sand to put out the fire? I think that saved my life."

"I did, and we're fortunate that dump truck was loaded."

Tanner offered his hand. Durand took it. After they shook, they each nodded at the other.

"Are your people chasing after Scallato?" Sara asked Durand.

"I called them off. The man had a Minigun; even if they cornered Scallato they would have been woefully lacking in firepower. I curse the Italians for not granting air support. Had they done so, we could have at least kept track of Scallato."

"What's our next move?" Sara asked.

Durand smiled at her. "You and I will do a little playacting for Sabella's benefit, so she will pass it along to Scallato."

"And what about Bruno?" Sara said. "That son of a bitch has to pay for this."

Tanner pushed back his damp hair to reveal eyes reddened from heat stroke. "I'll deal with Bruno in a way that won't alert Scallato that I'm still alive."

"You said he would stay loyal to Scallato, but then, they are related by marriage," Sara said.

"It's not just that. Bruno also fears Scallato more than he fears me."

"That will prove to be a fatal mistake," Durand said.

Tanner shrugged. "You can't fix stupid."

37

GREATLY EXAGGERATED

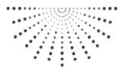

Sara checked her look in the mirror one more time before telling Durand to make the connection. Durand had his laptop open on a coffee table as he sat on a sofa, while behind him, Sara pretended to weep into a tissue as she sat hunched over on the side of a bed.

When the connection was made, Durand reminded himself to keep his anger in check, as on his laptop screen appeared the smiling face of Sabella Barbieri. She appeared to be sitting on a park bench. That was likely to make him believe she was being the good aunt and watching her sister's grandchildren. It was the excuse she had given for needing a few days off. The duplicity of the woman made Durand want to strangle her.

"Jacques, hello, I was going to call later to get a progress report. Is everything going as planned?"

"Sabella, there's been a tragedy. Tanner is dead and Scallato killed him. Our informant, Bruno Allende, he betrayed us."

Sabella's hand flew to her mouth. When she spoke

again, she asked Durand who the woman was in the background.

"That is Sara Blake. She is devastated by Tanner's death."

"So, they were lovers. I thought I sensed something between them."

"Bruno also said vile things about you, Sabella, but I want you to know that I never believed him."

"What did he say?"

"He accused you of aiding Scallato, which is preposterous, since you have every reason to hate the man."

"Yes, and thank you for not believing his lies. But Jacques, listen to me. You are in danger every moment you're around Sara Blake. She was helping Tanner, that means Scallato will seek her death."

"And mine as well, since I'm sure Bruno has told Scallato of my involvement."

Sabella looked genuinely upset as she spoke her next words. "I hadn't considered that. Oh, Jacques, you must hide, it is your only chance to live."

"I know, and Sara will be coming with me. Where we're going, Scallato will never find us."

There was silence for a moment. It was broken by a whispered question, spoken in a hesitant voice.

"Where, where will you go?"

"Just know that it's safe and far away from Rome."

"I wish you luck, Jacques, and I'm so sorry that things turned out this way… so sorry."

"Yes, Sabella, but look on the bright side."

"There's a bright side?"

"If Scallato is ever killed, I'll be able to write one hell of a book."

"He won't die," Sabella said. "That man is the devil."

"Goodbye, Sabella."

"Goodbye Jacques, and please, run far, my friend. And God's speed."

Durand ended the call and told Sara that it was all right to speak. She walked over and sat beside him on the sofa.

"That should buy us some time," Sara said. "And did you hear the bitch try to learn where we were headed? If we were really on the run and you had given away our destination, Scallato would have been our first visitor."

Durand released a great sigh. "I once loved Sabella, I think, at least a little, when we were both so very young."

"Once Tanner kills Scallato she'll be arrested?"

"Yes, and then she will rot away in a cell."

Sara took Durand's hand. "I'm sorry you're losing an old friend, Jacques."

"Don't be. She deserves what she gets."

"I still know it hurts."

"There is a French phrase you've probably heard before, 'C'est la vie,' it means, 'Such is life.'"

Sara smiled. "We have a similar phrase in English— Shit happens."

In the San Lorenzo District of Rome, Bruno Allende returned to his hotel room after buying a bottle of wine and a cheap cell phone with cash. He was still limping a bit after jumping from the van, but his injury wasn't serious. Bruno had to use his credit card for the hotel room. However, he figured that even if Emilio Degussa was tracking his charges, he'd be gone before anyone from Genoa could come after him.

After activating the phone, Bruno called a number he

had memorized years earlier at Scallato's insistence. When an old lady answered him in broken Italian that had an Irish accent, Bruno hung up, tried again, and heard Scallato answer.

"Where are you?"

"Yeah, yeah. In San Lorenzo."

"Have you enough money to disappear?"

"Yeah, yeah. I just have to get to Milan. I have enough money hidden there to last me a year."

"I'll see to your problem soon and put old man Degussa in the grave where he belongs. In the meantime, take a vacation."

"Yeah, yeah. How soon?"

"Let's say a month; I have other business to attend to in Sicily."

"Yeah, yeah. Okay, I'll contact you in a month."

"You can stop the, 'yeah, yeahs' now, Bruno. I get the message, it's safe to talk."

"Thanks, Maurice, but hey, the system came in handy against Tanner. He thought I had sold you out right up until the time I leapt from the van."

"About that, I heard on the radio that there were two bodies found in the van. Who was the second one?"

"Two bodies? Oh, wait, that was the corpse Tanner stole. He was going to make you think you killed him, so you'd drop your guard. Ha! The dumb bastard, he doesn't have to fake anything now. I bet there's not much left of him either."

"He dared to believe he was better than me; I had to make an example of him."

"What about his woman, and the Frenchman? Will you kill them too?"

"Someday, but for now let them suffer from fear."

"That bitch Sara will go gray worrying about you, but

that Frenchman might be trouble, he knows about your pet cop."

"I know, but Durand told Sabella that he never believed you. It appears that her cover is still intact."

"I hated to give her up, but I had to give Tanner something or he would have killed me."

"It doesn't matter. There is no evidence against her and she still has use. With the Frenchman on the run from me, I'll have Sabella work to get his position or to be the assistant to his successor."

"Good, and I'm so glad you killed Tanner. I only wish I could have done it."

"You told them about Sabella, Bruno. Did you tell them anything else?"

The letter he'd mailed, and that Tanner stole, flashed across Bruno's mind, but he pushed it aside.

Tanner may have known the town where Scallato lived, but he was dead, and his woman and the Frenchman were on the run. Besides, Bruno wrote that letter in a state of fear and told his sister to run from her home. But that was when he thought Tanner had a chance of winning. If he admitted that to his brother-in-law, he'd be his next victim.

"Bruno?"

"Oh, sorry, it's just that I heard voices outside the door; it was just a bunch of teenagers out in the hallway. No, Maurice, I told them nothing else."

"Then we have no worries and I will return to Sicily tomorrow. Remember to destroy that phone. Goodbye, Bruno."

"Goodbye, Maurice, and give Maria and the kids my love."

Bruno placed the phone on the floor and raised his foot to smash it. The phone was tougher than he'd expected it to be and he had to stomp on it repeatedly. On his last attempt, the heel of his shoe came loose. When he picked it up, he saw that something electronic was embedded in the heel. He was sure it wasn't part of the phone, but then, what was it?

"It's a tracking device," Tanner said. He had been standing inside the room's small closet. His sudden appearance so unraveled Bruno that he dropped the heel and let out a shriek.

"You... you're dead."

"As Mark Twain once said, 'the reports of my death have been greatly exaggerated.'"

"What? Who?"

Tanner raised the Taser he was holding and fired. Bruno shrieked again, this time in agony, and fell to the floor. Tanner placed a set of handcuffs on Bruno as he cuffed his wrists around the base of the room's steel radiator. It was low to the floor and didn't even allow Bruno enough slack to stand up straight. Once he'd recovered, Bruno stared up at Tanner with a furrowed brow.

"How the hell are you alive, Tanner? Maurice emptied a damn Minigun on you."

"I ducked."

"Maurice will just have to kill you again."

"He'll get the chance. I'll be paying him a visit soon in Sicily. And thanks to you, I know just where to look."

Bruno tugged at the handcuffs, then kicked the floor in frustration. "When I don't call Maurice back, he'll know something is wrong."

"I heard your side of the conversation; you said you'd contact him in a month."

"Are you going to kill me?"

"No."

"No?"

"I'm going to tell Degussa where he can find you."

"That's the same as killing me."

"Yeah, yeah," Tanner said, and slapped a thick piece of duct tape over Bruno's mouth.

Degussa answered the phone himself and said that he would contact associates who would pick up, "The package" and ship it back home. Tanner had to wait for nearly two hours, but then watched as two men exited a white van and rolled a large suitcase into the hotel. When they rolled the suitcase out, a keen observer could tell that it weighed considerably more.

With Bruno handled, Tanner drove to where Sara was waiting for him, and was amazed to realize that he couldn't wait to feel her in his arms.

"Yeah, yeah," he whispered, and drove faster.

38

HAIL THE CONQUERING HERO

MARIA SQUEALED WITH DELIGHT WHEN HER HUSBAND TOLD her he had killed Tanner.

Scallato held his hands up, as if to say, "What other outcome could there be?"

He arrived in Sicily the day before, but he had been three towns away looking at properties with a real estate agent. He was searching for something near, but not too near his home, to make it easier to visit Veronika. Once they had sons, and he was confident that Veronika could give him sons, he would be spending most of his time with his new family.

After kissing him, Maria promised that she would make him his favorite dish, but then remembered that she was out of garlic.

"Send the boy to fetch some," Scallato said.

"But don't you remember, Maurice? You told me that Antonio wasn't to run errands anymore."

"I know what I said, but he's good for little else, so send him."

Maria started to protest, but knew it would do no good,

271

and so she called for Antonio. He was outside in the field behind the house.

"What's he doing out there?" Scallato said.

"He's practicing his knife throwing and is getting quite good. You should go watch him."

"The boy had his chance to impress me. He failed miserably."

Antonio entered, when he saw his father he broke out in a huge smile. It faded when Scallato gazed back at him impassively.

"Antonio, we have good news. Your father has killed the American assassin named Tanner. I need you to go into town and buy garlic. We're having Busiate with the Pesto Trapanese that your father likes, for a celebration."

Maria handed Antonio money for his trip to the store, and he stared at it, then over at his father. Only weeks ago, Scallato had told him that he was a man, and that a man didn't run errands for women.

"Patri?" Antonio said.

"What, boy? Just do as your mother says and get the garlic. Perhaps you'll do that right."

Antonio hung his head and slunk out of the house. Maria watched him through the window and gave a little moan.

"You are too tough on the boy, Maurice, and he loves you so much."

Scallato stood up from the table. "I'll be in my workshop. Let me know when it's time to eat."

"Maurice?"

"Yes?"

"What about Tanner's woman, is she dead too?"

"Not yet, but there will be plenty of time to deal with her."

"I don't like her running around; she sounds dangerous

to me."

Scallato spun and pointed a finger at Maria. "I don't care what you like or don't like, and don't tell me how to do my work. I will kill the bitch when I'm good and ready. Tanner is dead, and the threat is ended, be happy about that."

"I didn't mean to question you. Maurice... do you blame me for Antonio's failure?"

"Maybe you babied him too much, or maybe it was me and I should have been home more, either way, the boy is useless."

Tears erupted from Maria's eyes. "No, Maurice, do not give up on him. Antonio loves you and will prove himself worthy someday, please, just have patience."

Scallato opened the door. "I'll be in my workshop."

As he stepped outside and closed the door behind him, Maria sank into a chair and sobbed.

ANTONIO ENTERED TOWN AND BOUGHT THE GARLIC HIS mother needed, and as he did so, he felt like a child. But he was a man, wasn't he? Hadn't he been with a woman, and hadn't that made him a man? And such a beautiful woman Yana had been.

But, he was a coward. His disgraceful behavior with the Martello brothers had proven that, but maybe he didn't have to stay a coward. He would prove himself a man someday, perhaps like his mother said, when he was older, then his father would love him again.

He was about to head home when he heard his name being called, it was his friend, Paolo. Paolo waved at him from the front porch of the town's cozy little hotel, that was more like a bed & breakfast establishment. Paolo's father worked as manager while Paolo's mother was the maid and cook.

Paolo had two puppies with him and was playing with them. They were the same dogs that Antonio's father had wanted him to kill. After leaving them to fend for themselves in the hills, Antonio found he couldn't sleep for worrying about them.

He had snuck out of the house that night, while his father had been in the workshop, and gone to tap on Paolo's window at the rear of the hotel. Paolo also snuck out, then, the two of them went to look for the puppies up in the hills with a pair of flashlights.

It took an hour of searching, but they found the pups. The small hounds had been shivering, and the next day, Paolo's mother talked his father into letting him take care of the dogs until he found them homes.

Antonio picked up one of the puppies and was surprised by how much bigger it looked than the last time he'd seen it. That brought to mind his first sight of the pup, and he asked Paolo a question.

"Do you think you could ever kill something like a puppy?"

Paolo gave Antonio a strange look. Paolo was a handsome boy with lots of curly hair. Girls were attracted to him, but he blushed and became tongue-tied whenever he spoke to one. Although he was a year older than Antonio, Paolo looked up to his friend.

"Kill it?"

"Yeah, like with a shotgun. Do you think you could do it?"

"Antonio, you would have to be mental to do something like that. Those are the kind of guys that grow up to be serial killers."

Antonio stared at the puppy as he held it up. "Why is it

so hard to do? It's about the same size as the rats that live down by the docks. I could shoot the rats. Anyone could shoot the rats."

Paolo smiled, as the other pup licked his face. "Rats don't know how to love, puppies do."

Antonio was considering the difference between rats and dogs when the puppy he was holding squirmed loose. The pup then went exploring beneath the floorboards, which were set high, due to habitual flooding in the spring.

Paolo pointed at his feet, indicating the floorboards. "Get the puppy, Antonio! Talk about rats, my father places rat poison under there. Don't let the puppy eat it."

Antonio scrambled onto his belly and crawled under the porch. He was familiar with the space; he and Paolo had played under there when they were smaller boys. He saw the puppy up ahead and to the left, but the creature eluded his first attempt to grab him. By the time Antonio managed to catch him, he was almost out the back side.

Someone was standing on the rear porch and talking, no, two people, a man and a woman. When Antonio recognized they were speaking English, he listened in. He understood the language, along with French and some German.

When he realized what he was hearing and who it was that was speaking, Antonio was stunned.

Sara looked over the scenery while sipping on a cup of coffee. She was in disguise again, but this time it was a simple one, just a blond wig and sunglasses.

Tanner wore no disguise, but was dressed in a suit, complete with a wide-brimmed hat. They had been in town for only an hour and were waiting for it to get dark.

"It's beautiful here, Tanner. We've been to so many gorgeous locations and could barely enjoy them. Once Scallato is no longer a threat, I want to take a few days and return to Rome to play tourist."

"Fine, I could use the down time, but first, Scallato has to die."

"He won't see you coming," Sara said.

ANTONIO CRAWLED BACK TOWARD THE FRONT OF THE hotel with the squirming pup beneath one arm. Tanner was alive somehow when his father was certain he had killed him. That was horrible. The man must know where they lived, or he wouldn't be in Raguso, and he was deadly, even his father had said so.

Antonio handed the pup back to Paolo, grabbed his bag of garlic, and ran for home as fast as he could. However, when he was halfway there, he slowed, then, he stopped.

His father had no idea Tanner still lived, and that meant his father had failed. Maurice Scallato, *Il Fantasma*, had failed. Somehow, Tanner had tricked his father into believing he had died, and if not for Antonio, Tanner would have the advantage and invade their home.

The thought of the American assassin sneaking into their home in the middle of the night chilled Antonio, but also enraged him. What if Tanner wasn't satisfied with just killing Antonio's father? He might also harm his mother, as well as Anna, Antonio's little sister.

The man had to be stopped from ever coming near their house. Antonio imagined the scene when he returned home and told them that Tanner was alive. Would they even believe him? Yes, his father would know he wouldn't lie about such a thing. But oh, how embarrassed he would be.

Would he blame me? Antonio thought. What was that saying, kill the messenger? Yes, he would be going home and proclaiming his father a failure. His father wouldn't like that, would hate it, and worse of all, Antonio would get no credit for alerting him. Antonio could hear his father's voice in his head.

"You were just lucky, Antonio."

"Only a boy playing with puppies would have been there to overhear them in the first place."

"If you were really a man, you would have killed Tanner yourself."

That last thought made Antonio cock his head. Why not kill Tanner? Oh, if he killed Tanner, killed a man who was said to be the equal of his father, oh, then, then his father would have to say he was a man. It would be easy too, all he had to do was go back to the hotel with a shotgun, and this time he would pull the trigger. One pull of the trigger and Tanner died, his family was safe, and his father would love and respect him again.

Yes! He could do it. Just one little pull of the trigger and the legend of Antonio Scallato would be born. He would be the man who killed the American assassin, Tanner, and he would at last be worthy to wear the name, Scallato.

Antonio rushed home, handed off the garlic to his mother, and ever so quietly, he removed the shotgun that sat above the fireplace.

After wrapping the gun in a blanket, he sneaked out his bedroom window and headed back to town.

Just one pull of the trigger and a legend would die, while another was born.

39

CATCH AND RELEASE

TANNER GUIDED SARA ONTO HER BACK AS HE MOVED between her legs. They were both fully dressed, in all but their shoes, and were waiting for darkness to fall. Outside, the last rays of the day's light were saying their farewells. Tanner and Sara knew that once they found Scallato's home, it would be like facing a lion in his den.

"What are you doing?" Sara said, and there was laughter in her voice.

"I think they call this sex," Tanner said.

"But we're fully clothed."

"Then let's just call it a dress rehearsal."

Sara giggled, angled her hips, then pushed Tanner off her with a knee. He settled beside her on his back and smiled.

"No sex, mister, not now, not when Scallato is so close. Maybe you could enjoy yourself with that sort of pressure, but I can't."

Tanner rolled onto his side and ran a hand along her body. "This will all be over soon. Once we talk to the priest, Father Rossetti, and learn where Scallato lives, I'll set up a sniper's nest and wait for him to show himself."

"What if he's with one of his children?"

"I'll still kill him."

"No, that's horrible. No child should see their parent killed."

Tanner kissed her. "The man wants you dead, Sara. I don't want to let him live a second longer than I have to."

"I understand the risk, but no. Tanner please? Only kill him when he's alone."

"All right, and of course, I'd prefer to do it that way. The last thing we want is for Scallato to get away again. I don't think he would resurface until he was firing rounds at us."

"You think he would abandon his family?"

"He's studied me. He knows that they would be safe and that I wouldn't use them as bait."

Sara turned toward him and supported herself on an elbow as she gazed into Tanner's eyes.

"Why not use them as bait, or threaten to kill them?"

"The family?"

"Yes, I've studied you too, remember? I know that you have a ruthless streak."

"Not against innocents, they're off-limits."

"I know that too. But why are they off-limits? Is it a rule you have, or is that a rule of the Tanner's?"

"It's both, although, a Tanner will do anything to survive. The first rule of being an assassin is to survive no matter what it takes. It's difficult to kill when you yourself are dead."

Sara gave Tanner a soft kiss on the lips. "You're a good man, do you know that?"

"I don't think I'd fit anyone's definition of good, Sara."

"You fit mine, and when I first realized that you were a

good man it redefined my beliefs about good and evil. You're not good in a traditional sense, because you don't behave within societal and moral expectations, but you are a good man, and you do good things."

"I'm going to do a good thing in this town and rid the world of Maurice Scallato."

Sara shook her head in wonder. "I still can't believe he has a wife."

Tanner held up a finger to correct her. "Widow, not wife, it's just a matter of time."

Sara laughed, pushed Tanner onto his back, then straddled his hips.

"Let's get back to that dress rehearsal."

At the home of Maurice Rizzo, who was actually Maurice Scallato, his wife Maria called out that dinner was ready. Little Anna came downstairs with her favorite doll in her arms. She was followed by her father, but there was no sign of Antonio.

Maria called him again, served the food, and looked over at the staircase. "Antonio get down here; it's time to eat."

"Maybe he's mad because he had to go to the store," Scallato suggested.

"Or maybe he's not feeling well; I should go check on him."

"No woman, sit down and eat. If the boy wants to sulk, let him sulk."

Maria sat, but called her son's name once more.

"Antonio, come eat!"

There was no response.

Scallato sent a backhanded wave toward the staircase.

"The hell with him. Now let's eat. The food looks excellent."

Maria smiled at the compliment to her cooking, but she cast a worried glance at the stairs. It wasn't like Antonio to sulk. Maria began to eat quickly. The faster she finished her food, the sooner she could check on Antonio.

"DRESS REHEARSAL" WAS WELL ON ITS WAY TO BECOMING A full-fledged performance when something nibbled at the edges of Tanner's awareness.

It was a sound, something akin to the creak of a floorboard, but less pronounced. It was the sound that wood made when a slight weight was placed upon it. When he heard it once again, he placed a finger to his lips and pointed at the door to their room.

Sara's eyes widened with alarm. She slid off Tanner, stood, and adjusted her clothing, when she looked over at him, she saw that Tanner was zipping up with one hand while slipping a knife out of its sheath with the other.

She arranged the bed so that it appeared to have been used, then tiptoed inside the bathroom and turned on the shower. She and Tanner had drilled on what to do if Scallato paid them a visit and they were both ready to kill anyone who entered the room. Sara opened the medicine cabinet, adjusting the mirror so that it showed her the door from her position inside the bathroom.

Another creak came, this time closer, and Tanner dropped flat and peered beneath the gap under the door. He saw a pair of feet clad in sneakers, and while they weren't tiny feet, they were too small to belong to Scallato.

Tanner went back to standing from his prone position with an effortlessness and speed that would be the envy of many athletes. After reaching over and soundlessly unlocking the door, he turned to find Sara peeking around the door frame of the bathroom.

Tanner mouthed the words, "Don't shoot," before flattening himself against the wall near the door.

More than a minute passed before the handle on the door began to turn. Tanner assumed that their young visitor had been steeling himself to make entry into the room. When the door opened, Tanner was behind it, as the boy who had opened it stood, listened, and panted slightly.

As the intruder edged toward the bathroom, Tanner pushed the door closed with his foot while yanking a shotgun out of the teen's hands. The boy spun around so fast that he tripped over his own feet and fell back on his butt.

Tanner aimed the shotgun at the boy's chest as Sara shut off the shower, then, Tanner introduced their uninvited guest to her when she left the bathroom.

"Meet Antonio Scallato, boy assassin."

Antonio had been glaring up at Tanner with a look of defiance, but at the utterance of the word, "boy", his face crumpled, and tears fell down his cheeks. He had failed yet again, and now his father would die.

MARIA FLEW DOWN THE STAIRS, RUSHED INTO THE KITCHEN, then grabbed her husband by the arm. "Antonio is gone! His room is empty."

Scallato had been enjoying a cup of coffee. It sloshed onto the table and soaked the newspaper he'd been reading.

"Relax, Maria. The boy probably just snuck out to see a girl."

"But what if he's run away?"

"Are his things missing?"

"I don't know. I'll go check."

While Maria was gone, Scallato tossed the soggy newspaper into the garbage can, then he stood and leaned back against the sink as he thought things over. Antonio running away could be a good thing, perhaps a few years out in the world would toughen the boy. But no, the boy just didn't have what it takes. If he had run off, the world would eat him alive and spit him out.

Maria came back with a smile on her face. "His things are all here. Maybe you're right, perhaps he snuck out to meet a girl."

Scallato ran a hand over his chin. "Why not eat dinner first? If he had gone out after eating, we might not have known about it for hours."

Maria's face became a mask of worry again. "Do you think something is wrong?"

"I don't know, Maria."

"Patri," Anna called to her father. She was sitting by the television in the living room. "The lights outside came on. I see Antonio, he's back."

Maria let out a sigh of relief and went to the door to greet her son. Antonio stood in the doorway with tears running down his cheeks.

"What's wrong, baby?" Maria asked, but Antonio could only cry.

TANNER AND SARA WERE STANDING JUST BEYOND THE reach of the floodlights of Scallato's home, as they watched Maria greet Antonio. Tanner held a Glock, while Sara carried the shotgun they had taken from Antonio.

Tanner had pushed the boy out of their room at the hotel and told him to go home and tell his father that he was coming for him in the morning. Antonio was too distraught and dejected to see through the lie and didn't realize that Tanner and Sara would follow him.

Now that Antonio had led them to his father's doorstep, Tanner knew they had to strike hard and fast. If Antonio got the opportunity to utter his name, Scallato would be instantly on guard.

As Maria draped an arm over Antonio's shoulders, Tanner sprinted toward the door. As Maria went to shut the door with her free hand, Tanner rammed into it, entered the home, and saw Scallato standing in the kitchen near a table.

Tanner aimed the Glock at Scallato's chest as Sara came in behind him and slammed the door shut. Little Anna screamed and ran to her mother, then Maria rushed to her husband's side, with her children clinging to her.

Scallato's face betrayed amazement at seeing Tanner alive. That was followed by a chuckle and a shake of his head.

"Well played, Tanner. I wouldn't have thought such a thing possible, but you truly are in my league. I see now that I was a fool to ever underestimate you."

"We all make mistakes," Tanner said, as he and Sara moved closer. "But don't make another mistake and put your family at risk. I have no desire to harm them or to torture you. Just walk toward me with your hands in the air and we'll end this outside."

"I want your word that you won't harm my family," Scallato said. As he spoke, he slid a knife free from the sheath on his belt. He also wore a gun in an ankle holster, but he knew that Tanner would shoot him dead if he tried to reach for it.

"You have my word, Scallato. Neither of us will harm your family. Now, get over here."

Scallato let out a deep breath as his face twisted into a grimace, when he looked over at his wife, he spoke softly, but audibly.

"I've failed you, Maria. Please forgive me?"

All Maria could do was nod, as emotion choked off her voice and tears leaked from her beautiful blue eyes.

After wrapping his arms around Antonio tenderly and placing a gentle kiss on his son's head, Scallato slit the boy's throat open, while angling Antonio's neck so that Tanner was blinded by the spray of arterial blood. As Tanner remarked earlier, the first rule of being an assassin was to survive no matter what.

Maurice Scallato was a survivor.

40

IN THE WIND

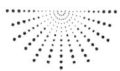

Scallato freed the gun from his ankle holster then moved behind Maria to use her as a shield.

Tanner, although blinded by Antonio's blood, fired off a shot at the spot where Scallato's head had been. Sara was frozen in utter shock by Scallato's casual murder of his own son, then was aghast and appalled as Scallato placed his gun to his daughter's head and pulled the trigger. The child fell to the floor as three more shots rang out. Scallato had fired a trio of rounds into Maria's back, before shoving her toward Tanner.

Tanner had been attempting to clear his vision of Antonio's blood. When he felt Maria's body collide into him, he reached out to take hold of it and mistook the female form to be Sara's.

"No! Sara no!"

Sara had been stunned into inactivity, but Tanner's voice brought her back to herself. She leveled the shotgun at Scallato, who was running to her left while looking over his shoulder. She fired the weapon an instant after Scallato dove to the floor. The shotgun pellets destroyed a window, and Scallato popped up from the floor and jumped through the splintered remains of the window frame.

"Sara, thank God," Tanner said. His vision had cleared, and he saw that Sara was all right. After lowering Maria's dead form to the floor, Tanner looked beneath the table and saw the bodies of her children.

"He killed them? All of them?" Tanner asked in a hoarse voice. He looked ghastly. His face was stained red with blood, as were the front of his clothes. He was not the only one covered in gore, as Sara had taken spray from wounds as well. Tanner grabbed the shotgun from Sara and passed her his weapon. "Stay here and use your phone to call Durand. If I don't come back, don't come out until sunrise or until Durand sends help."

Sara appeared to have barely heard him, as she gestured about at the carnage.

Tanner shook her shoulder with one hand. "Hey! Stay with me. You have to be able to defend yourself while I'm gone."

"Yes, right, I'm good, I'm good, just go and kill that bastard. Oh Tanner, please kill that monster."

Tanner left the home the same way Scallato had, by leaping through the damaged window.

He saw the light pouring out from the nearby shed, but he took the time to make a circuit of the home before heading toward the structure. The shed was empty, but there were signs that something secreted away behind a wall had been removed.

Tanner searched through the woods that bordered the home for an hour, then came upon the rope that had been buried in plastic at the base of a tree. The rope dangled over the edge of a sheer drop that ended in a landscape filled with boulders. Scallato must have rappelled down the rope and fled into the night. He was gone, long gone.

Tanner returned to the house, but called to Sara before entering, so she'd know it was him. She was in the living room holding a wet towel, which she had used to wipe off the gore, crime scene forensics be damned.

Tanner looked better than he had when he left. He had torn off his sleeves, wetted them in a stream, and used them to clean his face. A face that told Sara everything she needed to know.

"He's gone, isn't he?"

"Scallato's in the wind," Tanner said.

41

BEYOND PERSONAL

At sunrise, Tanner leaned against the back wall of Scallato's home and marveled at the man's inhumanity. Inside the house, Durand's people were wading through the carnage as they searched for a clue as to where Scallato might have gone

Sara was in Tanner's arms with her head resting against his chest, and every so often, she cried.

Durand's people had given them new clothing that resembled hospital scrubs and they had washed off the gore. However, the scent of Antonio Scallato's blood lingered in Tanner's nostrils. He guessed that the memory of it always would.

Tanner thought back to his early years, and of a conversation he'd had with his mentor. Spenser pointed out that even an assassin had rules, and that the Tanner's all lived by a code of conduct.

"A Tanner never kills the innocent, Cody. A Tanner kills the murderers, the butchers, or those who facilitate their butchery.

I won't go so far as to describe what we do as a force of good, but someday I'll stand before my maker and proudly proclaim that I never murdered anyone, but I killed them, oh yes, and at times with a righteous anger."

As Tanner returned from the memory, Sara asked him what they would do next. He took her by the hand and led her over to a tree. After pacing back and forth for a moment in an uncharacteristic state of agitation, Tanner gazed at Sara, and she saw that he looked worried, and appeared to be uneasy.

"What Scallato did in there… I… I hope you know I would never do that."

Sara had been leaning with her back against the tree. She took her weight off it to reach over and take Tanner's hand.

"I once hated you more than anyone and believed you were the scum of the earth, but Tanner, not once would I have thought you capable of… of… that, that slaughter. I mean, he killed his own children… that poor little girl. No, oh baby, no, don't ever believe that I equate you on any level with Maurice Scallato. You are his superior in every way and someday soon you'll put that monster in his grave."

Tanner took Sara in his arms. "It may not happen soon; it may even cover a span of years, but I promise you this, I'll track down Scallato and kill him if it takes me the rest of my life."

Sabella Barbieri was sure she was in trouble, but she had no idea what kind or how bad the evidence was against her. She had been tracked down in Rome overnight, rousted from bed, and driven to the airport. Once there, she'd been placed on a helicopter and flown to Sicily. Not once during any of it were her questions answered. When she tried to press the issue, she was told that she would be cuffed and possibly tasered if she didn't remain quiet.

The helicopter landed in a field near a secluded house that had multiple crime scene units parked nearby. A wide area surrounding the home was taped off and guarded by local and regional police.

What is this all about? Sabella wondered.

Her wondering stopped after she approached the home and saw Jacques Durand staring at her. To her amazement, Tanner was there, alive and without so much as a scratch. Standing beside Tanner was Sara Blake, and she looked enraged enough to claw Sabella's eyes out.

Sabella forced a smile onto her face as she was about to say how relieved she was at Tanner's survival.

The words turned into a gasp of pain. Durand had seized Sabella by the arm and dragged her to a coroner's wagon. Once there, he ordered a forensic tech to unzip the body bags and show her Scallato's handiwork.

"These are Scallato's wife and children. The bastard murdered them as a distraction so that he could escape from Tanner."

Sabella's face contorted as she shook her head in denial. Then, she ran to a tree, bent over, and vomited. It was so violent and sudden that she fell to her knees. As she attempted to get up, she felt the cold metal of a gun at her temple.

Tilting her head, she saw her longtime friend and past lover, Jacques Durand. There was a look in his eyes she had never glimpsed there before.

"Tell me where I can find Scallato."

Sabella said nothing. Durand knew the truth about her, and what he didn't know, he could guess. However, what could he prove? When Durand spoke again, it was as if he were reading her mind.

"I can't prove a thing, Sabella, but I know that you were the person Scallato called his, 'pet cop.' If you know where he is and don't tell me, I will kill you."

Sabella let out a wail, collapsed into her own vomit, and a sleeve of her jacket soaked up the vileness, after turning over onto her back, she stared up at Durand.

"I don't know where he is, Jacques. I swear it on Monique's grave."

Durand's face twisted into something unrecognizable as he leaned over and forced the barrel of his gun into Sabella's mouth. "Do not ever mention my wife's name again or God help me I will kill you."

Sara stepped closer to Durand and laid a hand on his arm. "Jacques, don't do it. She might yet prove useful in tracking down Scallato."

Durand's anger faded as he looked at Sara, and he removed his gun from Sabella's mouth. With Tanner and Sara beside him, Durand left Sabella lying on the ground.

ONCE SHE FINISHED WEEPING, SABELLA SAT UP, THEN stood. After wiping tears from her eyes, she looked around and saw a female agent staring at her. Sabella figured that the woman was there to keep her from leaving, and that Durand would soon take her in for an interrogation.

Sabella wandered up the hill where there was a view of the town in the distance. She was standing near the spot where Scallato had rappelled over a hundred feet down a rope to his freedom.

Sabella gained her freedom without the rope, as she stepped out into space and plummeted to the rocks below.

42

THERE CAN BE ONLY ONE

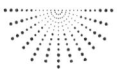

Maurice Scallato hovered the helicopter low over the house and scrutinized the snow that covered the landscape. There were no footprints other than those made by small creatures, while any animal hoof marks larger than that were all many meters distant from the home.

The whirring blades of the helicopter cleared most of the snow off the helipad, but Scallato planned to have its surface redone with heated coils someday. The important thing was that there were no tracks on the roof, not even those of a bird, and that's what mattered most.

Scallato purchased the luxury home under the name of Ivan Yenin, his new identity. His companion was his mistress, Veronika, who was now Mrs. Ivan Yenin, his new wife.

He had escaped Sicily and made it to Rome. Once

there, he told Veronika that Maria had shocked him by asking for a divorce, and that she was moving with the children to America. Scallato knew Veronika was smart enough to know that he was lying about at least some of that, but she was also wise enough not to pry.

When the news stations reported that a Sicilian carpenter named Maurice Rizzo was wanted for committing the vile and despicable act of slaughtering his own family, it caught the attention of many. When it soon followed that Maurice Rizzo was, in fact, a legendary assassin named Maurice Scallato, the story was the lead for days. It had been Durand who let the truth be known in his guise as a true crime writer, and he excoriated Scallato while calling him a coward and a despicable human being.

Durand revealed that Scallato slaughtered his own family to escape from another assassin who had tracked Scallato down to kill him. And while he didn't mention Tanner by name, those in the know, and within the criminal underworld knew of whom he spoke.

When asked if he would be writing a book about Scallato someday, Durand answered yes. By murdering his own children, Scallato had made himself into one of the most despised people on the planet. A sketch of the man was being broadcast all over the world, as a massive manhunt was on for him.

With so much attention on him, Veronika learned the true fate of Maria and the children. When she confronted Scallato about it, he told her that Tanner had backed him into a corner from which he had only one way out.

Veronika surprised Scallato by telling him that she didn't care what circumstances transpired to cause him to resort to such an extreme reaction. All she knew was that Scallato was hers now, the thing she'd always wanted.

Veronika promised Scallato that she would give him an army of sons.

That was when Scallato decided to marry Veronika under his new identity, and he promised her that he would triumph over Tanner in the end.

SCALLATO MAY HAVE ESCAPED SICILY, BUT HE WAS NOW A top priority of law enforcement. It was believed he would go into hiding, to someday emerge with a new face.

Meanwhile, in the small town of Raguso, Sicily, the murders of Maria, Antonio, and little Anna were the most sensational things that had ever happened. Add to that the revelation that they had been the family of Maurice Scallato. A famous assassin had been living in their midst, and it left the citizens of Raguso stunned and with many unanswered questions.

SCALLATO STEPPED FROM THE CHOPPER AND LOOKED around. The brick home was surrounded by trees, but they were all well over a mile away to prevent against their use as a sniper's nest. Other than the helicopter pad, there was only one road leading into the property. That road was blocked by a series of iron gates and was watched over by a 24/7 security service.

The interior of the home was alarmed, had motion, heat, and vibration sensors. Glass break alarms were near every window along with decorative iron bars. There was also a drone with night vision that flew over the perimeter at random intervals each day, and of course, a panic room on each of its three floors.

The house had been built by a high-ranking member of the former KGB and another such individual oversaw the firm that supplied its security. It was a perfect place for a man like Scallato to hide. He had bought it outright in exchange for many Russian rubles.

Scallato rarely thought of his family. They had become a liability and he used them as a tool for his survival. While he would have liked to have spared Maria, the woman had known him better than anyone alive. Under the proper interrogation she might have led someone to his doorstep before he could have fled to Russia.

Tanner, now there was someone Scallato thought of often, and to his consternation he realized that he feared the man. He had not lied when he told Tanner he was in his league, and that he was an equal. They would have to meet again someday and decide which of them was the best. Scallato wanted that day to be of his choosing; however, he had no doubts that Tanner was hunting for him. Given his new surroundings, Scallato thought Tanner would have to be a miracle worker to breach his security. Yet, he still worried that would happen somehow.

Scallato helped his new bride from the chopper, then got a laugh out of her when he insisted on carrying her through the snow to reach the door on the roof. His thumbprint was read by a scanner, followed by a retina scan, and he and Veronika were granted access to their home.

While Veronika undressed and took off her jewelry and makeup, Scallato made a quick circuit through the huge home with a gun. He was checking for intruders, he told Veronika, but there was only one intruder that concerned Scallato, and his name was Tanner.

Once satisfied that they were alone in the house, Scallato sat on the side of their huge bed and removed his boots. Veronika blew him a kiss as she disappeared into the master bathroom and into the shower.

Scallato turned on the television and watched the news. It was the same old crap they always reported, and only the names of the players changed over the years. Still, he needed to stay abreast of current developments. He'd been watching the TV for less than a minute when a thought occurred to him.

While he'd had a view into the bathroom from the bedroom, he had never checked the shower before Veronika stepped into it. After easing his gun off the bedside table, Scallato called out to her as he sat up on the side of the bed.

"Veronika!"

There was no answer, only the sound of running water.

He moved from the bed and crouched by the bathroom door, then reached up and turned the knob slowly. Steam wafted through the opening along with the pleasant scent of perfumed soap, while the sound of the shower grew more distinct.

"Veronika?"

Still no answer.

Scallato moved into the bathroom and crawled along stealthily on his elbows and knees. His eyes remained fixed on the shower door, as he attempted in vain to see what was going on behind it. The door's beveled glass was clouded by steam and streaked with soap lather. It allowed only an impression of a form, or, possibly, forms, moving within the spacious shower stall.

Once he reached the base of the shower, Scallato took a deep breath, then reached up and tapped twice on the door by using his gun. He had expected to hear a cacophony of sound as a barrage of bullets shattered the glass door, but instead, he heard only Veronika's voice.

"Maurice?"

Scallato cracked the door open an inch and saw her soapy back and perfect buttocks. After sighing, he stood and opened the door wider.

"Didn't you hear me calling for you?"

"In here, with the water running? Why? Is something wrong?"

"Tanner is still alive, that's what's wrong."

"And you were worried? Maurice, you saw the snow outside. If anyone had walked through that snow they would have left tracks."

"I was not worried; I was being cautious."

"All right. But now please close the shower door; it's getting chilly in here and I still have to wash my hair."

Scallato shut the door, stomped back into the bedroom, and cut off the TV. Veronika was right. She was right about the snow and she was right about him being worried.

Him, *Il Fantasma*, worried. It was disgusting. He had to get a grip on himself. Tanner was good, but he was no magician who could walk on snow and not leave a trace.

Scallato smiled as he fell onto the bed and wondered what he must have looked like crawling along on the bathroom floor. His mind had been filled with a vision of Tanner standing in the shower, looking like a ninja, with one hand holding a knife to Veronika's throat, and the other gripping an Uzi. He chuckled to himself. If he kept it up, he'd be checking under the bed at night for the man.

Scallato rolled over onto his stomach, fluffed his pillow, and closed his eyes.

The sound of four distinct, although muffled, gunshots reverberated throughout the room.

Scallato's eyes opened for what would be the last time, and he watched in amazement as Tanner slipped out from under the bed. There was a gun in Tanner's hand that had a sound suppressor attached.

The two men stared at each other wordlessly, although Scallato had many questions. However, a set of collapsed lungs along with the blood filling his mouth made Scallato's queries impossible to ask.

TANNER STARED AT THE BATHROOM DOOR AND HEARD NO disruption in the sound of falling water. Veronika was still inside the shower and apparently had not heard the muffled shots. Tanner was thankful for that. Veronika likely would have been a handful to restrain, and he saw no reason to harm her.

Tanner leaned over until he was eye-to-eye with Scallato. There was a look of immense disbelief on the Sicilian's face. Scallato had thought he was the best assassin who had ever lived, but he was now faced with the truth. Tanner was better, without equal, and the price of that knowledge was death.

Tanner straightened up. Maybe another man would curse Scallato or wish him a fine time in hell, but Tanner only wanted to watch the bastard die and know that their personal war was finally over.

Tanner did just that, as life faded from Maurice Scallato. And in his mind, Tanner ran over the events that led him to their final confrontation.

IN THE DAYS AFTER THE MASSACRE, TANNER BARELY SLEPT or ate as he searched for Scallato in and around Sicily, but it soon became apparent that Maurice Scallato had made it to a place of safety.

Durand's organization took most of the heat for the escape, because they had been watching the port and airfield, while other agents had surreptitiously observed the few vehicles that traveled in and out of the small town of Raguso. However he had gotten away, Scallato was gone, and Tanner, Sara, and Durand were back to square one.

That all changed two weeks after the funerals of Maria, Antonio, and Anna. That's when the man who ran the local hotel walked into the police station. Accompanying him was his son, Paolo. Paolo had been best friends with Antonio Rizzo, yet even he hadn't known that Antonio's father was the assassin, Maurice Scallato.

Young Paolo had a story to tell, one that was interesting and could be the key to finding Scallato. Tanner, Sara, and Durand met with the boy to hear the tale, but Paolo had a request before he would recite it.

"He doesn't want me here?" Sara said to Durand, who had asked her and Tanner to step out in the hallway of the precinct.

"I don't know the details yet, only that the story involves sex," Durand said. "Your presence might make the boy uncomfortable. At least, while talking about some aspects."

Sara laughed. "All right, it's being filmed anyway, and I'll watch the interview later. But what big sex secrets can a fourteen-year-old boy have?"

Very big, as it turned out, because Antonio had confided in Paolo and told him all about his visit to Rome. Antonio had been with a girl, Paolo told them, but no, more than a girl, a woman like Sara, and she was Russian too. His father had arranged it at the apartment of another woman named Veronika, and the blonde girl's name had been Yana. Paolo also knew that Veronika was the mistress of Antonio's father.

It took Durand's people only a day to find and interview Yana. The petite hooker was happy to help them. She had liked Antonio, and she disliked Veronika.

Information gathered from her led them to Russia, where a bribe to a relative of Veronika's procured an email with a picture of Veronika's fabulous new home, which resembled a fortress. There were no pictures of her husband, but Tanner knew the man's face all too well.

The Russian security firm that monitored Scallato's secluded home was obstinate in their stance of non-cooperation and said they would fight any legal action. They also threatened to inform their client, Ivan Yenin, of the authorities' interest in him.

Durand told the company's CEO they had reason to believe that Ivan Yenin was Maurice Scallato. The CEO said that his company was in the business of selling security. If they betrayed the trust of their clientele, even a man like Scallato, that they might as well close up shop.

Tanner convinced the CEO to make an exception. He made it past the chief executive's own superb security, into his bedroom, and promised him death if he didn't cooperate or alerted the man they were after.

The CEO agreed that there were times in business when you had to make compromises. He came to that decision with the barrel of Tanner's gun pressed against his forehead. An agreement was reached that they would allow access to the home while doctoring any surveillance footage of the time in question. All sensors within the home would be disabled and anyone viewing the home's cameras remotely would receive a feed of old video that made it appear all was well.

The final hurdle was the snow, and the question of how

to get inside the house without leaving tracks. A similar situation had happened to another Tanner decades earlier. That had been Tanner Four, and Tanner remembered from the memoirs of the man that he had figured a way around it.

Minutes after Tanner marched his way through two feet of snow, a team of firefighting airplanes covered the area around the home. The planes usually carried water or fire retardant, but instead, they carried snow. After several passes by the aircraft, Tanner's footprints were eliminated, while leaving the landscape looking pristine.

Then, the waiting game came.

Tanner had spent thirty-eight hours in the home before Scallato returned from a trip to the city of Barnaul. Thirty-eight minutes after that, Tanner stood over the man and watched him die.

Tanner's mentor, Spenser Hawke, once told him that if the day ever came that a Scallato and a Tanner went head-to-head, that their best better be better than that of the Scallato's. It had been, and now the long line of assassins known as the Scallatos had ended.

TANNER FELT A MIXTURE OF ANNOYANCE AND HAPPINESS when he saw that Sara had chosen to come for him at the designated pick-up spot. She was dressed in a fur coat and leaning against a Mercedes, while gazing out at the icy landscape.

She greeted Tanner without turning his way. "Congratulations."

He sighed as he walked in front of her. "What if I had been Scallato? He could have killed me, sent a phony message, and come looking for my ride."

Sara smiled. "That's not possible; I know it and so do you."

After sharing a kiss, Tanner drove toward the nearest town with a decent hotel.

Once he reached his destination, he stopped at a mailbox. There was one last thing to do.

EPILOGUE

GENOA, ITALY

Nurse Ginevra Valli smiled as she handed the padded envelope over to Carlo Scallato. Carlo was sitting up in bed inside his private room, and he was having a good day.

"Good" for Carlo meant that he was aware of who he was, and what day it was, at least, most of the time.

As he opened the envelope, Carlo saw that it held no letter, only a single item. It was a ring, an unadorned band of gray metal which had a storied history. It had started its life as a bullet.

Carlo gasped when he understood the ring's significance, and he realized who must have sent it to him.

The last of the Scallatos held a ring that had been a family talisman. If there had ever been any luck in the damn thing, Carlo knew it had all run out.

TANNER RETURNS!

WHITE HELL - BOOK 17

AFTERWORD

Thank you,

REMINGTON KANE

JOIN MY INNER CIRCLE

You'll receive FREE books, such as,

SLAY BELLS – A TANNER NOVEL – BOOK 0

TAKEN! ALPHABET SERIES – 26 ORIGINAL TAKEN! TALES

BLUE STEELE - KARMA

Also – Exclusive short stories featuring TANNER, along with other books.

TO BECOME AN INNER CIRCLE MEMBER, GO TO:

http://remingtonkane.com/mailing-list/

ALSO BY REMINGTON KANE

The TANNER Series in order

The Young Guns Series in order

YOUNG GUNS

YOUNG GUNS 2 - SMOKE & MIRRORS

YOUNG GUNS 3 - BEYOND LIMITS

YOUNG GUNS 4 - RYKER'S RAIDERS

YOUNG GUNS 5 - ULTIMATE TRAINING

YOUNG GUNS 6 - CONTRACT TO KILL

YOUNG GUNS 7 - FIRST LOVE

YOUNG GUNS 8 - THE END OF THE BEGINNING

A Tanner Series in order

TANNER: YEAR ONE

TANNER: YEAR TWO

TANNER: YEAR THREE

TANNER: YEAR FOUR

TANNER: YEAR FIVE

The TAKEN! Series in order

TAKEN! - LOVE CONQUERS ALL - Book 1

TAKEN! - SECRETS & LIES - Book 2

TAKEN! - STALKER - Book 3

TAKEN! - BREAKOUT! - Book 4

TAKEN! - THE THIRTY-NINE - Book 5

TAKEN! - KIDNAPPING THE DEVIL - Book 6

TAKEN! - HIT SQUAD - Book 7

TAKEN! - MASQUERADE - Book 8

The MR. WHITE Series

The BLUE STEELE Series in order

BLUE STEELE - DADDY'S GIRL - Book 7 & the Series Finale

The CALIBER DETECTIVE AGENCY Series in order

CALIBER DETECTIVE AGENCY - GENERATIONS-
Book 1

CALIBER DETECTIVE AGENCY - TEMPTATION- Book 2

CALIBER DETECTIVE AGENCY - A RANSOM PAID IN
BLOOD- Book 3

CALIBER DETECTIVE AGENCY - MISSING- Book 4

CALIBER DETECTIVE AGENCY - DECEPTION- Book 5

CALIBER DETECTIVE AGENCY - CRUCIBLE- Book 6

CALIBER DETECTIVE AGENCY – LEGENDARY – Book 7

CALIBER DETECTIVE AGENCY – WE ARE GATHERED
HERE TODAY - Book 8

CALIBER DETECTIVE AGENCY - MEANS, MOTIVE, and
OPPORTUNITY - Book 9 & the Series Finale

THE TAKEN!/TANNER Series in order

THE CONTRACT: KILL JESSICA WHITE - Taken!/Tanner
- Book 1

UNFINISHED BUSINESS – Taken!/Tanner – Book 2

THE ABDUCTION OF THOMAS LAWSON -
Taken!/Tanner – Book 3

PREDATOR - Taken!/Tanner - Book 4

DETECTIVE PIERCE Series in order

MONSTERS - A Detective Pierce Novel - Book 1

DEMONS - A Detective Pierce Novel - Book 2

ANGELS - A Detective Pierce Novel - Book 3

THE OCEAN BEACH ISLAND Series in order

THE MANY AND THE ONE - Book 1

SINS & SECOND CHANES - Book 2

DRY ADULTERY, WET AMBITION -Book 3

OF TONGUE AND PEN - Book 4

ALL GOOD THINGS… - Book 5

LITTLE WHITE SINS - Book 6

THE LIGHT OF DARKNESS - Book 7

STERN ISLAND - Book 8 & the Series Finale

THE REVENGE Series in order

JOHNNY REVENGE - The Revenge Series - Book 1

THE APPOINTMENT KILLER - The Revenge Series - Book 2

AN I FOR AN I - The Revenge Series - Book 3

ALSO

THE EFFECT: Reality is changing!

THE FIX-IT MAN: A Tale of True Love and Revenge

DOUBLE OR NOTHING

PARKER & KNIGHT

REDEMPTION: Someone's taken her

DESOLATION LAKE

TIME TRAVEL TALES & OTHER SHORT STORIES

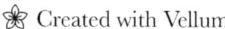

Printed in Great Britain
by Amazon